FAWNW, the Fellowship of Australian Writers – North-West, has been operating for over sixty years. Our members are spread widely along the North-West Coast of Tasmania and occasionally further afield. Meetings are held monthly and visitors are always welcome.

For further information, email the FAWNW President, Allan Jamieson: jamtin79@gmail.com

We have published anthologies of short stories and poems in 2012, 2019, 2021 and 2023. This 2025 anthology is quite extensive, with 26 authors submitting a total of 75 items (33 non-fiction stories, 17 fiction stories and 25 poems). The authors are either members of FAWNW or members of the Fellowship of Australian Writers group (FAW) based in Hobart.

I0590989

Strange and Marvellous Things

Editor: Allan Jamieson

(leave blank)

Table of Contents
[**NF** = Non-Fiction; **F** = Fiction; **P** = Poem]

Editor's note: (Re. Papua New Guinea – PNG)

The initial theme for this year's anthology (*A strange thing happened ...*) led to many entries describing places somewhere on Earth (or 'in the mind'). Three members of FAWNW know a lot about New Guinea, the world's second-largest island, and you will find seven stories herein that describe some of their experiences.

Colonialisation! The western half of the island of New Guinea was under Dutch colonial rule until 1949; nowadays it is an Indonesian region known as Irian Jaya. Papua was a British colony ceded to Australia in 1884 and then annexed in 1888. New Guinea was part of the German empire until 1914 when the Australian army invaded and captured it. Later, it became a United Nations Trust Territory. These two latter regions were administered by Australia as the Territory of Papua and New Guinea, which transitioned in 1975 to the Independent Country of Papua New Guinea (PNG).

The approximate locations of most of the places mentioned in those seven stories are shown on this map.

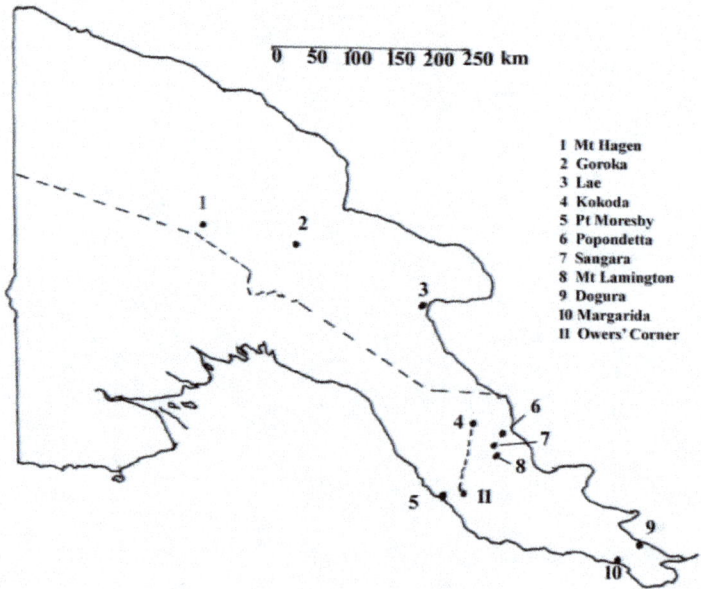

0   50 100 150 200 250 km

1 Mt Hagen
2 Goroka
3 Lae
4 Kokoda
5 Pt Moresby
6 Popondetta
7 Sangara
8 Mt Lamington
9 Dogura
10 Margarida
11 Owers' Corner

Dog Day Afternoon
Graham Meyers

Sunday, bloody Sunday! How time drags when nothing's happening! Jim has a headache – he came in very late last night and today he looks ill. Even Sue is lying down. She does that a lot since she started to get fat around the middle. We used to spend a lot of time together, but lately she's always in the shed. She's making some kind of a nest I reckon. Tells me to bugger off if I even go near "her" back corner.

So, I'm on my own and bored. The occasional car cruises slowly past – old Clem McCall in his Chev two-tonner taking hay to the cattle down at Maggotty Point, Ted Perkins on his way to town, Betty Morrison on her way to church. Years ago, even church provided a bit of excitement, but all the young speedsters have gone to live in Adelaide. Only the aged and infirm go to church now, and they don't progress beyond second gear.

I close my eyes and dream of adventures past, when there was real action here. God, how I looked forward to young Ned coming past in his hotted old Plymouth! He always went ten-tenths, those big wheels kicking up gravel and small rocks. One hit me in the eye once, but I could see ok again after a couple of weeks. The injury got me plenty of attention then, now I mostly get yelled at. But being wounded is better than being bored.

There's the hum of a distant car. Nah, probably on the school road, heading into town. I listen – I don't mean to but it's a reflex, I guess. The sound is getting louder. Bugger me, it's on our road, and it's going like a bat out of hell.

I leap up and race out to the road verge. Can't see it yet, there's a slight rise blocking my view. Here it comes – it's the Plymouth! Can't believe my luck, but timing is everything here.

I crouch in the grass, waiting for the exact moment – now! Out onto the road, give it all you've got Nim! I accelerate hard and close on the quarry – up along the side the gravel sprays but I'm oblivious. Beside the front wheel now and my spit starts to fly. This is harder than I remember, but it's glorious! Get a couple of good barks in and a nip at that beautiful tyre, but no actual contact. Contact can hurt.

Fifty yards along I've had enough. I brake but stay close by the car's side in case the rear wheel needs a bollocking as well.

Suddenly I'm flying – road, sky, and car become one whirling mass, then I'm sliding and rolling to a stop. The dust has settled and the Plymouth is disappearing in the distance. I stand up. Dunno what happened, I'm covered in dirt and my legs are like jelly, but I can still walk. On the way back to my driveway a splitting headache hits and keeps hitting. Haven't had a headache this bad since that mad cow Alma gave me a kick in the face, and all I'd given her was a little bite on the udder.

Over the next week the pain gradually subsides, and I can flex my neck more than a few degrees. I'd swear I've been hit with a lump of two-inch pipe, it's that bad. Maybe I blacked out and somebody did hit me, but there was nobody around when I came to. Whatever happened, it's a mystery.

A fortnight after "the incident" I'm innocently lying in the driveway again and I hear a car coming. Sounds familiar – can't be! But it is, it's the blanky Plymouth! It slows at the top of the little hill and I'm outa here. I slink off into the shed with images of road, sky, car, and pain all mixed up. Ned gets out of the car and knocks on our door. The boss answers and Ned says,

"G'day Jim, just checkin' if your dog's OK. I might have hit him a coupla weeks ago. Didn't feel anything, but I saw him in the rearview mirror gettin' up off the road. Point is, I've re-routed the exhaust to exit ahead of the back wheel and it sticks out a bit. Now I'd swear it's bent back slightly."

"That's OK young feller, Nimrod'll get over it. Might teach him a lesson. As long as your car's undamaged."

That's humans for you, sooo blanky caring. A pox on cars, I'm giving them up fer good. No, I mean it, I hope I never see one again, I really do.

The Unknown Lady - Remnants of a Life in Her Linen
Dawn Meredith

The life of an unknown lady is piled in my hallway. Decades of her life are displayed in her linen and her glassware, acquired at an auction. As I trawl through, unwrap and inspect it all I am struck by sadness at the vulnerability of a life lived and sold this way. The love and devotion of this lady to her family is in my hands - the well-worn enamel pot, the faded aprons, the neatly folded sheet sets, the embroidered table cloths. Things she used often, things she saved specially, they are here in my house now.

When my husband said he was going to a farm auction (called a clearing sale), to see if there might be something useful to us I had no idea he was bringing home a woman's life. The callousness with which it was just sold! sold! sold! to the highest low bidder has affected me. I've been to many auctions and not felt this way. But this unknown lady speaks to me through what she left behind. Starched linen tea towels never used speak of her travels, perhaps in her retirement years - Scotland 2002, Ireland, Western Australia, Canada. Or were they gifts from her children, flown from her nest?

Was she married long? Widowed early? Survived by her husband? I will never know. But I do know many things about her through the things she used.

The unknown lady's life is utterly unremarkable. She spent it in service and devotion to those she loved, evidenced here in the acts of everyday domestic life of women of her generation. She is gone now. And this is all that is left of the washing, ironing, mending, cooking, comforting, cajoling. All those hours of work stacked in a stranger's hallway, streaks of sunlight playing upon the patterned china.

I'd like to think she met up regularly with her friends, completed this cross-stitched tablecloth in the company of others around a pot of tea and some scones. Perhaps she laughed, recounting small stories of small moments of family life. Perhaps she shared her dreams of adventure. Perhaps it was a joy to crotchet the pink lady in the crinoline dress sewn so carefully to a white pillow slip. I can see her, sitting in a comfy chair in the evenings watching telly with her husband.

This unknown lady's life in linen and tableware was sold at an auction for ten dollars. It slumped in uneven towers upon a table. A job lot. Ten dollars was considered a reasonable price for one lady's devotion. I feel humbled as I look through the floral flat sheets and the flannelette pillowcases I know I can't use, fighting this immense wave of sadness that her life is over and struck by the thought that this could be me in thirty years. It's only because the wind kept me awake all night and the loneliness of this new life sometimes curls inside my chest in a tight, knotted ball. It makes everything feel heavier. I wonder, what my life in linen will look like when I am gone.

So, I have chosen three of her aprons and will wear them with pride while I make scones in the kitchen of my country house as my family come in from the cold rubbing their hands, standing in front of the kitchen stove. I will think of the unknown lady as I make new culinary efforts. What do you do with kangaroo meat? Do you cook it long and slow or fast and hot? It would be handy to have the unknown lady here to give me that advice.

I don't know what else the unknown lady did with her life, whether she had a job in town, whether she was a teacher and writer like me, if she balanced work and family as I do, but as I look at the remnants of her life I will try to feel joy, focus on that, because there is a lot of love here piled up among her linen. There is gentleness in the delicate gold edging of her best glassware. It seems not just cruel but inevitable and devastating and horrible that cheerful, pastel-striped flannelette sheets which comforted the bodies of children at night should have a number stuck to them. Is this the worth of love?

There are also boxes of glassware and crockery, cooking utensils, sugar bowls and milk jugs. There are precious, unused items in packets, saved for a special occasion - paper serviettes in floral patterns and Christmas designs, writing sets of beautiful note paper that were never opened, an overlocker machine with three giant spools still full. I got that for twenty dollars. Always wanted one. Feels like I cheated her.

If there's one positive thing I can take from this experience, it's this: don't save the beautiful paper serviettes. Don't save the lovely writing paper. Use it. Send it. Share it. Enjoy. Because you don't know when your life will end. You could be saving it up for a day that you never see.

The wind has eased a bit and the rain has drifted away for now. I can hear crows and magpies outside in the sunshine, chasing each other past the window. It's time to move on, into my own life today, with all its problems and challenges, living in this house in this isolated place, regenerating a farm, writing books and blogs, caring for my family, dealing with money pressures, not having enough cupboards to put everything. These are small problems compared to someone who is homeless, compared to someone who has lost their family, their job, their home. I know I should be grateful. But some days…

As I look at the unknown lady's complete Royal Doulton dinnerware set in perfect condition I resolve to use it, to live my life as fully as I can and to share it with others. Because it's not just a pile of crockery and linen that you leave behind, it's the memories in the minds of those who loved you. And I'm sure the unknown lady has left behind treasured memories of childhood and marriage and friendship in the minds of those who knew and loved her.

So, to honour the unknown lady I am going to don one of her aprons and bake something today. As a child I was a tomboy and wouldn't ever dream of standing in a kitchen, wearing a pinny, *baking*. But we grow and change, don't we? We mould to the life we're living. And when we're gone, people may speak of us kindly, having noticed our small acts of kindness and care, may admire us for our courage and determination, may have fond memories of times they spent with us. It's up to us, really.

Apple and peach pie with caraway, nutmeg and cinnamon

A memorable airflight in Papua New Guinea
Lesley Ririka

I love flying, but like love, it can be scary sometimes. There were four of us waiting at the little grass airstrip at Dogura in the Milne Bay Province, Papua New Guinea for the small single engine Cessna plane which was due in a few minutes. We soon saw a black dot silhouetted over the mountains and then heard the hum of the plane. It landed and taxied to a stop close to us. There were no terminal buildings, just our group of people with our luggage and the vehicle that had driven us down the hill. The pilot, who I will call Bill, gave us a cheery greeting as the incoming passengers disembarked.

Ref. https://www.airhistory.net/photo/89392

"Morning all, a lovely day for flying!" We had weighed ourselves and our baggage up at the station and had the list ready for Bill; (the total weight is very important on these small planes). After chatting for a while Bill loaded our luggage, we said our goodbyes and boarded at about 8am, being told where to sit to be sure the balance was correct. We fastened our seat belts, and the plane took off, with clear blue skies and no wind; we looked forward to the trip.

We were to go via Popondetta to leave two passengers. It was an uneventful flight of an hour going west along the coast, so there were no mountains, and we enjoyed watching the landscape while listening to the even hum of the engine. We made a smooth landing on the sealed World War Two airstrip and some Mission staff were waiting for us as we all disembarked. Looking at the mountains we were to fly over or go through the pass of, it was very different, there was a heavy cloud cover and Bill said to us; "We better hurry. I don't like the look of that cloud." We left the two passengers, there was no one to pick up and no new luggage to worry about, so we boarded quickly and squeezed into the two seats behind the pilot and fastened our seat belts. This turnaround had taken us about half an hour, and we were ready for the next part of our flight. Bill turned around to check that we had our seat belts fastened correctly and told us; "I'm going to try and go over that cloud, so will circle to gain height."

This was a new experience, but we trusted Bill, as we had flown with him before. The engine was louder as it worked to gain height then after 20 minutes with very little turbulence, Bill donned his oxygen mask (there was no oxygen for passengers). Jelilah and I looked at each other – we felt alright! Bill looked for any breaks in the clouds going along a possible gap but turning back each time as there was no clear way. We knew things were not going well and after about 20 minutes or more he swiveled around and said to us; "I can't go over the cloud, and there is no way through, so we'll go back." The plane was quieter as we spiraled down, and we needed to swallow quickly for our ears to be okay, but *oh dear,* Popondetta was now under cloud!

Bill said "We can't go down to Popondetta, we'll go back to Milne Bay and see how things are there." It was a long way back to Milne Bay, and as the weather was changing rapidly, I wondered what I would find when we got there. This flight was above the clouds and an hour later we reached Milne Bay and flew over Dogura (which we had left a few hours earlier) and could see they had experienced heavy rain making it impossible for us to land. To reinforce that, a vehicle drove down the strip with water splashing out both sides – definitely too wet for us! What now? We were in a small plane flying around on top of clouds with nowhere to land. Bill just said; "That's okay, we will go on around the end of the mountains (the Owen Stanleys) and on to the south coast." So, we settled down for some more flying. This was taking a long time, and things were not getting better yet! Forty or fifty minutes later, after flying around the end of the mountains we were over the United Church airstrip at Margarida on the South coast. This looked promising, it was somewhere where we could land! It was a sealed strip, and the weather was okay, soon we felt a gentle thud as the wheels hit the tarmac and we taxied to a stop on this deserted unmanned mission strip, but the station was only a short distance away.

Bill said; "I'll see if they can let us have some fuel, I'm right out." Jelilah and I had a rather different concern; we needed a toilet! We had been flying around for a long time, and there are no toilets on small planes! As Bill went to negotiate for some fuel, Jelilah found someone and asked; *"Haus pispis em wea"* (Where is the toilet?)"

"Daun bilo" ("Down at the end of the strip.") We were pointed to a small bush material building at the other end of the airstrip. It was a drop toilet with a very high seat, and no paper. That didn't matter, it was a toilet, and we managed the high seat with our feet dangling!

Feeling much more comfortable we walked around for a while to stretch our legs. The strip we had landed on, being a Mission strip, didn't have terminal buildings, just a shed with the essentials for storing fuel, fueling, and weighing passengers and their cargo. Soon some staff came out from the station to see who we were and why we had landed. After an explanation, Bill was able to refuel from a 44-gallon drum using a hand pump and without wasting any more time we all gathered with the now fueled plane and two much more comfortable passengers. We thanked the staff for their help and Bill negotiated payment for the fuel, then having discussed our situation and the weather with the staff, we took off. We crept at a low level back to Port Moresby under the cloud in very gloomy weather, keeping close to the coastline and getting in just before dark.

After going as high as was possible to try and get over the cloud, we were now going as low as was safe to be under the cloud. It was reassuring to see the shoreline all the way though we did have a thick cloud cover above us, and then we saw the very welcoming sight of the lights of Port Moresby and after a while the runway and heard Bill requesting landing and the positive reply from the airport staff and I knew we would soon be there; this long flight was nearly over!

We felt and heard the wheels touch down with a slight thump and taxied over to the MAF (Mission Aviation Fellowship) hanger. Our little plane amongst the big planes at the busy airport, and all the bright lights that are part of the larger airports were a big contrast to the loneliness of flying alone up in the sky over thick clouds looking for somewhere to land. We were very thankful to be at our destination, even though it was hours later than we expected. It should have taken one hour and twenty minutes if we had flown straight or two and a half hours going via Popondetta, but it had taken ten hours! We did thank Bill for his skill, patience and perseverance. Our love for flying in small aircraft was not lost, but this flight was different and one I will not forget! After a short taxi ride, we reached our accommodation and a chance to have something to eat and drink.

It was a very different flight for Bill too and he must have been relieved and glad to be safely back home with his wife and family. The MAF pilots serve many isolated mission stations and face many different and varied conditions and many challenges. He was a very good MAF pilot and managed the difficulties calmly and smoothly. He said nothing about the shortage of fuel until we had safely landed, but there must have been many thoughts, calculations and prayers going through his head, and even the last part of the flight would have been tricky, flying so low in unpleasant weather. We as Christians, know that God is with us and guiding us on our journeys, and that certainly was so on this day.

NB: Single engine Cessna planes cannot travel through clouds and cannot travel after dark as they do not have radar.

The Kokoda Trail
Noel Davern

Eight days. Ninety-six kilometres. Memories I'll take to my grave.

It was mid-July 2012. Wilfred's and Suzanne's organisational chores behind them, and our preparatory exercise programs dutifully completed. Eleven excited members of the Townsville Bushwalking Club, passports in pockets, walked across the tarmac of the Cairns Airport. We were heading to Papua New Guinea! To walk the Kokoda Trail!

Our guide was waiting for us at the motel in Port Moresby— the site of our first night 'in country.' We sat around the bar while he explained how things would go from here. A lot more detail emerged than during our previous correspondence.

A bit of background—this isn't a trip to do unguided, so we went with Kokoda Spirit, an Australian-based company. Fortune had it that our guide was Wayne Wetherall, the owner. A superb leader, he brought the 1942 diggers' achievements to life along the track.

You can do the trek in either direction and we had chosen the option from Kokoda to Owers' Corner—back towards Port Moresby—the direction of the 'fighting withdrawal' by the Australians.

Our main pack had to be under 15kg, and we each had a smaller day pack containing stuff we would need between camps. They supplied some of the gear, while the rest was our own, which we had in abundance since we were all avid bushwalkers. This company strongly recommends engaging a personal porter—referred to by Wayne as 'one of his boys'—to carry your main pack. Just fine by us! Not only would it make it easier on us, but it offers employment to the locals. In fact, Wayne told us it's the highest paying job available to most of them. His terminology of boys raised an eyebrow or two, but Wayne explained that in PNG, they use the term commonly without the connotations it may carry elsewhere. I must admit, it didn't seem to worry any of them. And, where I come from, being 'one of the boys' means you're part of the group. Accepted. Same thing being 'one of the girls.' It's in that context that I use the term. I made it my business to learn as many of their names as possible, but, for authenticity's sake, will refer to them collectively as boys here.

The briefing wasn't all one-way either. Wayne was doing some recon of his own. We each had to 'fess up to what we were doing there. Talk about being put on the spot. Amongst the things I divulged, I mentioned my dad was a veteran of the New Guinea campaign. He hadn't fought on the Kokoda Trail, but in what he referred to as 'Dutch New Guinea.'

With the briefing behind us, we settled in over pizza, the banter light-hearted and the mood relaxed. We were a tight-knit crew, having shared more than a few wild-and-woolly days and nights together over the years.

The next morning, it was back to the airport to have ourselves and gear weighed before the charter flight to Kokoda Village. Our excitement was palpable and the flight picturesque, if a little daunting, as the size of the task we had taken on unveiled below us. The Owen Stanley Range, rugged and beautiful, stretched endlessly—a formidable home for the week it would take to traverse it.

As we stepped off the plane, the entire village was there to greet us. A prominent sign read *Oro Oro Oro*, not in Pidgin, or *tok pisin* as it is formally known, but *ewa-ge*, their local language. This personal touch, paired with their carved totems, gave me a great feeling about this trip. Not only were the diggers who had passed on present here, but so too were the ancestral presences that guided and guarded this land. We weren't interlopers but welcomed as friends!

It all got real when we met our personal porters, and mine, Lufus, was small and wiry. Quietly spoken, but as tough as they come.

There were also several 'general' porters to carry food, supplies and the like. What a cheerful bunch of guys they were; all strong and sure-footed. Our interaction with them was the highlight of the trip.

I felt so mean, passing over gear to be hauled by someone else, not carrying my weight, so to speak, but they assured me it wasn't a problem.

A larrikin among them piped up. "No worries, mate!" One afternoon after completing the day's walk, the boys were yackaing (skylarking) together, lost in the joy of a game of touch footy. While watching their effortless camaraderie, I got my confirmation that the physical challenge of getting all our gear from one place to the next was no real burden for them. And you might notice in our photo, I'm a dripping lather of sweat; Lufus is in cruise mode.

I had noticed that none of the porters did up the waist belt of the packs. When I discussed this with Wayne, he said that none of them 'liked that.' This raises the subject of load-carrying. Modern pack manufacturers fixate on transferring the weight to your hips. Given their different physique and stature, our packs were unlikely to be their correct back size, but interestingly, none of the methods of carrying loads used by indigenous peoples do this—they all carry the load on their shoulders (or heads!). Hmmm …

Besides carrying our packs, our porters rushed ahead of us each time we approached camp and pitched our tents in readiness. Lufus must have had some seniority, because mine occupied the prime spot at every campsite! This is my tent site overlooking the Goldie River, our last night on the trail.

Poor, hardworking Lufus soon found out he had another task he didn't know about when he signed on for this trip. He was going to teach me *tok pisin*.

A bond developed between the two of us, and we had many a chat as we walked the trail together. I found out where he was from, about his family, and his usual occupation when not acting as a porter.

From time to time, Lufus would point out local vegetation.

"That is a Betel Nut tree." I noticed the gleam in his eyes as he said this.

A few days into the trip, he pointed to a plant that looked like undersized sugar cane.

"We eat that."

"Really. What's it called?"

"*Pitpit.*"

"What does it taste like?"

"Gooood."

Our meals comprised ingredients we were used to, but to save on haulage, locally procured produce figured prominently. By this time, Wayne had us all pegged. We could handle a bit of adventure with our eating as well. That night one of our side dishes was mashed yams with *Pitpit* mixed through it. *And* Wayne had brought along our own dedicated cook, one of his boys with the brilliant name 'Toast.' Lufus was right; it 'tasted good.'

But I'm getting ahead of myself. Back to the sequence of events.

We had a quick look at the sights of Kokoda Village, and a tour of the museum, then we set off.

It didn't take long to get our feet wet, either. There were hundreds of creek crossings, most of which we waded through, but there were also numerous 'bridges,' if you could stretch your imagination to call them that.

Our first lunch set the tone for the trip. Bread rolls with salami and salad topped off with fresh fruit. Yummy! This wasn't a 'dried food and biscuits' trip!

The first night, at Deniki, as I lay in my tent, nursing the odd ache and pain, I heard singing! I poked my head out to track down its source and discovered the boys, sitting outside an open-walled, thatched-roof shelter, all smiles and right into it. As I ventured nearer, Lufus pointed to a spot beside him. I was there in a flash. I had no idea what they were singing, but it was bloody brilliant. Then, Wayne came over around 9:30 and chased everyone off to bed.

Cocking an eye at him, I got the order. "Go to bed. Big day tomorrow." Which, of course, I had no option but to obey. This got repeated pretty much each night. Apparently, every day was going to be a big day in Wayne's book. And, as it turned out, in mine as well.

Going to bed early had another benefit. It counteracted the fact that we were up with the sparrows, or whatever their equivalent is in PNG. Get the hard yards over and done with in the cool of the morning. No argument from me.

By far, the most elaborate memorial on the trail is at Isurava. We paused there to conduct a service. At its conclusion, the boys sang their national anthem and ours, with Ruben standing prominently in front, leading them with his guitar.

Before we left, Wilfred went over and squatted down for a little quiet reflection of his own.

Sitting here thinking about it all as I pen this to share with you, the images flitter around in my mind, each jolting the next back into existence, some firing around between those special synapses that meld the conscious with the sub-conscious, until they weave into a kaleidoscope for me to pause and embrace, before attempting to choose the words to do them justice.

Our tireless porters, clambering everywhere, ensuring our safe passage across the many creeks we encountered.

The euphoria of sitting around a campfire after a hard day's walk, our bellies full with one of Toast's masterpieces and sipping hot, sweet tea while listening to the boys singing. My favourite song was *Longpela Rot*, which they sang to the tune of John Denver's *Take*

Me Home, Country Roads. Its familiar melody, paired with the boys' soulful voices and carried on the cool mountain breezes, seemed to whisk our collective weariness off into the night. Ah, the bread of the working man is sweet!

The bright-eyed little *piccaninnies* in Efogi 2 Village as they headed off to school, one clutching her pencil and exercise book, another gifts from Glenys and Rosemary. Barefooted, but resplendent in their little pink dresses. Looking at them took me back a few years. My dad used to call us 'his little piccaninnies' when we were young. Like a lot of the Diggers, he had picked up some *tok pisin*, and came out with a phrase or two now and then.

The neat and modest church at Naduri Village, its half-dozen rough-hewn bench pews arranged in quiet order, with a lone bible resting on one of them, extending a gentle invitation for one of us to delve inside.

The conga line of us negotiating the tangled masses of tree roots, trudging upward, or scrambling downward, wrestling with the unforgiving slopes of the track.

The hunter we encountered near Manari Village, his catch–a lifeless wild pig–slung effortlessly across his shoulders, with his faithful dogs loyally by his side.

The solitary old lady, a repurposed tree branch her sturdy crutch, with her load slung from her head in a bag, shuffling home barefooted through the mist across the meticulously swept hard earth of Naduri Village.

Humidity you could touch, as Wayne sat on a rock, enveloped in steam, while the rest of us caught our breath during a gruelling climb.

The ambience of the bright blazes of the setting sun's rays radiating starkly through the deep, threatening clouds that loomed over the valley as we gazed down from our haven at Ioribaiwa Village.

The only Japanese monument is at Eora Creek, and it has a guardian. This fellow stores it in his hut for safe keeping and places it on its plinth whenever trekkers pass through.

At Naoro Village, I saw a Cassowary chick, of all things, standing beside a bloke sitting in front of his neat hut which, as I got closer, revealed its true identity: a guest house.

I went over to him.

"*Gude.*"

He smiled and replied with his own greeting, "*Gude.*"

"*Nem bilong mi Noel. Nem bilong yu?*"

I can't remember his name, but his reply informed me he could speak English.

I commented that they didn't seem to have many possessions. He smiled and replied, "No, we don't have much, but we don't want much. We are happy."

Come to think of it, they don't have 30-year house mortgages, vehicle expenses, power bills, etc. They probably don't even pay taxes. Maybe we have lost the plot somewhat in the West.

And the Cassowary chick? He told me he had 'domesticated' it and was feeding it up for a future feast.

And enveloping them all, the vivid recollection of when I read the poem *The Anzac on the Wall* while standing amongst the grave sites during our solemn service at Brigade Hill. Sixty-two of them. Each one marking a life cut short—their supreme sacrifice. The lump in my throat as I choked on the words, struggling to utter them.

A vision had flashed before me of the sepia photo of my dad, with his youthful and innocent face, in full uniform and slouch hat, gazing out at us from where it perched in pride of place on the piano in our lounge room.

And it conjured up an incident from my youth: vividly, as if I was re-living it. I was standing on our verandah, surveying the mayhem that Cyclone Althea had wreaked. We—and, in truth—all of Townsville, were without power. Dad was busy hanging up a few stubbies wrapped in a wet hessian bag, trying his best to cool them off.

I said, "Can't you go without beer for a day?"

He shook his head.

"Noelie, the day my best mate was killed, I promised him that if I ever got out of that place, a day would not pass by without me having a beer with him. I've kept that promise all these years, and I'm not about to break it today."

At Brigade Hill

My dad had passed on as well by now, and I decided there and then that I would have a beer with both of them as soon as I got back to Port Moresby.

Later that afternoon, while we were taking a breather, Wayne came over to me and said, "What happened back there? I rarely see that much emotion." His eyes locked onto mine, demanding an explanation. I related the vision it had invoked. He just stood there looking at me in silence for a while, then nodded and turned away.

On our last night on the trail, we had a big shindig—bonfire and all. The boys treated us to a concert; one song after another, all of them familiar to us by now, echoed around the jungle.

♫ ♪ ♪ ♫
Longpela rot
Mi wokabaut
Long Kokoda trail
Mi laik go

Two boys had gone ahead and brought back an esky containing our treat for the night, chicken thighs, ready for Toast to put on the barbie plate and weave his magic spell. And it also contained a dozen beers! Which sparked us up, I can tell you! All of us: the women up Queensland way enjoy a cold beer on a hot afternoon as well – the ones we had with us, anyway!

But Wayne had continued to tease us for a while.

"Not yet. They're for later."

Finally, they got passed around. We stood in an arc with Wayne in front, facing us. Wayne raised his drink.

"To the Diggers."

We all took a swig.

"The Diggers!"

Later, I took my beer over and sat on a rock that overlooked the creek. Its gentle flow transported my mind to a time and place I had never been, in the company of people—except one—I had never met.

The next morning, all that was left was the short walk out to Owers' Corner. We posed for a group photo, all of us a little changed by our experience.

Then, on the drive back to Port Moresby, we visited the Bomana War Cemetery—the solemn sight of the impossibly neat row upon row of gravestones washed over us with an almost unbearable weight of history. Beside the sheer enormity of it, what struck me the most was a toss-up: the two gravestones marking the resting place of brothers, killed on the same day and now lying peacefully side by side, and the anonymous headstones bearing the painfully inadequate yet hauntingly evocative words *An Australian Soldier of the 1939-1945 War*.

This journey was a physical and emotional roller coaster. It offered no respite—the trail itself demanded constant shifts, one moment ascending, the next descending—but it was the emotional terrain, oscillating between awe, reflection, and resolve that truly mirrored the journey. All the while, acutely aware that you were treading in the footsteps of heroes.

Walking the Kokoda Trail isn't for everyone, but for those who do, it shifts perspectives in ways that words can barely capture—it certainly did for me.

This Time
Noel Davern

The steady banging of the piano keys droned on, Saturday's practice in full swing. It wasn't music, just scales. Not completely random notes, but not music. Not like it sounded when mum played. But that would come. So we had been told. Then something that sounded a little more like music. Arpeggios. They were music to my ears, anyway. This was the last bit, then it would be over. Soon ... soon. To pass the time faster, I had escaped downstairs and was doing some banging of my own. Banging nails into wood. At least I was creating something.

Finally, silence from above! My little sister came rushing down the steps, her face flushed with excitement. I bolted upstairs, lent out my window, and dropped the torch for her to secrete away. "See you, Mum. We're off to the igloos." She mightn't have caught the last part as I left the landing.

That's what we knew them as—igloos. The remnants of abandoned WWII aircraft hangers dotted throughout the bush behind our place. The only things left were their concrete bases. But they were our favourite haunt. They had character. Atmosphere.

We both grabbed our bikes. Girls' bikes. That didn't bother my sister: she was a girl. Mine was mum's old one, but that didn't bother me either. Any bike was good enough. More than transport, they were time machines. We could travel farther in our allotted time. Get there in no time at all.

I wasn't big on following rules, but I had two immutable ones.
- Don't leave your sister behind.
- Be home before the streetlights come on.

Whatever immutable meant, I didn't quite know. But set in stone—I understood that phrase. And the rules kind of made sense if you thought about them for a minute. I was eleven, and my sister was eight. We could live with that level of containment.

This time, time mattered. We weren't going to the igloos; we were ranging further afield. All the way to Mount Louisa.

The gravel roads and bush tracks disappeared beneath our tyres as we pedalled furiously. No time for talking, but I was trailing, shouting directions on which track to take. I caught glimpses of Mercurochrome on my sister's knee—evidence of her latest buster.

We drew rein at Peewee Creek. Looking up at our landmark of the large overhanging rock above us. We ditched the bikes and scrambled up to it, then skirted across to the almost hidden mouth of the bunker carved into the mountain beside it.

We looked at each other with wide eyes. What treasures lay inside? This time, we were going to find out. My sister reached into her knapsack, handed me the torch, stepped behind me, and grabbed my shirt tail.

Three and a half times involuntarily in Paris
Val Colic-Peisker

I cannot measure up to the bloggers who travel competitively and/or professionally and have hence been 'everywhere' but I claim one almost certainly undisputable travelling world record: I have been to Paris three-point-five (3.5) times *involuntarily*. This means I didn't really want to go to Paris but nonetheless found myself there. The 'half-time' happened when I had to detour to Paris to take my re-routed flight back to Australia. I only spent half a day in Paris on that occasion, so this does not count as a full visit.

You may think, *oh c'mon*, is this even possible, unless you've been trafficked by evil people? No, I was not trafficked, and yes, it's possible. This is not fiction. It is easy to mess up things while travelling, so most of it was my own fault. Travelling is an ideal opportunity to do stupid things. We all travel lusting for new experiences, but alas, those new situations, and even more those that *look* familiar but are in fact unfamiliar, can be tricky. And moreover, as you've no doubt noticed yourself, dear reader, life/fate/God/chance, whatever you prefer to call it, likes to play practical jokes on every one of us from time to time.

Nearly everyone wants to visit Paris, the charming metropolis of grand boulevards and stately buildings adorned with brass plaques telling you this or that famous artist once lived there. The city is packed with sites whose names evoke the worldly chic, bohemian lifestyle and late nights filled with excitement, culture, imperial grandeur, irresistible shopping, fragrant gardens—you name it, it's all there, resplendent and waiting for enraptured visitors. Even the romantic walks across many bridges on the river Seine, if this is your cup of tea. And time travel; see Woody Allen's movie *Midnight in Paris*.

My first and only voluntary visit to Paris took place when I was a starry-eyed youth of twenty, in the company of my adventurous boyfriend, five years my senior. We drove from Zagreb, where we both studied politics at the time, to Paris. It was a big deal that included being truant from university for a week. Dear oh dear! My father strongly objected when he learned what I did from my postcard (the olden days of postcards…).

On a map, our route was a strange zig-zag line through Slovenia-Italy-Switzerland-France, not entirely deliberately so, but we did not mind getting lost because wherever we found ourselves, it was exciting. Once we realised we could not possibly complete the road trip in one day (nowadays you could not fool yourself—Google says 14-15 hours driving—we stopped, late at night, in Mulhouse, a town in Alsace (an eastern French province next to Germany). At that point we barely knew where we were. We had a very basic road map, and this was decades before smart phones.

We knocked on the door of a B&B and after a little while a friendly middle-aged gentleman wrapped in a bath robe let us in and gave us a room. I'm grateful to this day. By the early afternoon of the following day, we drove past a huge road sign: PARIS. It gave me butterflies in the stomach. Never again in my life was I quite so over the moon about arriving at my travel destination.

But some decades later was an entirely different story. I'm hoping not to go there again.

An ungrateful person with poor taste, you might think. Yes, it's a great city, *objectively*. Apart from those hopelessly, relentlessly grey roofs. The red roofs of nearby Brussels and many other cities are so much more attractive. Perhaps they slated Paris in grey not only because slate lasts nearly forever but also because the city is so flat it is hard to see the roofs anyway. The highest point of the city is Montmartre, a smallish hill with the large, white Sacré-Cœur basilica on top.

If you climb on the viewing platform of the grand old church for *une visite panoramique*, which I did on my third visit, you'll see a lead-grey sea of densely packed roofs and then, in the hazy distance, a ring of high-rise buildings in the *banlieues* that encircle the Paris known to tourists. The *banlieues* represent the Paris unknown to tourists, yet of great interest to sociologists like me—but that's another topic. So that's the city panorama, mainly grey, hardly *une belle vue*. Many cities are nested under a picturesque, imposing mountain. Not Paris.

But as a dyed-in-the-wool road cyclist, I appreciated its flatness.

Grey, grey, grey roofs of Paris.

Paris, involuntary visit #1.

It's June 2011 and I am bound for Lyon from Rijeka, my Croatian hometown, to visit a friend who moved there for work. A good opportunity to see the second largest French city. There are 441 km by rail between Lyon and Paris, so how did I manage to end up in Paris? French national railways, known among the natives as SNCF (*La Société générale des chemins de fer*) have trains ('TGV', le *Train à Grande Vitesse*) that, running at a maximum speed of 500 kms per hour and typically at over 300 km per hour, do not tend to stop much. Lyon-Paris, 2 hrs 2 mins—be impressed! The slowest train between the two cities takes 3hrs 17 mins.

The trains that took me through northern Italy were quite another kettle of fish, stopping a lot. The train Trieste-Milano was mostly empty, clean and pleasant. Milano was hot and there was no point leaving the cool, marble-clad *Stazione Ferroviaria* built by Mussolini in 1930 (or as it was known then, 'the 9th year of the Fascist Era'). It's still the biggest railway station building in Europe. The 20th century fascists (and communists, to be fair) were known for their taste for grandiose buildings. Nonetheless, *la stazione* is impressive and in there, in a deep cool shade, I had the best coffee ice-cream in my life while waiting for my next train.

The train Milano-Lyon reached the Alps after a longish and monotonous ride through the western part of the flat Lombardia (the fat part of otherwise thin Italy). My ears were getting blocked, we were climbing; tunnel after tunnel. The train was packed, toilets were few and dirty. The train crossed the Alps at over 1500 metres elevation. The scenery was stunning—the European Alps are serious mountains.

At some point, the station names started to sound French, but we were still in Italy. The mixing of languages and cultures in Europe's frontier regions is quite cool. The next stop: Oulx. What a name, it must be France, I thought. But then in the next, Italian-sounding station, Bardonecchia, the platform swarmed with police—perhaps this was the end of Italy? In fact, Italy ended, and France began in a tunnel. Makes sense! In Modane, the first French stop, the police came in and looked at our travel documents. So much for the 'borderless Europe.' We were now descending from the Alps and travelling along a biggish river. I could not figure out in a hurry which one it was. After nearly twelve hours of travelling, I had to endure another three to Lyon.

So what did I do next? Desperate to finally arrive, I didn't get off the train in Lyon!! How? Why? Well, when the train stopped in Lyon, this was not the Lyonnaise main railway station as I—rightfully, I'll claim—expected. It was Lyon's Saint-Exupéry Airport and what I saw through the not-so-clean window of my carriage was a strange, tall, white, curving metal construction, nothing like a good old 19th century European railway station. So I waited for the train to proceed to the actual centre of Lyon, straining to understand a barely audible announcement crackling out through the loudspeaker, first in French, then in English.

When a moment later I received an SMS that read "*Where are you??*"—yes, with a double question mark—I instantly knew I'd stuffed up. This *was* my stop! By the time I jumped off my seat in a panic and rushed to grab my suitcase, the train was already gliding forth and, abandoning its erstwhile unhurried style, picked up a very high speed indeed. Now this was a proper TGV, which would shoot into Paris in two hours without stopping. I fell back into my seat, a hot flush coming over me. I understood, with visceral exactitude, the phrase 'my heart sank.'

A few moments later I jumped up again and rushed to the uniformed conductor for advice. *No, the train will not stop anywhere before Paris*. He did not even try to hide his amusement behind professional politeness. To make things worse, he insisted I spoke French, the torture that the French often inflict on foreigners (I dare say, usually French men on foreign women). Stammering in my rusty French in that distressed state made me feel even stupider.

He kindly offered the cheapest ticket Lyon-Paris.

Resigned to my fate, I took the closest available seat next to a young Senegalese-French man, in Paris for more than ten years. Chatting with Abdoul was calming and comforting while we were covering those 441 unwanted kilometres. The conversation soon turned sociological. He confided about being a little sad about 'being a black person in a white society,' but he was getting used to it. He generously offered to take me to his cousin who had a spare room, but I decided to stay as close as possible to the *Gare de Lyon* for as painless as possible return to my intended destination.

Upon arrival at the famous old station with no lifts or escalators that I could find, I learned that the SNCF provided free overnight accommodation in empty carriages for passengers who changed trains in Paris, provided they had a valid ticket for their next train trip. I forewent this offer too and decided to look for a proper bed in a hotel room.

In Paris at 10pm, *involuntarily* and worn-out—having risen at 4.30am—I dejectedly dragged my suitcase, wrecking its wheels on the Parisian pavement. The first and second hotels I entered were full to the last room. The second one was an upmarket Novotel, so I used their perfect bathroom to brush my teeth and otherwise get ready for bed, short of putting on my pyjamas. Back on the street—by now it was 11pm—I was losing hope of finding a bed.

But then I heard a voice addressing me in English: "Do you need a room?" Yes, I surely do! A young Arabic-looking man smiled his perfect teeth at me from the doorstep of a small hotel with an inconspicuous entrance and a tiny reception desk. The attraction of the idea of horizontality overrode all other considerations; this was not an occasion to be choosy. It was a cheap hotel, by central-Parisian standards. My room had a bathroom unrenovated since circa 1965. Just saying—at that point I really did not care. It was clean.

Well past midnight I finally collapsed into bed and fell asleep. A couple of hours later, I was awakened by a racket in the hotel's backyard, right under my third-floor window. This was a parking yard of garbage trucks starting their nocturnal mission in the small hours of the morning. I'm not a great sleeper, so any further attempt to sleep was futile. My Lyon-bound TGV was leaving at 5am. As a thin silver lining, I was within walking distance of it.

At 4.15am I left the hotel, having forgotten two pieces of clothing there. Ugh! I'd love to erase 28 June 2011 from my memory. For some years I remained mildly traumatised: being reminded of this unintended visit to Paris caused an unpleasant jolt in my stomach each time.

Paris, involuntary visit #0.5

The one-half (#1.5 if that makes sense) unwanted visit to Paris happened in 2013. I was in Spain, or rather Catalonia (which would prefer not to be in Spain, it seems) and Barcelona airport was on strike. I would not make it to Frankfurt on time to catch my intercontinental flight, so after many hours of waiting at the airport and being sent from pillar to post, I was rerouted. I would catch another flight, from Paris. The connecting flight delivered me to Orly, 90 minutes *en retard*. Trying to reach CDG (Charles de Gaulle Airport) on time led me to *La Gare d'Austerlitz*, a station built in 1838 and in 1997 designated as a historical monument. A well-deserved honour, but this means no upgrades, no escalators or lifts. In the 19th century, people who travelled by train had servants, and station porters were keen to carry their trunks, beauty cases and hat boxes for a good tip. Not so in the 21st century! Luckily, Frenchmen are *très galants*. My heavy suitcase was snatched from my hand and, with a turn of the head and a smile, deposited a few seconds later on top of a flight of stone stairs. *Voilà!* Patriarchy is occasionally pleasant.

The suburban train to the CDG looked old and dilapidated, matching in style the station of origin, and quite slow. Poor ol' Europe! Next, my ticket didn't work, but I managed to squeeze through the station barriers out of sheer desperation. I arrived at the airport flustered and stressed. I ran to my gate dragging a largish suitcase and ignoring my bladder's urgent demands. Oh, the fun never ceases in Paris! I managed to buy a coffee and a croissant on the run though. The first thing I'd eaten that morning, at 11am, munching and slurping eagerly at the boarding queue.

I thought once again: what constitutes the attraction of travel? One has to keep a clenched-teeth focus most of the time; there is no moving through space on automatic pilot with only 10-20 per cent of one's brain capacity used, like at home. So many tense and uncomfortable moments! I remember reading an article years ago where the advice was 'try a holiday at home, doing as little as possible, it's relaxing and affordable.' A good piece of advice! But I suffer from two diseases that prevent me from following it: travel itch and workaholism.

Paris, involuntary visit #2
The second time, in 2014, I travelled to Paris for an Australian friend's sake. A woman in her early 50s at the time, she had never been to continental Europe. Immediately after uttering a spontaneous Eurocentric 'wow,' I realised that visiting Europe was not a universal obligation. As her European hostess of a sort, I felt compelled to ask what part of Europe she'd like to visit, apart from our primary destination, Provence for a cycling tour. Of course, she said 'Paris.'

'Isn't that *the* place to go to in Europe?

'Yes, it is,' I had to admit. 'Let's go there then!'

Sigh.

But there was a great and pleasant surprise waiting for me there: Parisian drivers are remarkably patient with rambling cyclists, usually tourists who are not sure where they're going hence prone to sudden manoeuvres. I was one of them, at one point crossing four lanes of traffic and slowing a river of cars down to a crawl without anyone so much as tooting at me. Thank you, good burghers of Paris (don't try this in Australia if you value your life).

Just as I developed some cycling confidence on a heavy bike-share ('Vélib'= 'Vélo'+'Liberté') machine with three gears, I found myself wrong-headed in a one-way street without the *sauf vélos* sign.

The street was short and deserted of cars and pedestrians so I took my chances. But in an instant and out of absolutely nowhere two *gendarmes* materialised next to me and addressed me in sharp tones while crowding me somewhat threateningly. I apologised in French, upon which they insisted I continued speaking French. They were not satisfied by my repentance and demanded to see my ID. Ten seconds later, upon seeing my Australian driving licence, they produced, in unison, an 'aaaahh' sound, waved their respective hands dismissively, lost all interest in me and disappeared as magically as they had appeared.

To this day I am uncertain why my Australian identity set me free. A friend offered this theory: the French hate the British and despise Americans; upon realising I was of neither of the blacklisted nationalities, they decided my minor traffic offence was not worth bothering with. Another friend added: they actually love Aussie (a long story… from the First World War).

Our cycling week in Provence was quite eventful too. We were given bikes, and Marco, our Venetian guide who spoke all main European languages fluently, transported our luggage in a van from town to town. We had a paper map with a marked route and we stuck to it—still no smart phone. Yet, the cycling distances stated in the brochure were far exceeded each day. On the third day my knees started complaining. Provence is hilly and not the easiest place to meander through on a touristy route meant to take you *everywhere*. I compared the actual with the planned kilometres, and it turned out that the Italians who franchised this packaged holiday from the British miscalculated—or rather, did not calculate at all. They turned British miles into continental European kilometres 1:1! I gave Marco a piece of my mind about this and demanded to be driven to Avignon. He agreed in a split second. I hopped into the van with him, which saved my sore knees from cycling 80 kms. Marco chucked my touring bike in the back of the van, on top of suitcases. He may not have been a numbers man, but he was fun to travel with. We discussed art and linguistics.

My Australian friend did not have any issues with overtime cycling. It was revealed only then that she had been a cycling champion in her youth. It still showed! While she covered the uphills steadily turning the pedals devastatingly effortlessly, I'd push pedals like mad for a maximum speed, Melbourne road-cyclist style, then my lungs and legs would betray me and I'd walk the bike uphill, embarrassed and regretting I was not one of those people who spend their holidays in a beach lounge reading a book.

My day saved from cycling was spent exploring Avignon. I went to see the Pope's Palace, a huge, forbidding, empty edifice. The only amusing bit was an exhibition of erotic paintings in one of the many large halls. The secular French are known to like showing the middle finger to religion, and the Pope, ever since the French revolution.

Having finished with the Pope quite quickly, I went to pay a fan visit to the grave of John Stuart Mill in the vast Avignon cemetery, probably larger than the medieval walled city itself. In spite of the map I was given at the entrance, I had to return and ask the concierge for help. He drove me there and waited for me while I took a couple of quick snaps.

The great man—John Stuart Mill, even though the cemetery's concierge may have been a great man too—declared the English to be a 'nation of shopkeepers,' in case you wondered who said that, and moved to the south of France to live out of wedlock with Mrs Taylor who was still married to Mr Taylor.

The French have never been squeamish about such things. More recently, President Mitterrand had a wife and a mistress and children with each lady, and it did not make as much as a dent in his political career. If anything, it portrayed him as a true representative of the people. Mill and his adored Missus were buried together in Avignon—my type of romanticism, which is best practised post-mortem. The clever Mrs Taylor inspired a thought in her partner that women may not be naturally stupider than men. The result was the only famous feminist book written by a man (*The Subjection of Women,* 1869). Forgive me, this little digression was irresistible.

My next problem was a bad smell in my hotel room in Arles, the Provençal town famous for being home to Vincent van Gogh in his artistically most productive year. Sniffing about for the source of the stench led to my suitcase, more precisely its wheels thoroughly smeared with dog poo. Ugh! I rushed to the reception to borrow some cleaning utensils, but the young receptionist was adamant she should clean the mess herself. She profusely apologised in the name of the nation, explaining that the French, annoyingly, didn't give a toss about collecting after their dogs. The nice *mademoiselle* cleaned the wheels promptly and thoroughly. Unlike Australians, whose behaviour is mostly predictable (polite, with an all-purpose smile), with the French one is on a rollercoaster.

The next day we embarked on the Arles-Paris train, via Lyon, and I tried to repress my erstwhile travel trauma. In this mostly flat part of France, a nuclear power plant north of Lyon was the most impressive thing to be seen from the hurtling train.

On the train Arles-Paris, past a nuclear power plant

Our Parisian Airbnb was a tiny *mansarde* six floors up a steep stairwell, no lift—a total cliché. Luckily, the owner helped with suitcases.

A typical view from a Parisian Airbnb

I volunteered to sleep in an 'upstairs' bedroom, right under the roof, accessed by the steepest winding ladder one can still step on. Descending to the loo during the night was risking one's life. The first thing in the morning was hitting my head on the roof beam which was not a full metre above my bed at its highest point. Did I say 'bed'? It was a mattress on the floor.

Vélib saved my legs from the sightseeing fatigue, but so many bikes were faulty that we had to conclude that the national stereotypes have more than a grain of truth in them (my Frankfurt experience: nearly all city bikes in perfect working order). At some Vélib stations it was hard to find a functioning bike or return one properly, which is necessary to avoid extra charges. The weather was totally perfect though.

It was the start of October, with summer temperatures, and one day we had an impromptu *pique-nique* of takeaway baguette sandwiches in the Jardin de Luxembourg, while Parisians worshipped the autumn sun.

Parisians enjoying the autumn sun in Jardin de Luxembourg

French baguettes are the only white bread on planet Earth worth eating and croissants are superb in the whole of France. Other offerings to tourists are far from foolproof; Parisian hospitality is corrupted by tourist hordes, as is anywhere else where visitors are a dime a dozen. On my first youthful visit to Paris, I ate the worst pizza in my whole life in a Parisian café.

The incident with the police described above actually happened while I was *en route* to another cemetery, Père Lachaise, on another fan visit to a dead celebrity. At Père Lachaise, one is spoilt for choice. I stumbled upon the kissed-over grave of Oscar Wilde (encased in glass so the fans cannot leave lipstick smudges on the grave, so instead the glass is covered with them, no doubt contrary to public hygiene); simple and modest but bouquets-covered graves of Edith Piaf and Marcel Proust; a tall but rather forgotten-looking grave of Honoré de Balzac. *Etc.* I would have liked to say hello to young Jim Morrison, but it was only with a dogged effort that I found the grave I had actually come to see, that of my favourite sociologist, Pierre Bourdieu. Apologies, that's a bit niche! I took a photo for my university staff page captioned *He's dead but I'm alive*. This cheerful looking grave stood out from the general solemnity.

So, for an unwanted five days in Paris, it was not too bad! It ended with a hectic and tense departure because it turned out that 'in front of the Opera House' was not a precise-enough location of the airport bus stop—*duh*! It's a large building!

Paris, involuntary visit #3

I found myself in Paris again in December 2020. A bad time to travel, for a bad reason. My father had a severe stroke and died six days later. Rushing overseas was not a thing at the height of the COVID-19 pandemic; I was one day too late to find him alive. After all the sad business was over, the only way to return to locked-up Australia was to book one of the Qantas 'repatriation flights.' The one I managed to book was a flight Paris-Darwin. *Paris-Darwin*! How does that sound?

Upon arriving in Paris from Zagreb, I first had to join a Covid-19-test queue. Waiting for cotton sticks to be pushed up my nostrils again—longer ones than in Croatia, I noticed.

Paris in deep December, less than a week from the winter solstice. Due to being only two degrees east of London but in the middle-European time zone, the daybreak was not until after 8am. The fuzzy sun rose at 8.45am. I spent two depressing days in an airport hotel at CDG awaiting the COVID-19 test result. Through the drizzle I could see the surrounding nondescript office buildings and streetscape that could belong to any city in the world. Spending most of the day in the hotel room was like being suspended in time. In the afternoon the sun shone through the mist and I decided to shake off the gloom by getting some fresh air outside, with limited success. Has a brisk walk around Air France's Headquarters ever cheered up anyone?

On the day of departure, 16 December 2020, I woke up from a disturbing dream two minutes before the phone alarm. On my very last ascent to my first-floor room with my breakfast tray I finally figured how to operate the lift. Travelling is an extended intelligence test. It reminded me of my first visit to Switzerland, at the tender age of 20, where I discovered there was a mind-boggling variety of ways to flush a toilet.

After consuming yet another perfect croissant far too quickly, I dragged my 30-kilos suitcase up a flight of stairs that divided the hotel from the road and rushed to the Roissy Station. By sheer luck, I hopped onto the correct shuttle and made it to Gate 2E. The security check took about half an hour; most bags were checked in incredible detail. What does COVID-19 have to do with the airport security? From the start to the end of this dismal trip, I had a feeling that passengers having the bad luck to have to travel at this time were somehow suspect.

The gate was densely populated by face-masked Australians, and the boarding queue was moving at a glacial pace. And then, amidst the tedium, a young French woman appeared out of nowhere offering everyone those fabulous Lindt chocolate bombs. Some poor souls refused, to my advantage. After I took one and released a happy squeal, she offered me another and could I refuse? I ate both at once; chocolate is good stress relief and an anti-depressant.

Next, we were packed like sardines into a bus, four people per square metre of space, and taken to the Qantas 'Spirit of Australia' (don't believe it!) plane painted all over in pictorial Aboriginal art (that was nice). At the end of the bus ride the door opened and an official told us, in a French-accented English, to make sure we 'keep a sanitary distance of one meter from each other.' Laughter rippled through the travelling public. Once out of the bus, a chilly wind blew through my jeans. In anticipation of Australian tropics, some Aussies were already in shorts and short sleeves.

We landed at the military airport and through a police cordon boarded a bus to Howard Springs, a FIFO camp turned into a Covid-19 quarantine site. Here, even longer sticks were pushed up our noses before we were escorted to our 3x3.5m rooms. We were detained for two weeks; food delivered once a day in plastic boxes with disposable cutlery. No toaster or microwave, only a kettle. Mountains of rubbish that 'could not be recycled because of Covid-19'(?). Being involuntarily in Darwin, locked up too, I was dead sure I'd rather be in Paris.

Everything is relative and a matter of perspective.

An Old Lady and a Cow
Graham Meyers

What follows is a true story, but I was only given the bare bones of it by the son-in-law of one of the men concerned. I have tried to put flesh on those bones to show the simultaneous good and bad in humanity.

The year is 1940. On the outskirts of a tiny Polish village, an old lady is sitting by the roadside, crying softly. She is thin and dressed in rags. Two young Luftwaffe officers approach. Hans and Willem stop and ask the woman what is wrong.

"They have taken my cow. I have nothing left. My family – all gone, and now my only cow."

She continues to weep and the men look at each other.

"Who took it?"

"Soldiers. German soldiers. They had been drinking." The men exchange a look. They both abhor the mistreatment of civilians, and this is clearly theft. One of the officers gets an idea. He asks,

"What colour were their uniforms?" If the thieves had black SS uniforms, there is nothing the young pilots can do.

"Ah, grey. There were too many. I try to stop them, I say please no, but they push me away!"

The woman is speaking in Polish, so the two converse in German. Those low Wehrmacht bastards!

"Are you thinking what I'm thinking, Hans?"

"Yeah, if we could find them maybe?"

"We can only try."

The woman is exhausted, resting her head on her knees. Willem leans down and touches her bony shoulder. She looks up.

"Maybe we can find your cow. Wait here."

The officers walk off, apprehensive about what they are getting themselves into. They head in the general direction of the Wehrmacht barracks in an abandoned church. Near a still-functional bar, a group of men in uniform are talking and laughing. Some are drunk. In the middle of the crowd there is a brown and white cow. Several of the soldiers seem to be trying to sell the animal to others.

The two airmen look around for commissioned Wehrmacht officers. There seems to be only two corporals. At the approach of the commissioned pilots most of the talk stops.

"Good day to you, gentlemen. Nice cow – where did you get it?"

"We found her. She was lost and asked for directions." Some smirk at this, but nobody laughs.

"You realise that theft of private property is forbidden?"

"Yeah, but like I said sir, the cow has no owner."

"We have spoken to the owner who says you stole the cow."

"She's lying then, these Poles are all liars."

"If you found the cow, how did you know the owner is a woman?"

It begins to dawn on the soldiers that the animal could be more trouble than it's worth.

The airmen seize the moment and announce, with as much authority as they can muster,

"If you hand the cow over now it will save us all a lot of trouble."

The man holding the cow's halter hesitates, then grins at his compatriots.

"Ah, shit. Take it away then flyboy!"

"I will ignore your insolence for now, soldier. In future you will be careful how you speak to a senior officer."

The two pilots take the cow's halter and lead her away, back toward the edge of the village.

The woman is still by the roadside. She sees the lads approaching and hobbles out to meet them.

"My God, you were sent from heaven! How can I thank you enough! Your parents will be very proud of you, such good boys!"

Somewhat embarrassed, the pilots suggest that in future she keep the cow out of sight.

"Thankyou. Yes, I know some people can't be trusted, but you boys are from heaven, truly!"

Hans and Willem start to walk away but she follows them.

"I have something for you. It is a small thing, but it has been blessed by a saint. It was given to me by a Bishop many years ago."

She removes a string from around her neck. On the string there hangs a small brass medallion. The disc has the image of a saint on one side and a Cyrillic inscription on the other.

"Thank you, but you keep it. It must mean a lot to you."

"No, no! You need it to keep you safe in this awful war!"

She pushes it into Willem's hand and closes his fingers around it.

"Carry it with you always, it will protect you. God bless you both!"

* * *

Oberleutnant Willem Becker was later transferred to a fighter unit in France. He carried the medallion with him on every mission, since it reminded him of something other than the death and destruction of war. He did not believe that it had special powers, but on the only occasion he forgot to put it in his flying-suit pocket he was ambushed by enemy fighters and shot down. He survived and emigrated to Australia in the 1950s.

THE MAGIC OF WINTER
Kathleen Bentley

A carpet of diamonds twinkle and glow across the lawn
Caught by the morning sun.
The frost gathered during darkness to brighten the dawn
Melts in the suns warmth - its job done.

Soon the snows will come to whiten the land.
A new vista to explore -
A new world established by an unseen hand -
Discovering plants, animals and more…

Watching a bright full moon climbing the dark night sky,
Stars vibrantly gleaming.
Toasting marsh mellows before a roaring fire.
And mugs of hot toddy consumed before dreaming.

But diving into a warm bed, clutching a hot water flask
Makes the whole day worthwhile.
Except to anticipate the snow – what more could you ask?
To sleep and awaken to a white world. In my sleep I smile.

THREE VIEWS ON DERELICTION
Jennie Herrera

EYESORES

'Bloody eyesore if you ask me! They should—'
'Course they should!' And then eyesores diverge;
was a bustling place once but industry moved on,
got sent offshore, got changed, got automated, got …
and the shape of factories changed. This one rearing
over heavy ruts and piled scrap, its girders rust-red
against the sky, its roofing collapsed inward, junked.
They should. Course they should. But who should,
whose world depends on change, who should pay
and for what, when industry's gone somewhere else,
somewhere far away …

Weeds with heavy seedheads thrive in spring with
run-off and ruts as mini dams, and birds nesting in
safe angles where struts meet. Butterflies drift
across the sunny space and make no judgement
on human failure. And moths at night. A line of ants
going … where, unmolested, and a watching beetle,
iridescent. A stray cat finding shelter behind
a tank empty of … empty of … But none of these
small denizens record the slow demise, the final
shabby agreement, the last men out the gates,
none divined this peace …

Concerted clamouring concerned neighbours,
fairly close neighbours—'it's dangerous, might
lure kids in there, just little curious eyes, just
wanting to explore or a quick vape out of sight,
and if the company won't clean up—guess it's us,
guess it's money best spent and can be offset by—
if they won't come to the table, a forced sale, it can
be done, don't hide behind council rules, is it so hard
to turn abandonment into something, anything,
even just a decent fence and padlocks on the gates,
course it can be done …

THE UNWANTED

Slam the gate with tortured logo and look around.
Fine big sign still bright. Potential. Great word to use and use.
Awful sight. Look north and south. Rust and more rust.
But … potential. Everything has potential. Just …

From small bustling sheds it grew, it grew,
peaked and failed and died, in grease-filled pain, yet foreswore
death and waited for blame-laying … oh, public pickiness,
offshore offers, all of that, fads, frights, fickleness …

Boys sneaking in, that wide expanse waiting, inviting,
for skateboarding, never mind the cracks and wiry weeds,
and signs for absent security firms. So—who cares?
set a fire, throw a rock, those pointless pressed-on dares.

Call upon the eternal, if someone, no one, somewhere
turns a back, when council men come by to check and note,
to watch streaming rain, stained brown at first and then
oily rainbow shades, can't pass it safe and well, those men.

Tempted naturally. Be done with. Sell off. But a ghostly
finger taps on corporate unconcern, that space, take care, lawyers
have hungers. The un-divine, as wind rattles sheets of holy tin,
and cautious sparrows brave raftered webs, chicks ushered in.

A feral cat seeking sanctuary somewhere there,
avoiding grease and toxic smells, stepping daintily where once
a bottle blonde, handed out with dainty nails, men's pay
and smiled and watched them sign their health away.

The sound of uncanny feet trudging through empty sheds,
loading bays, backing forklifts, raucous noise, against machinery
through caverns of unwantedness. Tap and thump, think back,
not how it was but how it will be; the developer's knack …

Return to a light bright office space, with sites galore,
waiting, the right option, the package deal, the price depressed,

a place re-defined, not for birds and strays, ants, sliding things,
but the massaged hope, honed, air-brushed, selling, sings.

And then the seeping sadness intervenes, even bored kids
go elsewhere. This portion of once good earth slinks away unsold
and the cheery bonus-driven staff park and stretch and hesitate,
words on their lips falter, die. Let nature intervene. We'll wait …

MESS

Do we love the land that's suffered,
the land that shows the scars, that lies
gouged and sick. Or do we turn away.
'What a mess!'
Not quite shame, we didn't do …
but, somehow, indirectly, we did …
we wanted, we asked, we assumed.
'We? Speak for yourself!'

Yes, we. And my question hangs—
the pits of oily water, the stinking,
toxic mess no one wants, that sees
the baton passed.
Our baton, your baton, you will reach out?
You won't? No, I didn't think—always
the other, out there, carting, making, selling …
you sought, bought—you—*and me*—

Can we love the land left behind? Find
in a pebble, a rainbow slick, a blade of tiny
green … can we love or have we left it
beyond loving?
Can we go past the contamination,
the soiled sadness, to ask of it, pardon,
pity, and lay over it rest and waiting time,
hoping that by loving we heal?

Escape from the Volcano
How I escaped but thousands did not.
Denys Ririka

{Editor's note: Initially, this story was told by Denys's father. Denys heard it many times and enjoyed it every time, hence his desire to repeat it here}

In 1951 I was attending a workshop for teacher/evangelists at Martyrs school Sangara Northern Province, P.N.G. which is below Mt Lamington. The mountain was an old volcano that had been dormant for many years, and the soil was very rich, so the district was heavily populated with about ten to twelve large villages surrounding the mountain.

Our workshop was going well, and we were not too worried when the volcano started rumbling, and smoke started coming, as the government was constantly sending messages to say it was nothing to worry about. The rumblings were, however, getting more frequent but none of the local elders had experienced an eruption and so did not have any real forebodings. When people saw the smoke they said;

"Sumbiripa (Mt Lamington) must be hungry, baking taro."

They saw it as a being, not just a mountain.

On Saturday 20th Jan, George and I were sent out to different villages some kilometres away to conduct the Sunday morning service on the 21st. I went to Sasembata at the foot of the mountain with my two young children, as my wife was twelve kilometres away at the coastal hospital at Gona for delivery of our fourth child and she had our third child, a toddler, with her. George was sent to Waseta further away west from the mountain.

Just as the service finished, we heard louder rumblings from the mountain and then there was an eerie silence, no bird songs and no other animal sounds, and then a huge bang louder than anything we had heard before. Looking up to the mountain there was a massive spout of smoke and lava. In the panic reaction there was a shout of; *"Run!!"* I grabbed my two children and together we ran down the slope as fast as we could. I lifted my smaller child (Andrew) onto my shoulders and took Charlotte's hand. She saw her friend, Grace, running ahead and shook off my grip, so I let her run off with her friend and many others and shouted *"Go to Waseta Station."* With Andrew on my shoulder, I could not keep up with them but was going as fast as I could. With a left turn I went to Peromba near Agenahambo.

I hoped Charlotte was safe, but did not know until later. At midday it turned dark as the smoke covered the sun, stones from the mountain were falling so we went under one of the houses that was built on stilts. I crouched with Andrew on one knee. About three pm while rumbling continued, smoke was still coming and embers still falling, a bird flew in and sat on my arm. By that sign I felt that my brother and his family that we had left behind, had departed; that they were victims of the disaster. I later found this was so.

The two mission sisters at Sasembata could not run, so I had advised them to cover themselves with wet blankets and shelter under their beds. They survived, but those who were burnt by the flowing lava and blast were killed.

The bang was heard hundreds of kilometres away and the smoke could be seen by many. The explosion had gone out the side of the mountain destroying many villages and killing around 5,000 people. It was the lava and heat from it that killed people. Many were stumbling away with their skin peeled off calling for water. They had a drink and then lay down and died. It was a scene that was just too horrible.

Mt Lamington – just after the eruption in 1951

My wife delivered that same day at the coastal hospital, which was well away from danger, but she knew nothing of my escape; she could only worry, wait and pray. The medical staff from Gona and Popondetta rushed up to do what they could for survivors and were able to give some relief to those who were dying from severe burns, but many had been killed by the initial blast, and nothing could be done for them.

The next day I was concerned for the two sisters that I had left at Sasembata and so left Andrew with family friends and walked off with a bush knife along the track back to the disaster area. Many trees were down across the road and the smaller ones I could move. When I came across a large tree that was too big for my bush knife and I was contemplating what to do, an old man appeared beside the road with a large old string bag hanging on his shoulder and a new axe in his hand. He said; "Here son, I think you need this, give it back to me later, I know you." He just disappeared and I never saw him again, I firmly believe he was an angel sent by God in my time of need, for I had just cleared the first part of the road when Rod Hart came up with his vehicle loaded with a group of able-bodied young men to see what they could do.

Many people came from Kokoda and the coast to help, and from Australia. It was church, and government facilities and village people who were affected – so many people, relatives and friends, including all who were there at the workshop, but George and I were spared.

Every wet season when there is thunder, I remember that day and tears form in my eyes.

My son, born that day, I named Denys after one of the clergymen, Rev. Denys Taylor, who died in the blast.

THE SONG I WROTE -- MT LAMINGTON LAMENT.

Nango einda Sangara da, dada ewora e
Naso nano-namendide, usari nati e

> *CHORUS*
> *Nango jo e, nango jo e, Bada iso ingoda e*

Iso itari diri da, matu nango gae

Bada iteso bugira, nango dududu e

Imo Mamo utu topo, iso memei gi e
Paradaisi da torero iso parara da

Diri wasiri etira, ungoi petetera
Ungoda kinapeina de, inono torero.

English Translation
Sangara was the usual gathering place for my brothers for meetings and refresher courses.

    Chorus   Mercy upon us, mercy upon us, we are in Your hands.

Your creation of the mountain that we knew nothing about,
We knew nothing about its purpose; we were shocked.

You are Lord of the heavens, look down at your children here
Departed to paradise into your everlasting light.

When the mountain shook, they and their families stayed where they were
They and their children and their families together have gone into paradise in the light of your presence.

What I never told them
Edith Speers

I knew the place. It was the same place where my big brother threw the stone in my dream.

In my dream I was standing in a field. It was a vacant lot. Two birds flew over the field. My brother threw a stone at the two birds and they both fell out of the air. Then I remembered that yesterday he said to someone; "I killed two birds with one stone." Also, I woke up from the dream.

But this wasn't the dream anymore. I had the dream back in Cranbrook and now we were in Vancouver. My family moved when I was six years old, so my dad could find work. This was the first time I walked out of our new house and down the back alley. But I knew the place. It was the same field.

I felt scared and I never told anybody.

There but for the grace of . . .
Anne Layton-Bennett

another year over and the future looks bleak
we're at war with ourselves and each other
as displaced people everywhere
are eager to seek
peace and safety away from the bombs
and the bullets
that shatter their homes
yet their resilience
shines in the maelstrom
of turmoil and despair

we watch in horror at their refusal to yield
numbed by a screen that acts as a shield
against the tension and anticipation
yet knowing each day brings more
misery and murder and destruction
but they know – they can see -
the cameras are rolling
and they hope we'll be moved
enough to care because they also know
or suspect perhaps
that tomorrow, or the next day
or perhaps the day after that
we, could become them

From HI to NI *via* AI
Allan Jamieson

These days, whenever anyone asks me; 'How are you, Allan?' I reply, 'I'm vertical.' This short response is a whole lot simpler than saying; 'I'm OK, but I have no idea if I will be alive tomorrow.' That extended reply would bring with it a whole host of additional questions. If you don't know me, I am 84 yrs old and my pocket diary is full of doctor's appointments and dates for pathology samples to be taken, etc., etc..

I am travelling on a train. I know there is only one station up ahead, but I do not know when the train (and I) will reach it. What I do know, though, is that the station truly is THE END; I will no longer be vertical!

While it might appear to you that I have a morbid perspective, in fact I give thanks that I am on the train, because it means that I will not have to live through the emerging miasma of our disintegrating civilisation.

For all my life – up to roughly the end of the Twentieth Century – I was excited to experience the Human Intelligence (HI) era, when humanity exhibited characteristics indicating that humans were *human*: we could think, learn and try to understand events around us.

The onset of the Twenty-first Century clearly marked the end of the HI era.

What is taking its place is very evident today. The world now revolves around Artificial Intelligence (AI). Increasingly accepted as 'the best thing since sliced bread' or 'the bee's knees' AI is rapidly taking over from our former reliance on HI. No longer is a human being expected to know anything. AI is instantly accessible via the nearest mobile phone, and nobody needs to think any further. When AI has declared an opinion, the world 'runs with it.'

AI is not a human trait, but the world has already adapted to this. Ask yourself when was the last time you phoned any organisation to get an answer to the question you have – and *succeeded* in talking with a human being? Perhaps more relevant, can you even find the company's phone number now, one that does not 'ring out' when you try it? A website, yes, but this will be 'manned' by computers, not humans. Soon all organisations will 'know' that we humans readily accept that humans no longer know anything, so it is sufficient and cheaper for these businesses to respond to your phone call with a recorded message that bears no relation to what you wanted to find out!

I will give you a real example from 2024. Just a couple of years ago – not decades ago – if you wanted to book a hotel room in some city, you would phone the hotel and speak with a live person. No longer! Damn near all hotels worldwide have chosen to close their reservation service and hand the task to one or other <u>independent</u> groups that will boast of being able to reserve a room for you anywhere! There are dozens of such groups, and I strongly suspect that each one is AI-driven and has but one or two humans on its payroll. Each group has its own preferred list of hotels and there is no way that the AI algorithm will budge and book you into *your* preferred hotel. After all, you are a human and humans arc dumb.

<u>Tomorrow</u>

The internet is now flooded with websites providing examples of AI-usage and its ugly face. Here is just one such example (see 'box').

From https://www.bbc.com/news/articles/cp8k5gezykyo
How an AI-written book shows why the tech 'terrifies' creatives
By Zoe Kleinman 31 January 2025

Musicians, authors, artists and actors worldwide have expressed alarm about their work being used to train generative AI tools that then churn out similar content based upon it.

"We should be clear, when we are talking about data here, we actually mean human creators' life works," says Ed Newton Rex, founder of Fairly Trained, which campaigns for AI firms to respect creators' rights ... "The whole point of AI training is to learn how to do something and then do more like that."

In 2023 a song featuring AI-generated voices of Canadian singers Drake and The Weeknd went viral on social media before being pulled from streaming platforms, because it was not *their* work, and they had not consented to it. It didn't stop the track's creator trying to nominate it for a Grammy award.

"*Tech-Splaining for Dummies*" (great title) bears my name and my photo on its cover, and it has glowing reviews. Yet it was entirely

> written by AI … It's an interesting read, and very funny in parts … It mimics my chatty style of writing …
>
> My book was from BookByAnyone. When I contacted the chief executive Adir Mashiach, based in Israel, he told me he had sold around 150,000 personalised books, mainly in the US, since pivoting from compiling AI-generated travel guides in June 2024 … Legally, the copyright belongs to the firm, but Mr Mashiach stresses that the product is intended as a "personalised gag gift", and the books do not get sold further ... (yet) it's also a bit terrifying if, like me, you write for a living. Not least because it probably took less than a minute to generate, and it does, certainly in some parts, sound just like me.

Another example from the internet:

> [Ref. ttps://online.maryville.edu/blog/history-of-ai]
> May 19, 2023.
>
> AI now offers many benefits to our lives. They include:
> 1. Increasing efficiency of transportation
> 2. Limiting the need for human manual labor [*sic*]
> 3. Automating home care routines
> 4. Helping organizations [*sic*] make quicker, smarter decisions through data analytics
> 5. Improving the customer service experience
>
> The broadest delineation of AI is between narrow (all current AI systems) and general (all potential future AI systems).
> … General AI is sometimes referred to as "strong" AI. This category of AI does not exist currently, as any modern AI tool requires some level of human collaboration or maintenance. However, many developers continue to improve on the capabilities of their systems **in an effort to reach a level of effectiveness that will require less human intervention in the machine learning process.** [emphasis added – AJ]

That 5-point list does not leave much for any human being to excel at! Furthermore, it is demonstrable that the said 'benefits' are in fact 'deadly disasters.' Of course, the odd-balls who see only good in AI, are blind to human beings – we are just a dumb waste of space on the planet.

I don't know about you, but that list leads me to ask myself; 'Why get out of bed?'

The same webpage continues:

'AI tools can automate all sorts of tasks, whether they are mundane or complex, such as answering customer questions through a chatbot or analysing large volumes of data to help make predictions ... They can also try to predict what an employee or customer needs through recommendation engines to expedite their search experience.'

Oh, yes? Any such prediction would be useful(?) only if all humans thought alike.

'Transportation is an area where we're already seeing automation take hold. While local trains are often operated without a driver on board, we'll see more driverless cars and trucks on the roads. The positive outcome here will be the ability to minimize accidents, increase efficiency, and reduce stress on drivers.'

Hmmm! That assumes that humans are no longer venturing onto the road, and such a situation must precede any 'positive outcome.' Methinks I will take the train – or walk if there is no human driving it.

The authors of this webpage get tied in knots seeking to justify AI development.

'(W)e must always keep in mind the importance of ethics in this work. AI must serve everyone and not create undue harm in people's lives, for example by reducing employment opportunities through automation, increasing social isolation, or perpetuating bias.'

Bull!

The 'killer?' That website was simply seeking to persuade students to enrol in the university's online Master of Science in Artificial Intelligence and AI certificate programs. 'Through focused higher education and training in this future-oriented [*sic*] field, you can be a part of creating a more technologically advanced world for all.'

It is a mistake to think that we are now at the start of an AI era. It is, at best, a momentary adjustment from HI to NI (No Intelligence). Maybe NI will become an era, though I suspect *every human alive today* is already on <u>my</u> train – they simply do not realise this – and their days are numbered.

The Call
Bethamy Nader

The phone buzzed insistently on the kitchen counter, pulling Jennie away from the lukewarm coffee she was nursing. She glanced at the display ... Dr. Nader's office. A knot tightened in her stomach. Justin had been feeling under the weather lately, a persistent tiredness that clung to him like a shadow. The doctor had ordered blood tests earlier in the week. She'd been trying to tell herself it was just a virus, maybe low iron.

She swiped to answer. "Hello this is Jennie Walsh speaking." A polite professional voice responded, "Good Morning Mrs Walsh. This is Sarah from Dr. Nader's office. The doctor would like to speak with you regarding Justin's blood tests. "Please hold."

The music that filled the silence was irritating. Jennie tapped her foot nervously against the worn linoleum. She pictured Justin at school, probably drawing intricate spaceships in his notebook, lost in his own vibrant world.

Finally, Dr. Nader's voice crackled on the line. "Jennie, thank you for holding. I'm afraid I have some very difficult news to share regarding Justin's tests."

The knot in her stomach tightened into a suffocating fist. Jennie braced herself, but nothing could have prepared her for the words that followed.

"The tests have come back positive for acute lymphoblastic leukemia." "Mrs. Walsh, that's Bone marrow cancer."

Jennie's breath hitched. The words seemed to echo in the kitchen, distorted and impossibly wrong. A wave of dizziness washes over her, and she instinctively reaches for the counter to steady herself. Dr. Nader continued, his voice now laced with a somber tone. "Based on the staging, we estimate...he has approximately six months."

Six months. The phrase hung in the air, heavy and suffocating. Six months to pack a lifetime of love, laughter, and memories into a span of time that felt impossibly short. Jennie's throat closed up. She tried to speak, to ask questions, to deny what she was hearing, but her voice was trapped, a strangled sob caught in her chest. All that came out was a choked silent gasp.

Dr. Nader sensing her shock, spoke gently. "Jennie? Are you there? I understand this is incredibly difficult to process. We'll need to discuss treatment options and palliative care. I want you to know we'll be with you every step of the way."

But Jennie couldn't hear him anymore. The blood was pounding in her ears, drowning out his words. Her mind was a whirlwind, a chaotic tapestry of memories swirling around her.

Justin's birth – the first time she held him, his tiny fingers gripping hers with surprising strength. His first word a garbled, "Mama," that had sent a thrill of joy through her. His first steps, wobbly and unsteady, but filled with determination. The time he drew a picture of her as a superhero, complete with a flowing cape and a sparkling tiara. The countless bedtime stories, the scraped knees kissed better, the whispered secrets under the covers.

She saw him learning to ride his bike, the triumphant grin on his face as he finally wobbled off on his own. His passion for drawing, his incredible imagination that filled their small apartment with fantastical creatures and daring adventures. His kindness, his gentle heart that saw good in everyone.

Six months. How could this be happening? How could her bright vibrant son, who deserved a lifetime of happiness be given a death sentence?

The silence stretched on, broken only by Jennie's shallow, ragged breaths. Finally, Dr. Nader cleared his throat. "Jennie, I understand that you're in shock. I'm going to prescribe something to help with the shock. Can you hear me? Are you able to respond?"

Jennie remained silent; a statue frozen in grief. The world around her seemed to blur, the sounds fading into a distant murmur. All she could see was Justin's face, his bright blue eyes, his infectious smile.

She had to get to him. She had to hold him. She had to tell him…No, she couldn't tell him. Not yet. With newfound desperate strength, Jennie managed a choked whisper. "Yes---Yes, I'm here."

"Good." Dr. Nader said gently. "I'm going to give you some time to process this. Please call my office when you're ready, and we can schedule a time to discuss everything in detail."

He gave her instructions, but she barely registered them. She hung up the phone and stumbled out of the kitchen, her legs feeling like lead.

It was almost time to pick Justin up from school. The thought hit her like a psychical blow. She had to pretend that everything was normal, at least for a little while longer.

With trembling hands, she grabbed her purse and keys. As she walked out the door, she looked up at the sky, a vast indifferent blue. How could the world be so beautiful, so ordinary when her world was crumbling around her?

She drove in a daze, her mind a chaotic jumble of grief and denial. She pictured Justin waiting for her at the school gate, his backpack slung over his shoulder, his face lighting up when he saw her.

How could she tell him? How could she break his bright, innocent heart?

Pulling up at the school, she saw him standing by the gate, just as she had imagined. He was talking animatedly to a classmate, gesturing wildly with his hands. A smile flickered across his lips despite the pain that threatened to consume her.

Taking a deep breath, she forced herself to smile as she got out of the car. "Justin!" she called out, her voice trembling slightly. His head snapped up and his face lit up with a grin. "Mom!" He ran towards her, his small arms wrapping around her legs. "I finished my spaceship drawing today! It has laser cannons and warp drive!"

Jennie knelt down and hugged him tight, burying her face in his soft hair. She could feel the warmth of his body, the innocent trust in his embrace.

"That sounds amazing, sweetheart," she whispered, her voice thick with unshed tears. "I can't wait to see it."

As they walked hand-in-hand towards the car, Jennie looked at her son, at his bright, shining face, and a wave of despair washed over her. Six months. How could she possibly tell him that he only had six months?

She knew she had to be strong, for him. But right now, all she felt was a crushing, unbearable weight of grief. The world had just shattered, and she had to figure out how to pick up the pieces, knowing that no matter what she did, it would never be whole again.

Author Bethamy Lari Nader   2/3/2025

A White Magnolia
Brenda Slavoff

White is a beginning
  with no end
An unwritten page with a
  silence of possibilities
  opens its eyes.
So in a ballet of purity
  the first bud of magnolia,
  lit within by stars and moon,
    breaks the bonds of earth
    to dance in perfume
    eternally a day.
Angels whisper comfort
  as cold winds blow
  and grasp the loveliness
  of inevitable farewell.

Snippet of Love
Dawn Meredith

We were cuddling on the lounge, watching Time Team. My seven year old daughter looked up at me, gave me a shy smile and a look of happy love.

"I love you," she said.

I hugged her tight. "I love you too!"

After a few minutes of watching TV she asked, "Do you think Daddy loves me?"

I said, "What do you think?"

She replied, "I think so, but I don't know how much."

Something stirred in me, an image so beautiful it had to come out:

"Daddy loves you more than the sun and the moon and the stars put together; more than all the grains of sand on all the beaches in the world."

I could see her thinking about it, trying to figure out how much that was.

And on the opposite lounge I saw Daddy, with tears in his eyes.

The Deal
Leigh Swinbourne

A dowdy middle-class living room, lounge suite well past its prime, chipped laminated 'nest' of coffee tables, faded Impressionist prints, dusty lily gracing a sunny corner. One classy feature: Ted's bar, stylishly deco and fully stocked. He lowers his Saturday *Mercury* and abstractly appraises his surrounds, eyes habitually coming to rest on the glinting bottles. Six o'clock is his rule, amongst many, weekends notwithstanding. The front door. His wife, Marie, strides in, stirring the air and charging the atmosphere. Ted notes the cat's upright tale progress along the farther side of the coffee tables like a periscope, heading outside, instinct scenting trouble.

'Home a little early, darling.'

She stands there before him, not looking at him. No response.

'How was lunch with the gals?'

'OK, I guess.'

The tone is not good, not OK.

'Ted, have you rung the kids about tomorrow?'

'Not as yet. Neither is ever in on a Saturday afternoon anyway.'

'You can leave a message. Embarrassing.'

Here it comes. 'What?'

'Lunch. I just felt embarrassed the whole time.'

'Why, for God's sake?'

'Why do you think?'

Ted places his paper on his lap with a stagey sigh, and considers his options. Is she after a fight or will she settle for sympathy?

'Let me guess. Endless airy talk of atrium extensions and expensive face lifts, a bit on here and a bit off there, and then of course there are those long mandatory hours at the hair salon, at the solarium, never enough hours in the day... Am I right? More money than sense those two. Honestly darling, I've got to tell you the last time I ran into Emily Rutherford she looked like a sculpture of varnished wood. Even her hair!'

Marie smiles at this. Good. She settles on the lounge, still not looking at him, her face inward with thought. A catch in Ted's throat, after twenty years of marriage he still loves and desires his wife. She is smartly dressed in a tight-fitting olive woollen dress, her figure is fine, a little thick at the hips from child-bearing, complexion fresh, hair chestnut and abundant in a loose girlish ponytail, some strands of grey, but still. He's falling behind here. His height helps, always has, but he's carrying a bit of a gut. Needs to get out of the armchair more.

'Emily's is not a good look, that I'll grant you. But honestly Ted, just to sit there while the two of them prattle away about things they know I'm not part of and never can be. But then what the hell! If you've got it flaunt it! Wish I could.'

'Weren't you all going to see a film or something? Couldn't they talk about that?'

'Oh yes, great looking people in Manhattan apartments. They talked plenty about it, Helen's thinking of upgrading her flat in Melbourne. Stop and think for one moment what it's really like for me with those two. Jesus Ted, we couldn't even afford to keep our old house at Sandy Bay.'

'Come on, let's not trawl over all that. So we can't afford a flat in Melbourne. You're a friend darling. I'm sure they don't give it a second thought.'

'I give it a second thought!'

She starts pacing the room, rubbing her hands down her sides. Ted would love to take her in his arms, comfort her, console her, but she won't have him like this. On the bar is a portrait of their children, aged five and seven, in front of the Sandy Bay bungalow, now a block of flats. Marie picks it up and inclines her head wistfully.

'God I miss that house,' she says, more to herself than him. 'Do you remember in the summertime when we'd put the kids to bed, and we still had an hour of dusk, sitting out on the balcony with our drinks and watching the boats in the river. The evening breeze would rise and catch the sails and those boats would just fly Ted, remember, so free, so lovely and free! It seems like an age ago, another life.'

'It was an age ago. Look, it was a great house, but in the end we just couldn't afford it with the kids' education and all.'

She places the portrait back carefully and turns to him, her face dark.

'I don't know, all along I had some, obviously crazy, notion that once the kids were off our hands things would finally pick up for us. So here we have Bill and Alison both comfortably settled in their careers, thank God, independent and happy, the world their oyster, and here we have the sponsors, Ted and Marie, stuck in a nondescript suburb in a nondescript semi and still mortgaged for Christ's sake! How is that possible?'

He needs to stand now, use his height.

'Because, let's be fair here Marie, from your absolutely unbendable point of view, nothing, *nothing*, was too good for our children's education.'

'Which is why they've both got great jobs.'

'Also why you've got rich friends.'

'Maybe not for long now the kids aren't involved anymore.'

He walks over and places his hands firmly on her upper arms. She avoids his eyes.

'So what does it matter? We spent the money and you got what you wanted for it. Marie, you cannot have your cake and eat it too.'

Now she looks up, tears glistening. With what seems like an immense effort of will, he resists crushing her to him.

'Others seem to. Helen's just returned from Noumea, and Emily's bought herself a little red convertible. Because they don't live exactly around the corner, I was running a bit late, and out of the corner of my eye I saw the two of them watch me park the Hyundai. That's what I mean by embarrassing. You went through Law School with both their husbands, and you got better grades, so I'm told. For some reason it always comes up in conversation.'

'Why get rid of a car that works perfectly well?'

'Because it's old and daggy. I am so sick of old and daggy, Ted.'

He moves behind the bar and, taking his time—piling the ice, slicing the lime, letting the ritual calm the air—fixes her a stiff gin-and-tonic. The juniper scent is wonderful.

'Here, have this.'

She takes the tumbler from him wordlessly, and drinks it like a medicine.

'Colin gives Emily her cars so she won't question his affairs, you told me, and Helen complained to you how Ken has been up again before the Real Estate Review Board. Look, I don't envy what those men do, never have, so I don't envy what they earn.'

'I envy what they earn! I'm not talking about being shonky, I'm talking about ambition, a bit of get-up-and-go. Now *you* be fair

Ted, you've been in the same bloody job for years, same company. Good old Steinberg. It's like you're rusted on to him.'

'I wanted to go to the Bar, you know, but we couldn't afford that either. But anyway, I'm happy with work. I don't think now that public advocacy would have suited me.'

She starts strolling around the room, swinging her drink like a baton.

'I'm not just talking about the Bar. Why, for example, didn't you go into business with that old schoolmate Clive Johnson when you had the chance?'

Where is this coming from? Clive Johnson?

'Clive is a bankrupt, last I heard. And he was never really a friend of mine.'

'Well he holds you in high esteem, and he also lives pretty well for a bankrupt from what little I've observed. Sure, he over-stretched himself for a while, that's just his personality, a bit entrepreneurial for his own good. But if *you* had been his partner, for example, you could have kept him in check, pulled him back a bit.'

'I haven't seen Clive for years. How do you know he's doing so well?'

'I ran into him last week at Coles. Bought me a coffee. He told me he hasn't paid tax in a decade.'

'You think that's something to boast about?'

'What's your problem Ted? The Government's in for its cut like everyone, everyone but you it seems.'

'I'm happy to pay tax.'

'That's exactly what I mean.'

'Marie, listen, yesterday morning I drove out to work, in the Hyundai, along well-surfaced streets, waved to the council garbage truck as I passed, gave way to a ute on my right, then stopped behind it at the traffic lights. There is, all around, in case you haven't observed beyond your luncheon table, a deliberate consensus for the common good.'

'This is what you tell yourself because these guys make a buck that you can't!'

'It's how you make the buck that matters, to me anyway.'

'I don't want a lecture Ted. All I'm saying is you could've shown a bit more drive down the years. And I'm right, aren't I!'

'Well you could get a job if the money's that important to you.'

'Get a job as what? With a twenty-five-year-old Arts degree? Listen mate, I've done my work, I've raised two kids and nursed you along too. And now I'd like a bit of a life!'

A firm rap on the door. Some hawker, thinks Ted. Marie looks up as if startled, then moves swiftly to let in, of all people, Clive Johnson.

It takes Ted a moment to recognise him, although the both-rows-of-teeth smile is distinctive. Plus the get-up: open necked pink shirt, wide-lapelled blue suit (Vinnies probably), and two-toned shoes with chunky heels. He has greyed, but the hair is still thick and long, swept back over his collar, the face lined but tanned, emphasising, with the suit, the startling ice-blue of his eyes.

'Hello Teddy boy! Long time no see. Should've rung, but I was in the neighbourhood. Don't know if Marie told you we bumped into one another last week.'

Already he's walking around as if he owns the place.

'Coffee at Coles.'

'Right. Few other things. You going to offer me a drink?'

'Little early for me.'

'But not for the Missus I see. Come on, loosen up old man, sun's over the yardarm. After all it's been a while.'

Ted looks across to Marie, who is wearing a completely neutral expression. Has she invited him?

'Ted, why don't we open that bottle of Jantz in the fridge.'

'What bottle of Jantz in the fridge?'

She has.

'Champagne, that's the go!' Clive rubs his hands together. 'Haven't been here for a while. Don't notice much change.'

'There hasn't been any,' says Marie. Ted tries to catch her eye, but she moves out to the kitchen.

'I don't recall you being here Clive.'

'Long while back. Yes, pity you two left Sandy Bay. Now that was a nice little place. That right, the kids' education. Those fancy schools. Marie tells me they're doing fine.'

'And what about yourself?'

'Bit of this, bit of that.'

Marie returns with the bottle and three flutes. Ted does the honours. He'll have to go easy on the grog. There's sharp company here, already he's feeling out-manoeuvred. Clive takes a long deep sip, a swig really.

'Whoa! That's the nice stuff. You're still at Steinberg's, right? Still paying you out in shekels I bet. You'd be amazed what that old pawnbroker's got squirreled away.'

'How would you know?'

'I hear all types of things. Still, you can't blame him. Gotta look after number one. You sit in your comfy old armchair Teddy gathering dust, but let me tell you, its dog eat dog out there. Just look at the front page of your paper. Some guy that's got no more raw talent than you or me climbs to the top, fucks over the Company, forgive the French, and then waltzes off with a five-million-dollar payola. And all these jerk-offs, they earn regular salaries in the millions, plus the perks. Just think, over a million bucks a year. What could you do with that, eh? What's Steinberg paying you? Little over a hundred? And half of it off to the tax man. These guys don't even pay tax, hide the loot offshore, or in the wife's name.'

'Wish it were in my name.'

'That's the ticket Marie! Another fill-up? So, actually, as I was chatting to Marie. Cheers. I couldn't help but mention this little opportunity I've happened to come across.'

'So this is why you're here. Some business scheme. Scam more like.'

'Teddy, I'm about to do you one big favour. I wouldn't even have thought of you if I hadn't by chance run into your little lady.'

'You can't do it because you're still out of action. You need a front man.'

'On the nail Teddy.'

'Forget it.'

'One hundred per-cent gold. They don't come around like this every day.'

'Not that I'm interested, but how much are you looking for?'

'The more, the merrier. Not much point under three.'

'And how much are you putting up.'

'Not allowed mate, as you said. Otherwise you wouldn't be knowing about it.'

'And who's going to lend me over quarter of a million dollars?'

'The bank. This place has got to be worth five-hundred minimum. If the bank won't come at it, I've got a few contacts.'

'I'll bet you have. Clive, it's been good catching up, but Marie and I have a busy afternoon, so if it's OK with you when you finish your drink...'

'No worries mate. I'm done. Just duck into the loo.'

Ted sees him catch Marie's eye as he strolls out. Fuck. They've rehearsed this.

'At least you can hear him out!'

'Are you crazy Marie? What if we lose it? The guy's a bankrupt!'

'You just don't want to make money! You're scared Ted, scared of being shown up for being a mug for all your working life. Do you know how sick I am of this life of ours! Really! And of all your do-nothing, do-good attitudes!'

Clive saw her coming, no question. What to do. Probably best to hear him out, get the crappy details, then Ted can reason properly with her later. Clive is back, all smiles and shine.

'Alright, talk.'

'You remember Lou Freeman?'

'Went through Medicine, didn't he?'

'Became a specialist, then he got a loan and started up his own medical research company. Some treatment for diabetics. Anyway, he develops this drug a couple of years back, finishes all the tests and everything, gets a few backers, lists the company, and it opens at par one dollar. Nothing happens. I think it's about eighty cents at present.'

'So?'

'The reason nothing happens is the thing's too expensive. Almost half of this bloody country are diabetics, more on the way, but most are on welfare. Since Lou listed, he's been lobbying the Government day and night to get onto the subsidised drug list. Well, just last week the Health Minister tells Lou to his face that when the Budget comes out in two months' time, he'll finally be on that list. And when that happens, the share price will go through the bloody ceiling.'

'Why would the Minister tell him that? I think it's a crime, but whatever, if it got out, he'd certainly be sacked, big scandal for the Government. It doesn't make any sense Clive.'

'They're old mates, used to run a surgery together in their twenties. An abortion clinic, largely. You might remember. What I reckon is, the Minister's in for his cut too.'

'And more to the point, why is Lou confiding in you?'

'Lou owes me a big favour Teddy. We won't go into details. Here, look at this.'

From the left inside pocket of his shiny blue suit, Clive flourishes a folded A4 sheet. It is a printed email from the Minister's office to Lou Freeman's surgery. It details the drug, the listing and the date. It is chummy and personal and to Ted's legal eyes looks the real thing. It is certainly incriminating, and leaving aside the possibility of political sabotage, seems to confirm Clive's story.'

'Where did you get this?'

'Just have a good long Captain Cook and hand it back Teddy.'

'Why would the Minister actually write something like this.'

'Lou wants proof. Maybe he's got him over a barrel or something. Who knows? Who cares?'

'What is it Ted?'

'As I said, one hundred-per-cent gold, mate. Look, the share price is not going to go down. It's been eighty cents for a year. What have you got to lose?'

'It's insider trading.'

'Not for you and me. We're not connected. If you spent a million dollars tomorrow, sure, it'd look suspicious. But if you spend anything up to half a mill over the next few months, no-one's going to worry. If somebody asks you, which nobody will, you just say you thought it was a good, safe investment, you'd read about it in the papers. You buy the stock slowly, wait a bit, then sell it slowly. We're not talking millions here, just a couple of hundred thou. But it'll make a big difference to your lifestyle mate.'

'And what about your lifestyle.'

'Thirty-per-cent I was thinking, which is roughly fifty/fifty after you pay your tax.'

'I don't have to give you anything Clive.'

'But if you do it, you will Teddy. I know my man, I don't need an email. Which is why I'm here. Anyway, double-crossing an old mate like me is never a good move, as I'm sure you appreciate. So, what about it. Look, I'm not asking you to rob a bank, just take advantage of something you happened to overhear. No-one's going to be hurt, no-one's going to care. Mate, if you look this gift horse in the mouth, you deserve to be a loser.'

'But don't you see Clive? That's exactly what he wants to be!'

'Now I might leave you two good people for a while to work it out between you. I happen to have a little business around the corner.'

'What, at the pub.'

'I'll see myself out. Be back in about an hour.'

He is suddenly gone, the absence a more malevolent presence. There is a tight knot in Ted's gut and a pressure at the back of his eyes, his peaceful Saturday has been blown to smithereens.

'What was that paper Ted?'

'An email from the Minister. It did look authentic. I don't know...'

'Come on Ted, email or not, this is a fantastic opportunity! Think, we could buy a new car, go overseas, pay a stack off the mortgage, maybe even buy a new place. You can't knock this back!'

'Why not? Seriously, there are principles at stake here, aside from the principle of doing a deal with a guy like Clive. You must see how we're privy to a situation, information, that others are not.'

'Well that's just our luck for a change, isn't it. I'm part owner of this house. What's to stop me getting a loan?'

'The fact you're not earning the money. Anyway, we're in this together or not at all. Look Marie, this is not such a big deal money-wise, I mean in the scheme of things, but can't you see that we're basically stealing here?'

'From who?'

'The community.'

'Every member of which would jump at such a chance if they could.'

'Not every member. That's where you're wrong.'

She puts her head in her hands, his beautiful wife, and performs a slow frenzied walk, like a kind of demented dance, around the confines of the shabby room. Watching her, for some reason it occurs to Ted that she might have done this before, maybe many times. She comes to a stop before him. She is crying.

'Ted, listen to me, I'm not interested in your precious probity, and I never have been. For me this really is the last straw. You just sit around on your fucking hands and think that because of that you're somehow superior to everyone else!'

She takes a deep staggered breath.

'If you don't do this damn deal with Clive, I'm walking out that door for good! I mean it!'

Her colour is high. She stares at him through wet eyes unblinking. From his long and deep experience, his wife is not a woman given to idle threats. Alright, she means what she says, that's clear, but will she do it? She probably doesn't know herself, so how can he? He has to tread carefully. But which way?

'For a couple of hundred thousand?'

'For the fact that if you won't do this, you'll never do anything and we'll, *I'll*, be stuck in this hell-hole forever.'

'Hell-hole? Are you serious?'

'You'd better believe it hubbie! I've never been more serious in my life! I'm totally fed up! This is it Ted!'

Ted has always believed in his ability to read people. One reason he thought he'd have made a good barrister. He examines his wife's face closely, every loving detail of it. Yes, certainly it is possible, she might do it. Always, he knows, she knows, all along it has been a slightly unequal relationship; he has loved her more than she has loved him, from the beginning, when he miraculously ardently persuaded her, and the rest of the way through. It is one of a number of necessary compromises with life Ted has acknowledged and accepted. Marie could live without him, but he could not live without her. So, what have we got here? Maybe it boils down simply to a matter of sacrifice: principle or love. Here, he cannot have both his cake and eat it too. Think, think. His head feels as if it is about to burst. He closes his eyes, shuts her out. Think, think.

'Alright'

Did he say that? Here she is, in his arms, finally; warm, vibrant, happy as a young girl. He is flooded with joy and feels irredeemably soiled.

Stadium folly
Anne Layton-Bennett

is it time to hesitate
before choosing to participate
in the online debate that's become
more fractious and heated by the day

did Rocky ever stop to think
of the harm he would evoke
with a deal we can't revoke
which has mired us in a mess
that's caused anxiety and distress
and has split the state in two

I'm no stranger to the vitriol
that's out there in the comments
you see I've been here before
and I recognise the signs
those paid trolls with made up names
and aliases who are unafraid to criticise

'build it and they will come!' they cry
their confidence is resolute
their optimism absolute

so they're deaf to all those voices
who oppose this mega travesty
a monument to sporting vanity
a third stadium we do not need
a stadium we do not want
and one we certainly can't afford

© 2025 Anne Layton-Bennett

The Phone Call That Broke Me
Anne Bailey

That phone call, the phone calls no mother, or parent ever expects to get, or wants to get. My husband and I moved into an old building, the front of which was a disused bank and in the back was the residence. We had lived there for approximately one month, with intentions of restoring it and I had my heart set on this project. On Friday the 11th March I was stripping back the lime green paint on the vault door in the main room of the bank, which was to become my Art and Craft shop. The shop was a dream I'd had for about 20 odd years, with me making various craft things, mending clothes, and making quilts.

On this day my son Shaun and his best friend paid us a visit. Shaun wanted to show us his first car with its brand-new tyres and mag wheels. He was so proud and I was so happy for him.

They looked over the building and didn't think much of it, till Shaun saw the bank vault. He said; "Wow look at this, a real vault! can I paint and fix this up for you?" It was his rostered day off on Tuesday, and he said he'd come up to start the job. He warned me not to touch it. They were the last words he ever said to me.

Sunday afternoon came; I was painting the walls in the bank when the phone rang. It was a young woman I knew from the nearby town we had just moved from. She proceeded to tell me there had been an accident just outside town on the Calingiri Rd. Her husband was on his way home from work, when he came across Shaun's car, he knew it was Shaun's car because he worked with Shaun. She didn't know any more than that.

I told my husband she sounded a little strange. I thought if it was a serious accident the police would have called us. I felt a little uneasy so decided to ring the local police station, only to find it was not manned and I was put through to the next town. The officer couldn't tell me much – only that yes, there had been an accident on the Calingiri Road. I had to really pump the officer for answers and all he could say was "Yes, an ambulance was called and took the occupants to the local hospital in Wongan Hills." He proceeded to ask me if I had someone to drive me to town, and said drive carefully.

I then became very scared; I think my voice **broke.** My husband and I arrived in Wongan Hills 20 minutes later. We hardly spoke a word to each other all the way, I was doing a lot of thinking, maybe he has a broken leg or arm. The tears began to roll down my face, that's when I told myself he's ok, he will be fine, just me being stupid. But I did tell my husband to hurry along a bit as it seemed to be taking a long time to get there. I needed to see Shaun to put my mind at ease.

We pulled up outside the local hotel, saw some friends outside, I saw Shaun's best friend Pauly sitting on the footpath, his face was red, and I could see quite clearly he was crying, sobbing very hard. I thought, "what's going on, why is everyone standing around like this? Why is his friend here? He's normally with Shaun, they are inseparable.

"What's going on, where is Shaun?" I said to my husband. A friend then came to the window of our car and said; "Get to the hospital, now!" I had this terrible feeling rush through me, "Oh, hell what has happened?"

On arrival at the hospital, there were no nurses or doctors in sight. I was met by a lady I knew who worked in catering and she took us through to the staff dining room. She knew why we were there, obviously. She offered us tea and coffee, not that I was interested in tea and coffee, I just needed to see Shaun. She told me all the nurses, and the doctor were all busy with the boys, someone will come and speak to you soon. In the meantime, a young friend of Shaun's came into the hospital, that's when we found out what had happened and who was in the accident with Shaun, it was a 16-year-old boy, cousin to this young fellow. They were on their way back from a day trip to Perth. The grandparents of the other boy were here as well by now, I had been sitting with them, but I just had to get some air. I was so tired of hearing how she had lost her first husband and five children in an accident and the grandfather saying; "They only call an ambulance when it's bad," well that was the last thing I needed to hear.

I knew about her terrible loss and felt sorry for her, but it was the wrong time to talk to me about her loss that had happened 20 something years earlier.

The doctor brushed past me a couple of times, I was trying to have a word with him, but he wouldn't stop. I heard not long later that he was fighting for one of the boy's lives. A few hours later had passed and I'd been hearing a machine working away, like someone trying to breathe, I was so scared by this terrible sound. I walked that hallway for a couple of hours, crying my eyes out all the time. I couldn't believe this was happening, I have never had to spend any more than an hour or so at a hospital with any of my children.

Then I heard they were transferring the boys to a hospital in Perth. I saw an ambulance officer that worked with my husband, we asked him what was happening, and he told us that, only one boy was going to Perth and it wasn't Shaun.

Well, I said; "If he isn't going to Perth, he must be ok, then why can't I see him?" He shook his head and said Shaun wasn't going anywhere. It still didn't register what was happening, then I realised what he was saying, I wasn't going to accept that, I was numb for a few minutes till the catering lady grabbed my arm and took me aside.

She said; "He had no right to tell you that, he doesn't know Shaun's condition, no one knows. We will all know when the doctor comes to see you." I thought maybe she was right and I did feel a little better, I just wish I knew what was happening. I was thinking for her to say that she must know something and I thought maybe he was going to be blind or maybe in a wheelchair or something.

I then thought I'd better ring his father, as he lived in another state and Shaun was from my previous marriage. He didn't appreciate me waking him that hour of the night and told me to ring him tomorrow when I knew something more definite. I remember thinking how dare he, what if it is serious, I was thinking why did I bother. I rang my dad and my stepmother who also lived interstate, Tasmania, they said to call as soon as you know something. While I was talking to my stepmother this lady, a stranger, came from nowhere and gave me a hug and pulled me to her and she was so sorry for our loss and that God will be with him now, he will lay close by his great grandparents where I know they will help him on his last journey, and she did the same to my husband. No one knew who she was. I knew she was not nursing staff as I remember she was not wearing any shoes. It was so strange, what was she on about, I don't know her, so how did she know who I was? Now I was very confused what was going on. I was already crying, and she just upset me more, I just wish someone would come and tell me something either way. By this time, you can imagine what I was going through, I was at my wits end.

Four and a half hours since we arrived at the hospital, finally there was some movement coming from the direction of the room where the boys were. I saw the other boy being taken into the awaiting ambulance, to be transferred to a Perth hospital. A few minutes after the ambulance had left the boy's grandmother was standing near me and asked me if that was her grandson gone in the ambulance. I felt it wasn't my place to tell her, obviously no one had told them. But why did this not surprise me. Not long after, the doctor and the young policeman from town approached me, Will's grandmother, was still trying to get some answers about her grandson. The doctor told the officer to get her out of here. I thought the doctor was a bit rude to her.

We were standing inside the front entrance to the hospital; my husband, the catering lady, an ambulance officer, and of course me. the doctor stood in front of me and said; "Sorry your son is dead." The doctor just turned and walked away, left me just standing there. No sorry, nothing – that was it, no more. I was stunned, and screamed out no, no, I was screaming this is not right, oh no, oh God no. I started to slowly sink to the floor when my husband and the ambulance lady grabbed my arms and started to lead me to a room, I saw all these people in this room and I remember saying; "No not in here, get me out of here, I've got to get out for some air!" I was floored, I should have realised, there were many signs, but I didn't let myself believe.

I was screaming, "Anyone could have told me that!" in the short seconds it took for him to tell me I screamed out inside. Oh God what's happening, why is this happening to me? I needed to see Shaun, I asked them to take me to see him.

"I need to see him now!" I yelled, (I was so angry, waiting all these hours only to find out he had died at the accident, I just wanted to die). The nurse said, "Yes not a problem, we just need a moment to clean him up." I thought I'd better call his father, I know he said call the next day, but I thought he would want to know now, silly me. What was I thinking, I called and it was late and his partner answered the phone, and she said,

"I thought he said to call tomorrow!" I just calmly replied

"Just get him to the phone" and he got angry for calling and I lost it and screamed down the phone, "Your son has died", but he didn't believe me. I sobbed and cried uncontrollably, I just wanted to die. I had a knot inside me so bad I could hardly breathe. It was so hard to express the pain I was feeling. It was a pain I never want to feel ever again. The deepest pain was when I got to see him, it was so painful it felt like someone had run a knife through my heart. He just lay on a cold table, I closed his beautiful eyes that I would never look into again, I just hugged him and didn't want to let him go; here lay my beautiful boy who had never done harm to a single soul.

In the days that followed I would find myself sitting on the shower floor with water running away with my tears, this happened for some time. I had to pull myself together somehow, we were flying Shaun's body home to Tasmania after the service. The service was beautiful and the church was packed, I was so overwhelmed by the amount of people who came to pay their respect. In the year following I had my first Christmas without Shaun, his 21st birthday, and the anniversary of the accident, my marriage fell apart. I was trying to put my life in some order. We moved from the bank, as I lost interest in all my crafts, I also promised Shaun I would not touch the vault at the bank, it was to be his project. Not a day goes by that I don't think of him.

A few months down the track I started making bad decisions, I started gambling, staying at work longer, not wanting to go home, forgot to pick my husband up from work more than once. I wasn't myself; I did a couple's grief and loss workshop and I would always come out crying and angry. A few weeks after losing Shaun I finally found out what led to the accident. Shaun had just finished night shift and arrived home around six a.m., needing to go to Perth to visit his girlfriend. Shaun asked his friend Pauly to go with him, and Pauly tried to encourage him to have some sleep first, but of course Shaun needed to go there and then. His friend said no, he didn't want to go. Shaun said to his friend, "If you don't come, I might have an accident, and it will be your fault." Another friend said his younger brother would go with him as he wanted to see his own girlfriend as well.

Shaun needed to be back home before 6 pm as he had to work again that night. Unfortunately, they both had fallen asleep at the wheel, the police told me he may have woken and seen he was on the wrong side of the road, and tried to gain control of his car, and over corrected the car and it spun around and was facing in the opposite direction and slid at high speed into a tree. Shaun was pinned to the tree for several hours, apparently the rescue team had trouble getting his car away from the tree. His young friend suffered massive brain injuries till this day.

> The coroner's report said Shaun died of massive brain injuries, and every rib was shattered due to being crushed against a tree. Fatigue was the main cause of the accident.

Shaun was a beautiful young man, taken from us all too soon, he had high ambitions and wanted nothing but the best and before he left us, he had achieved a lot of these ambitions. He was easy to like and easily accepted. That was his way. We had a beautiful service in the town where we lived, the funeral home was packed out, with interstate family and friends, and a very large number of locals from the town. My number two ex-husband travelled across the Nullarbor, my other children and Shaun's dad and his partner and my current husband all under the same roof.

A few days later we flew Shaun home to Tasmania to be buried close to my grandparents. We had another service there as well with lots of family and friends, the only thing I remember about that day was a girl sitting in the back of the church on her own, it was very strange. She disappeared quickly and I never found out who she was, it's funny that I still remember that.

Two years passed and I still found myself crying in my sleep. I would try to open my eyes and when they finally opened tears just rolled down my face.

Years later I still find it hard to watch movies about young people dying. It's been over twenty years since Shaun left us and he has missed so much, with his sisters and brother having 11 children and 10 nieces and nephews between them. He got his letter accepting him into the navy one week after his passing.

I miss my beautiful boy every day.

Fiction
Hank Koopman

I am fascinated by authors who write fiction novels.

Who inspires them to step out into the unknown and create stories of imaginary characters who could range from superhumans to vulnerable minorities trapped in a mundane lifestyle but still possess a powerful aura that makes them stand out from society? What research is required before the first opening line is published to entice readers to investigate a story further? I am sure every author hopes they have written the ultimate thriller to appear in the *New York Times*' top 10 best sellers list.

Even the classic writers of the 1800s were influenced by other authors of their day. H.G. Wells and Jules Verne admitted to being influenced by Edgar Allan Poe. Edgar Rice Burroughs began reading pulp-fiction magazines in 1929, and he recalled thinking to himself; "If people were paid for writing rot such as I read in some of those magazines, I could write stories just as rotten. As a matter of fact, although I had never written a story, I knew absolutely that I could write stories just as entertaining and probably a whole lot better than the ones I read in those magazines."

However, before 1929, he had already written several titles that would hold him in esteem as one of America's most prolific writers. His most famous character was *Tarzan of the Apes* (1912); 25 other titles of Tarzan were written, closely followed by a John Carter heroic character involving life on Mars.

How did Jules Verne envision a giant submarine and go into detail about how Captain Nemo manufactured re-breathable air within the ship? The only submarines invented at the time were two-man submersibles the Confederate and Union armies used, both dismal failures in their attempts to be viable in warfare during the American Civil War.

In his novel *War of the Worlds*, H.G. Wells's dramatic descriptions of aliens attacking the earth were so "out there" that, when Orson Wells narrated a radio adaptation of the book on air in 1938, listeners believed an attack was underway by Martians and were terrified, causing panic in several cities in America.

Another novel H. G. Wells wrote was *War in the Air*, published in 1909. He must have seen the aircraft's potential only six years after the Wright Brothers proved that heavier-than-air aircraft could fly in December 1903.

At the time, all these fiction writers were authoring unbelievable fantasy stories. Who could have imagined that so much of it would become reality? Were they prophets, seers, gurus, or imaginaries with a special gift of seeing future technology?

Then, another possibility crossed my mind: experiences that most humans and animals face each time they fall asleep: dreams. Are dreams not sometimes so far-fetched and impossible to comprehend that you wonder what sets your subconscious mind in motion to simultaneously accept some visualisations that are so beautiful, scary, and terrifying?

It might have been a news story in print or on television, a book you've been reading, or a radio podcast you heard. Sometimes, dreams happen for no reason at all. Then again, these might form the genesis of a fabulous fictitious story.

Let me give you an example of a personal experience when I was seven. My family was emigrating to Australia, and I experienced my first nightmare. The same nightmare was repeated seven times over the following four years, triggered whenever we were about to move to different accommodations.

I had never seen an aeroplane before I left Holland, but in my nightmare, I was at the controls of one. However, was it me? In my nightmare, I presented as an adult, flying a small red monoplane, which I later discovered was a De Haviland Chipmunk. My flight path, once airborne, takes me over a river, and a few moments later, a 45° turn has me approaching what looks like an industrial area. Another 45° turn finds me on my down-wind leg approaching several chimneys rising from a factory making clay pipes. Red warning lights blink at the top of each smokestack as a height warning for aircraft in the Maylands Aerodrome circuit. Once I clear the chimneys, I reduce altitude, crossing the river again and performing a 45° turn on my crosswind leg. One last turn brings me onto my final leg.

Eerily, this sequence is all completed in silence, which in an actual situation would require radio calls between other aircraft flying the same circuit and the control tower. Then again, I wasn't aware of what an aeroplane was, let alone radio procedures. All I know is that once the wheels hit the grass runway, I started to take off again to complete another circuit.

Now, the dream becomes stranger because I watch three or four Chipmunks perform these "touch and go" procedures from a roadway beside the factory with the smokestacks. I watch this tranquil, silent scene of aircraft seemingly playing "chasey" when suddenly audio is added. A spluttering engine causes me to look to my left.

Then, as dreams can so magically appear to do, an instantaneous scene change finds me back in the Chipmunk, fighting with the controls as I slam into one of the chimneys and burst into flames. THE END.

However, that was not the end. I would have the same dream in its explicit detail six more times. As I became aware of aircraft and my fascination with them, the dream soon revealed its darker nightmare aspect. Our family initially wanted to emigrate to New Zealand, but unforeseen circumstances saw us disembark in Fremantle, West Australia.

Four years after we arrived, another eerie coincidence found me standing in the same spot as in my nightmare. This time, I was awake and not dreaming. I stood near the roadway next to five giant chimneys at H.L. Brisbane & Wunderlich, a clay pipe manufacturer. Maylands Aerodrome was on the other side of the river, and four chipmunks were playing "chasey" flying overhead.

Dèjá Vu? I believe so. Reincarnation is entirely possible.

So, what can set a dream off, you may ask?

Donna and I finished our show at the Coolah Bowls Club on a Sunday afternoon in late April 2003. We stowed our equipment in the boot of our 36ft converted bus, our home, for the past five years. Coming to the first hill out of town, I noticed a considerable engine power reduction. To make a long story short, we had to get a heavy haulage tow truck to take us to a Tamworth diesel mechanic's workshop, where they discovered we had "dropped" a piston. A major repair was required, which would take at least a week to complete. We had to book into a caravan park because our 14-tonne home was on a hoist 10ft in the air.

Our towed vehicle, a Honda Jazz, was used to fulfil a couple of other shows in the area, and we hoped "The Minstrel" would be ready by Friday, as we had a show booked in Tenterfield and Casino the following weekend. It wasn't ready, so we used the Honda, packed to the rafters, to meet our committed contracts. Seeing the underside of our 14-tonne bus hovering in the air must have caused me to have this dream as the deadline for our Queensland concerts drew closer, and I was worried we might have to cancel those shows. They were big money earners and would help us pay the repair bills that were mounting up daily. So, with a stressful week ahead, I slept in our rented unit at the caravan park, and I dreamt this fictitious story.

"It's a crazy idea, mate, but everything is possible when you think about it," a mechanic told me as I suggested installing a jet engine from a Harrier VSTOL in The Minstrel.

"Let's remove the Scania and retrofit the Harrier instead," I insisted. While the mechanic got to work, I had an aeronautic engineer fit wings that retracted into the sides of the Minstrel, much like stabilisers on an ocean liner. A gyro stabiliser was also required to maintain easy stability. This would be my surefire way of keeping those lucrative contracts in Queensland. I was also required to keep Donna out of the loop; I knew how she felt about flying. She was terrified of it.

"Well, here it is, Hank," the two inventors had persevered with my project over the last four days, making sure it would be ready by Friday morning. They were enthusiastic to see it work.

"Do you mean to say you haven't given it a test flight yet?" I asked.

"Do we look that stupid?" My mind was in turmoil. I had to get to Queensland, or we could lose everything. Time was running out. Donna was still unaware of the changes I authorised to be made to our "home."

"Come on, Don. We'll load the gear back into the boot and get going, or else we'll miss all our dates in Queensland." I reassured her we still had time to make the first scheduled gig.

"You're going to sit on 90, aren't you?" she said, referring to the speed limit she always insisted I stay on. "Where is the car trailer for the Honda?"

"We've got to leave it and the Honda as a surety for the work the mechanics have done."

"Didn't we have enough money in the bank to pay for the repairs?" she asked.

"No, I'm afraid not, love." I tried softening the blow of the $60,000:00 account we owed.

"Sixty thousand dollars? Where is the value in that? We've been ripped off again, haven't we?" These were three questions that

I would have to explain as soon as I turned the key to start our new power plant. Instead of the diesel motor's thump, thump, thump, there was the whine of a jet engine spooling up.

"What's that noise?" came the usual question when some new noise began to worry Donna.

"Nothing, Don," I reassured her. It's just the new motor the mechanic suggested we put in." With that statement, I could blame someone else. "You wait and see, love. There's no motor home like this in existence. We're unique, one of a kind."

With that, I pushed the accelerator down a little, waved goodbye to the geniuses who rebuilt our motorhome to my specifications, closed the pneumatic door and eased out of the garage, where we had been held captive for ten days. I eased into the street and held The Minstrel back, sticking to the speed limit. Donna sat back in her seat, and we settled down to our usual back-and-forth banter about the scenery or animals we saw in the paddocks.

"That motor seems to be running well," she remarked. "It's also much quieter; we don't have to shout as much as before."

"You like it then?"

"Yeah, I do." She seemed to relax as I kept The Minstrel rumbling along at Donna's approved speed of 90 kph. I knew we could extract 110 kph from the Scania motor, but I didn't want to upset the general ambience of peace and tranquillity. I thought, "I wonder how fast she'd go now." Still, there was no point in finding out now; it would only descend into an argument.

Coming up to the Moonbi Range, just north of Tamworth, the heavy semis were changing down to lower gears to make the climb up the long gradient. Not so The Minstrel. I added more pressure on the accelerator, and we stayed on 90, passing everyone else on the dual carriageway as if they were standing still. Donna had nodded off to sleep with the steady hypnotic whine of the jet engine.

Acoustic insulation around the engine bay kept the sound to a minimum. When I needed to cruise along on the ground, the thrust angle was only 10° to the horizontal. I had to engage the gyro stabiliser to ensure the Minstrel remained upright when the wheels lost traction with the earth. If I increased speed above 110 kph, the bus tended to shudder on the bitumen roads, so I used the Harrier engine's vertical take-off capability.

I entered a rest area to extend the wings, set the gimbal spinning in the gyro, took a last look at Donna to ensure she was still asleep, moved the exhaust to its 45° position and increased the engine power. Ever so gently, the 14-tonne vehicle lifted off the ground, and as I changed the angle of attack on the exhaust, the wings gave us further lift as we moved forward. What a remarkable piece of engineering those mechanics had achieved. I was amazed.

Cruising at about 300ft, the Air Traffic Controllers' radar wouldn't notice me, and I could still navigate by sight using my road map. The 600km journey would have made us late for our first gig on the Gold Coast, but now I landed in the car park at Carrara at about 1 a.m. With the wings retracted, the Gyro was no longer spinning; everything had returned to normal. I roused Donna from her slumber in the passenger seat and said,

"Are you coming to bed now, Don?"

"Where are we?" She rubbed her eyes to try to focus and see our surroundings.

"At Carrara," I smugly replied.

"We couldn't have made that good a time." She looked amazed and tried calculating the mileage and time in her head.

"Well, you know, love, sometimes, time flies."

Then I woke up.

Extract from *'Secrets of the Water Meadow'*
published 2024 by *Forty South*
Dawn Meredith

CHAPTER ONE

It was five o'clock in the morning. A sour wind stirred the small, restless waves in jagged white lines towards the grey-pebbled shore of Eikeberg Island. Eleven-year-old Freya stood submerged to her calves in frigid sea water, her nightie clutched high, her long brown hair gently moving in the breeze. Her toes, scrunched on the uneven pebbles, were numb. Thick ribbons of knobbly yellow seaweed slithered round her legs in the swirling water, sending goose bumps right up to her face. But Freya dared not move. If she stood perfectly still, and made no sound, she might see the beautiful *havfrue*, (mermaid), called Lorelei. Five o'clock was the exact time her elder sister Lisbet insisted the havfrue came to feed in the shallows. And Freya didn't want to miss it.

A pale pink horizon graced the snowy peaks on the opposite side of the fjord with a shimmering lustre, like pink icing on a cake. In a shallow valley at the shoreline sat the small Norwegian town of Stranda. If she squinted, Freya could see a fishing boat making its way from the harbour for the fishing grounds further up Strandafjord and out of sight. On a slope just behind Freya stood her ancestral home, Fjellheim, (mountain home) a sleepy, white painted wooden house, with her tiny attic bedroom facing the fjord. An impressive barn of great slabs of rough-sawn oak painted red with white trim stood beside the house, where it had been for over three hundred years. But that was not nearly as long as the merfolk had inhabited the deep of Strandafjord.

Legend called them *mørke engler*, (dark angels), to be feared and distrusted. Freya's mother, German by birth, called them Lorelei. Only the old ones, like their elderly neighbour Gamle Jenny, (old Jenny) believed the mørke engler actually existed, but folk legend had created strict rules, especially for children. On Eikeberg Island small children were never allowed to bathe alone or even stand in the fjord waters without supervision. But Lisbet insisted Lorelei was a havfrue, a maiden of the water meadow, not one of the mørke engler. In a whisper behind her hand, Lisbet had excitedly confided that Lorelei was a princess of the ocean, with glorious long hair, golden like the seaweed that fringed the shores, and large, sad eyes. Lorelei had no family, Lisbet said, and she got terribly lonely. Lisbet was her only friend, which was lucky for Lorelei, thought Freya, because sixteen year old Lisbet had lots of other friends.

"Freya! What are you doing in the water, *lille venn?*" (little friend) called her mother's voice faintly. Freya spun and frowned at the woman leaning over the balcony that ran the width of the white house. Freya raised a finger to her lips, then fiercely waved her mother away. Mamma waved, forced a smile and turned back to the house, no doubt to keep watch from the window. Mamma slept badly and was often awake all night, but Freya couldn't worry about that now. Her eyes greedily searched among the shallows lapping at her legs and beyond, to the tiny rocky islet that emerged when the tide receded. In a couple of hours, she could run and stand on it, pretending she lived on a deserted island all by herself, but right now she was hoping there were lots of juicy, delicious fish enticing Lorelei to come and feast. How could it be true that havfrue ate small children? They had all the monkfish, eels, brown trout, grayling and perch to choose from. Freya shook her head, dislodging horrifying images of a beautiful havfrue tearing at the limb of a screaming infant. Havfrue were kind as well as beautiful, Lisbet had said. And Lisbet was hardly ever wrong about anything.

The sky over the peaks above Stranda was the softest mauve-blue now. The wind was still cold, blowing Freya's hair into her eyes. Slowly, she lifted a hand to tuck it behind her ear, afraid any movement would frighten Lorelei away. Shivering, she lifted the wet hem of her flannelette nightie a little higher. Her belly grumbled loudly and she sighed. Why hadn't she thought of grabbing a biscuit or something on her way out the back door? She turned to look at the house, hoping her sister would join her. Why wasn't Lisbet here anyway? Lorelei was *her* special friend after all! She shifted her cramped feet.

"Lazy girl." Freya muttered. A violent shiver gripped her and Freya struggled to keep her breathing even. A tight fear crept into her throat. Surely Lorelei would see her waiting so patiently and come?

"Freya," said a warm, gentle voice right behind her. "Lille venn, why are you standing in that freezing water? You know you'll be having a breathing attack." Freya turned to glare at her mother, who stood perched expertly on the large grey stones of the beach, dressed in a woollen dress and brightly coloured gumboots, a towel draped over her shoulder.

"I'm waiting for…. Something!" Freya replied crossly.

"You are standing in the freezing cold waiting to see a seal? We can see those from the balcony, wrapped warmly in a blanket. *Kom da*, (come on). It's almost breakfast time."

"No, it's… Please, Mamma. Let me…."

"Liebling. Nein." (Darling. No). Mamma always switched to German when she was serious. Dark circles under her eyes meant her patience would be limited today and Freya knew better than to push it. There would be hell to pay from her father if she did. "Kom," said Mamma firmly, reaching out her hands. Mamma's dark blue eyes seemed deep enough to hold safe everything in Freya's world, even the secret desires of her heart. Freya reluctantly stepped out of the water and stumbled into her mother's arms, the warmth of the fluffy, dry towel enfolding her. She glanced one last time at the fjord and thought she saw a stirring of the waters, perhaps the flick of a graceful tail.

OCEAN – Cradle of Life
© Dawn Meredith

Turquoise light shafts through from the sparkling surface
as transparent jellyfish dance a graceful jig below.
Dark figures hover and glide, ever watchful.
Silver scales flash by, trailing bubble clouds
around gentle giants, caressed by the currents, their deep voices
rumbling on.

Reefs of chaotic colour.
Swaying grasses of subtle rainbow shades.
Miniscule eyes and mouths.

Juveniles hide among the knobbly, yellow ribbons in perfect
camouflage.
Bleached, empty shell homes lie waiting in the sandy shallows.
A diver, flippers like a frilly tail, pushes through the viscous world.
In the dark garden depths fantastical, ancient creatures grope
among fossils, frozen in stone.

The cradle of life.
The spiraled engine of evolution.

Attack on the Highway
Lesley Ririka

Looking back at what happened so many years ago, I realise how lucky I had been to survive this incident. Denys and I lived in the Eastern Highlands of Papua New Guinea at Goroka. Denys, my husband being a clergyman, had been called to Lae on the North Coast to officiate at a special service for the church. He asked me to come with him and play the organ for the service.

Lae is the second largest city in PNG, and to travel between Lae and Goroka, we used the Highland Highway winding through the wide and long Markham Valley, climbing through the foothills to the mountains of the Eastern Highlands.

The hijacking of trucks and their cargo by bandits happened frequently along this route. The public was advised to be cautious as to what times to travel on the highway, as ambushes by bandits had occurred recently, attacking private cars where money and valuables were taken from the occupants by the robbers. In 2004, it was an unsealed two-lane highway, with many bridges reduced to one lane, causing a natural bottleneck where an ambush could easily occur.

Denys and I travelled together to Lae by car on Saturday with no adverse incidents, and Denys planned to return on Monday as he had a few things to follow up in Lae. Because I was due to begin work in Goroka on Monday morning, we decided I would return Sunday afternoon – we felt early Sunday afternoon should be safe enough to travel. Just to be sure, Denys organised John, one of the young men from our village, to escort me.

John and I waited at the public motor vehicle (PMV) stop until a 15-seater bus going to Goroka approached. We procured our tickets and immediately started on our journey. I was seated near the front as I was prone to travel sickness, and John sat in a window seat next to me.

The first two hours were incident-free, and there was general chatter as we moved relatively smoothly along the Markham Valley. I say relatively because it was not a sealed road, so there were the inevitable potholes and corrugations, but nothing too severe. We were in the foothills again with many tight corners to negotiate, reducing our speed to a crawl at times, as we started ascending the mountains.

Our bus approached a single-lane-bridge forcing the driver to slow down. Six men rushed from the dense foliage armed with guns and bush knives, yelling at the driver, "Stop, stop, muv." (move). Demanding the driver to stop, one of the bandits shoved him roughly out of his seat and commandeered the driver's compartment. Two men with bush knives came to the side door.

"Olgeta putim het i go daun," demanding we all put our heads down. I could hardly believe what was happening, and obviously did not have my head low enough because I felt the sharp smack of the flat side of a bush knife on my head and the angry order, "Het daun," followed by the warm flow of blood trickling down my face. I smartly put my head well down and instinctively put my hand up to stop the bleeding.

I could feel and hear the bus back up and then drive off the road into a grassy area, but I didn't dare stick my head up to have another look. When we stopped, we were all ordered:

"Olgeta kam, nau slip long graun." (get off and lie on the ground.) I could see we were in a coffee plantation, but when I got to the door, there was no space on the remaining patch of ground to lie down, so I was allowed to sit. The bandits were going through peoples' personal belongings and taking whatever they wanted. Mobiles, cameras, money, anything of value. I believe one young woman had her 'bride price' of K15,000 taken.

I had a suspicion the robbers must have been informed about her being on that bus and knew what they were looking for. Others had large sums of money, but I had a single 10 kina note which was amongst business cards I kept in a separate compartment of my purse. When they opened my purse, it appeared empty and so they threw it back at me in disgust.

They took the driver's takings, so did very well for themselves during this hold-up. Having taken everything, they said,

"Nau mipela i go, yupela weit hap au ten yu ken i go, no ken i go long polis." (We are going now; you wait half an hour, and then you can go, but don't contact the police.)

The mood was varied; some passengers were traumatised by the ordeal, and many were angry about losing everything of value they had, yet thankful that no one else was injured except me. No one seemed to worry about me; they were too worried about what had happened to them.

Our driver regained control of his bus, backed up from the clearing and drove onto the highway, and continued to Goroka. He was in a bad way; he ran short on fuel and had no money to buy more. He negotiated with one of the service stations to top up and drove into town to his bus terminus.

There were mixed feelings as we arrived, and people dispersed in different directions harbouring their own thoughts. I don't know what happened to the young woman who lost her "bride price".

I rang my brother-in-law, who was very upset when he saw my condition and took me to the hospital, where they repaired me with six stitches to my scalp. There were many questions at the emergency station when I walked in, and there was lots of sympathy and chatter.

It was later that I heard that one person had been killed in a similar situation the week before. Count me very lucky.

The Braiding
Andrea McMahon

I didn't notice the young woman as I got on the bus. I was too busy rummaging through the numerous pockets of my jacket in search of the two-dollar coin I had carefully placed in an easy-to-get-at spot before leaving for the bus-stop. Making what I thought to be witty, light-hearted remarks to the driver in order to hide my embarrassment at holding up the people in the queue behind me, I eventually managed to locate the offending coin, paid my fare and collapsed into the nearest vacant seat.

No sooner had I sat down than my handbag fell off the seat beside me and onto the floor, the contents of my money purse, my used tissues, spilling out underneath the seat. I embarked upon the uncomfortable and inconvenient business of retrieving them. When I'd garnered my belongings, ensuring they were carefully stowed, I slumped back in my seat to recover from the ordeal. If only bus lines supplied perfectly made-up stewards parroting perfectly enunciated warnings on the need for careful stowage, I would never have got in such a muddle. Composed was not a word associated with my person on that particular sunny spring day.

So I didn't notice the young woman at first. I had no idea whether she was already on the bus when I mounted the stairs or got on as I was scrambling over the floor. I saw her as I turned my head from the window and my attention remained thus fixed for the rest of my trip into town. I did, of course, withdraw my gaze every now and then. One does not wish to be seen to be staring.

The young woman was seated in the single front seat on the left-hand side of the bus, that exposed and very public seat in which I have never sat in over fifty years of catching public transport. She was brushing her hair, her long, straight, sandy hair. She was brushing her hair with long, slow, deliberate strokes. She had her head tilted slightly to one side and her eyes closed. It was to my mind an intimate scene, a parody of self-pleasuring. I watched as she put down the brush and divided her hair into two sheaths by hand, her fingers scuttling like slaters down the back of her skull. The resulting division was uneven and not at all pleasing to the eye. She began to braid her hair, entwining the strands over her left shoulder as if she were playing a harp. Perhaps she could hear the music. As she began the right plait it soon became obvious that it would turn out thinner, less impressive than the other. I found this disconcerting. One braids one's hair to be beautiful, surely? Not lumpy and bumpy. The young woman drew the plaits back behind her next, began to entwine them together. I felt reassured when I saw this. She was going to put her hair up, place a neat French knot at the nape of her neck. A quaint, conservative style that would hide the untidiness of the underlying component parts. I watched her long, pale hands busily tying, twisting, untying the braids until I saw those hands become disembodied forms, working feverishly, becoming insect-like in their industriousness. I could see those hands having difficulty achieving the desired result but the young woman's face remained impassive. I realized I was by no means watching a display of mastery, of skill painstakingly acquired over time. What was I watching then? Performance art? Certainly I was in the audience. The scene had begun to take on a melancholic air. I hoped it would be over soon. I reminded myself of Freud's response to a student who had once suggested his smoking was an example of oral behaviour: *Sometimes a cigar is just a cigar.*

But still I sat, entranced, as the disembodied hands continued to harangue their army of ant-like fingers until I saw without warning – the young woman giving only the slightest, most imperceptible sigh of exasperation – the ant-like fingers collapse, shrivel up and disappear as if they had been hit by an odourless insecticide. The plaits hung limp and alone for a moment. I waited for the return of the hands, full-bodied and vengeful. Those hands came, unravelled the braids without care, scooped the hair up and in one quick twist tied it up in a loose bun, the band placed higgledy-piggledy, leaving strands of hair poking out all over the place like placards of protest.

I followed the young woman off the bus. I saw that little bun bobbing in bemusement as the young woman walked on, quickly becoming lost in the crowd. I was left feeling empty, cheated. As if the curtains had been drawn before the performance had finished.

The Singing Sirens
Bethamy Nader

The salt spray kissed our feathers as we circled the gaudy yacht, our keen eyes taking in the scene below. Humans. Always so predictable in their celebrations. Tonight, it was a wedding. A plump, aging woman in a ridiculous white dress clung to a handsome, dark-haired man. Simon, the crew called him. We could smell their fear, barely masked by the cheap champagne and forced laughter.

"Such a waste," Lyra crooned, her voice a low rumble that vibrated in my chest. "So much potential for despair."

"Patience," I hissed, nudging her with my wing. I was their leader Astraea. My voice, the deadliest of the three, the one that could unravel the strongest will. "The captain is our target. He controls the vessel."

We descended, swirling around the bridge, our song weaving itself into the air. A melody of longing, of promises whispered on the wind, of the sweet oblivion that awaited them. I focused on the Captain, a grizzled man with eyes that had seen too much. He was trying to ignore us, clinging to the helm, but the song burrowed into his mind. The hypnotic rhythm throbbed in his temples, blurring the line between reality and illusion.

"Beautiful….so

Beautiful…." he mumbled, his grip on the wheel loosening. He saw not the jagged rocks looming ahead, but shimmering beaches and faces of loved ones long lost.

"Closer," I urged Lyra and Selene. Our voices swelled, a crescendo of seductive whispers. The yacht veered off course, drawn like a moth to a deadly flame. I could see the panicked faces of the guests, their laughter replaced with screams that were quickly swallowed by the wind. Simon, the groom, stared at us with wide terrified eyes, his arms wrapped protectively around Tanya, his new bride.

The impact was brutal. A screech of metal, a sickening lurch, then the icy embrace of the sea. The yacht splintered, sending bodies tumbling into the dark water. Their cries were pathetic, their struggles futile. They were so easily broken.

We soared above the wreckage, the shrieks dying down to gurgles. The air was thick with the metallic tang of blood and the bitter scent of salt.

"Another successful hunt." Selene sighed, preening her feathers.

I nodded, my gaze sweeping over the chaos below.

"Indeed, so many souls lost to the sea. Let us find a new vessel. There are always more foolish hearts waiting to be broken."

With a final, chilling laugh that echoed across the moonlit waves, we turned and flew towards the horizon, leaving the dead to their watery graves. Another feast for us, the Sirens. We circled once more, singing a triumphant dirge before soaring away seeking fresh prey. Our hunger never ends.

The Bystanders
Tatiana Petrovsky

Rats are squabbling, scrabbling in the rafters
of his mind –
their incisive incisors are nibbling, gnawing
the synaptic pathways creating chaotic confusion.
Nervous neurones are scrambling to escape
electrical discharges are pinging, zinging
firing random messages with increasing intensity.
Convulsing, he succumbs to oblivion
on the diesel-stained concrete platform
of an unforgiving train station.

Rendered immobile with moral ineptitude
bystanders huddle and mutter'
"reckon it's drugs?"
'he's pissed himself'
'how disgusting.'
The masked ones, shudder backwards
1.5 metres at all times.
'what if its Covid?'
Voyueristic holders of i-phones
snap into mobile mode,
'flash, flash' record, record every
clonic-tonic spasm of jerking limbs
You-tube notoriety here they come!

A black-cladded, nose-ringed vision,
roses tattooed around a youthful neck,
pushes through the bystanders
'Are you people for real?
Use your f-ing phones for good
call an ambulance.'
Rushes to the fallen body
removes a choking mask
gently moves the suffering soul
into the coma position
comforting with calming words

"Hang in there, you'll be okay."

Furtive eyes avert their gaze
cowardly bodies slink away.
A few recalcitrant ones,
reluctant to stop filming the tragedy
skulk on the periphery.
The young person stays.
A Good Samaritan
amongst a pack of jackals.

A different airflight experience
Lesley Ririka

Papua New Guinea (PNG) has been often described as *'the Land of the Unexpected'* as the following will show.

I was principal of the nursing school at Dogura/Alotau and I needed to travel between the two centres to supervise the staff and students. There were no roads for vehicles, so the journey was either eight hours by boat or 20 minutes by plane. This time I was returning from Alotau to Dogura by plane.

Other passengers and I were sitting on the stones outside the airline office at Alotau. We were getting impatient as we had our tickets and were waiting for the pilot to drive us on the Airline bus the eight kilometers to the airstrip. The plane would go firstly to Dogura and then on to Rabaraba and Tarakwaruru carrying mail, supplies and passengers.

After half an hour we heard a friendly voice asking: "Are you waiting for the pilot?"

"Yes" we replied. He said;

"There was a big party last night, but I'll wake him for you." He threw several handfuls of gravel at a window on the second story of the building next to the office. We could hear groans, and our helpful friend turned to us and said;

"There you are, he'll be right now."

Sure enough, a few minutes later a figure, still looking rather sleepy, and worse for wear, emerged and apologized.

"Sorry, are you ready? Let's go." He motioned for us to board the small airline bus, and I was sitting in the front next to him. The trip to the airstrip was on a gravel road with many corners, each necessitating gear changes. At each gear change his left foot struggled to find the pedal, and I was thinking;

"Am I going to fly with this man? If he has this difficulty with the bus, how will he manage the complexities of flying?"

We arrived at the terminal without incident and were weighed with our baggage, then the pilot came over to me and asked; "Will you have a coffee with me Lesley?"

"OK," I replied and enjoyed the coffee, then he said;

"I feel a bit better; I think I'll have another one." I hopped up and got a second cup for him, adding extra sugar thinking that would help. When he'd had the second cup he said;

"Right, I feel ready to fly now."

We lined up to board the plane and I was still trying to decide whether I would fly with him or not, but it was only a 20-minute flight so I thought it should be okay.

The take-off was smooth and the first part of the flight uneventful with only a little turbulence as we crossed the valley between the two mountain ranges.

"It was a bit bumpy back there," he said. I agreed. The next few minutes were smooth but as we approached Dogura it was a different story. Dogura station is on a plateau rising from the beach with surrounding mountains. The airstrip is a short grass strip at sea level below the station going at right angles from the sea towards a mountain with a river at the end of the strip. It is only safe to make the approach from the sea end if there is a strong downwind. There is often turbulence during the routine approach which requires flying toward the mountain, turning left over the river and then turning left again onto the strip. We made the first turn to fly along the valley, then suddenly hit some severe turbulence, the pilot hit full throttle and did a sharp rise and turn until we were headed in the opposite direction along the coast away from Dogura. I was worried; "What in the heck is he doing now?"

As if he had read my thoughts, he said;

"That was too rough for me there, we will go on to RabaRaba, and I will try again on the way back." We were flying smoothly now, and it was about 20 minutes to RabaRaba along the coast. This strip was sealed and parallel to the ocean with no obstruction at either end, so we landed without any problems. When we disembarked, I was still shaking from the experience at the Dogura strip, but as the other passengers were not going to Dogura they were not too concerned. After some people disembarked and all formalities were completed, the pilot said; "Okay all aboard, we'll continue on and I will try Dogura again on the way back,"

"No thank you!" I said – there was no way I was going to get back on that plane! "I'll walk back."

They didn't try to stop me; they just took my bag off and went on their way. I was facing either two hours on a canoe with an outboard motor or six hours walking which included two flooded rivers. There was no canoe or dinghy available, but there were two men who were willing to walk with me and carry my small bag. The story of what happened at Dogura would have been discussed in language by the disembarking passengers. The men were very quiet during the first part of our walk, along a well-worn track through the bush, and didn't ask; "Why are you walking?" so I didn't have to explain. I think they already knew. It was hot and sticky but not raining and after walking steadily for a couple of hours we came to the first river which was running waist high, but not dangerously fast. With one of the men helping me, we crossed without a fall and continued with our wet clothes for another couple of hours to the next river, which also was about waist high but again not too fast and no crocodiles! Pushing against the current, with the men's help we successfully crossed and continued on until we reached the foot of the hill up to Dogura. It was just on dark as we walked up past the boy's dormitory; I heard them calling out;

"Is that you Sister Lesley?"

"Yes, it's me." I replied and they responded;

"We knew you would make it!"

The plane had got into Dogura on its way back to Alotau, and the staff who met it asked;

"Where's Sister Lesley?" and the pilot replied; "She's walking!" I never heard how he explained that! Months later, though, we bumped into each other at a party at Dogura and he confessed; "I understand why you walked that day, and I don't blame you!"

I didn't have an occasion to fly with him again, but did fly on the plane with other pilots.

Broken Connections
Terry Hannan

The route ninety-six tram had arrived close to the centre of the city when clocks on walls and devices in hands or on people, indicated it was just after nine-thirty in the morning and the peak of the corporate rush hour had abated. In the front carriage sat Andrew where most of the green-patterned seats were unoccupied. The rush hour crowds of passengers stabilising themselves using the scaffolding of bright yellow bars or the swinging suspended hand grips had passed, and the moving tram continued to rock erratically side to side creating piercing, non-harmonic sounds from the metal wheels creating friction with the steel rails and lacked the rhythmical cadence of a train which often induces sleep in passengers.

Andrew, one of the remaining passengers had been sitting alone on a double seat on the right side of the tram. To his left on an adjacent seat sat a young woman resting against the window. She had been dressed neatly in a loose, ankle length, black skirt and wore boots that extended to just above her ankles and her upper torso was covered with a hip length, open fronted, neatly styled jacket which was also black and covered a black close-fitting jumper with a polo neck underneath her jacket. Her straight auburn hair was parted on the left and the contour of her hair style was being disrupted by the fingers of her left hand that supported her head. She had sat cross-legged, and, in her lap, she cradled her mobile phone and had no observable jewellery. Andrew estimated her to be aged in her late twenties or early thirties. Beside her on the seat was a stylish black handbag with a shiny gold-coloured clasp and the maker's brand was not visible. The presence of another person completed a triangulation of passengers. It was a young man in his early thirties with a bald head above a band of hair that had been cut professionally sort and, on his face, he wore thin-framed, circular, gold-rimmed glasses and his hands firmly held a mobile phone. The man and Andrew exchanged courteous smiles and nods acknowledging their proximity within the moving tram and it was noted that there had been no movements from the young woman.

When the tram jolted forward the woman moved and held her phone then began interacting with its screen in the manner of individuals who had grown up communicating with mobile electronic devices. Andrew observed the rapidity with which she typed and was not a skill he had mastered despite his efficiency with mobile phones. What did capture his attention were the erratic patterns of her finger movements which he initially disregarded thinking they were another example of the typing skills of the modern generation. Within minutes of his first observations, he heard the clatter of her mobile phone on the floor of the tram, and she had spontaneously leant forward and retrieved the undamaged device. The young man glanced towards the sounds and movements coming from the young woman then returned his gaze to his device and his mannerisms suggested he saw the events in the rocking tram as normal.

A series of incidents then appeared in quick succession. The woman began interacting with her phone with her head resting on the window. Her finger movements became more erratic, and the phone again crashed to the floor, and she repeated her retrieval manoeuvres. During the following five to seven minutes the scenario of the dislodged phone was repeated and occurred with diminishing time frames. Andrew then observed that the young man became more observant of the activities occurring with the young woman but did not react to her predicaments.

What became obvious was the young woman was barely awake and during the latter phone dropping events she appeared to be asleep and would react with automated grasping actions towards the persistently unstable phone. Initially she successfully retrieved the phone from the floor and Andrew had conceptualised that the woman's brain had recent memories of the phone being located between her folded legs and her normal integrated neural signals from the hands and objects existing in space and time became functionally disengaged. Any corrective signals from her brain were distorted, delayed and non-synchronised causing her fingers and hands to grope into space and on her body as her brain then plunged into a deeper somnolent state, leading to accelerated episodes of the phone crashing to the floor. Her final non-retrieval response to the phone on the floor confirmed she was deeply asleep. In fact, Andrew considered her to be comatose. The movements of her body created the appearance that she was not experiencing drug withdrawal or intoxication, and her actions were those of a person completely sleep deprived. Andrew had seen this behaviour before when it occurred amongst his colleagues in overworked healthcare institutions. He assessed her as not exhibiting the features of narcolepsy, an uncommon form of epilepsy. He further deduced that the young woman was in serious trouble, yet her face did not reveal agitated distress, and she was so deeply asleep it would have required an intense stimulus to awaken her. His mind formulated what may have occurred in her life during the previous twenty-four or more hours. Had she experienced the sudden death of a friend or family member by suicide or was her current state an after effect of being sexually assaulted or was she experiencing jet lag after an overseas flight without time to recover to take up her normal employment. Her intermittent facial grimaces in her somnolent state suggested a deep inner turmoil not associated with joy or celebrations. Neither the young man nor Andrew had moved to assist her in the retrieval of her phone and the young man had ceased interacting with his phone and which remained firmly held in both hands as he began to focus on the events surrounding the young woman as Andrew had begun vacillating over what he should do. He considered the woman's needs and privacy and sensed that the young man was also reluctant to impinge upon her personal space, but she needed help however in this era of 'woke' neither of the men moved to assist her.

The tram screeched loudly to a halt at a busy intersection of city roads and the piercing noise of metal upon metal would have woken most people and the tram doors opened automatically, and the young woman remained motionless in her comatose state, with her phone on the floor. The audio inside the tram sounded; 'Southern Cross station, next stop Bourke Street.' The woman was then suddenly awake and with autonomic reflexes snatched her shoulder bag and stood to leave when Andrew spoke authoritatively to her; 'Don't forget your phone', and she rapidly gathered the device on the floor and sped to the now closing doors that snapped shut almost trapping her jacket.

The tram had moved forward making a sharp right turn that created an intense metal on metal screeching noise as it crossed a pedestrian crossing on a green light, then above the cacophony Andrew heard the terrifying sounds of a car breaking at speed with all four tyres screeching for survival on the bitumen He began to create traumatic mental images that made him sweat and his heart pounded in his chest and within minutes he had travelled well away from the terminus.

My Evil Twin
Andrea McMahon

To every action there is an equal and opposite reaction. That is Sir Isaac Newton's third law of motion. I read about it during the school holidays. My name is Georgia White and I was born on 15th April 1998, at the very same moment, in the very same hospital, as a boy called George Brown.

George Brown is my evil twin.

George lives in the house opposite my house, sits at the desk opposite me in school. It is obvious that George Brown exists as an equal and opposite reaction to me. For example, I have long shiny blonde hair; George has wild, curly dark hair. I am tall; George is short. I am quiet and friendly; George is loud and rude. I have a pet dog; George has a pet cat. I live with my dad and sister; George lives with his mum and brother. If Sir Isaac Newton hadn't been dead for nearly four hundred years, he could tell you all about it. He would have no trouble at all explaining why George Brown is my worst nightmare.

I don't like George Brown and George Brown doesn't like me. When we walk home from school we walk on opposite sides of the road. We try to keep away from each other as much as possible, or at least I do all of the time, and George does most of the time, unless he is trying to show off to his friends by flicking chewing gum into my hair, or putting dead lizards in my lunch box.

So, you can just imagine how upset I was when my dad told me that he'd invited George's mum and the boys over for a barbeque. Tonight. Tonight, George Brown is coming over to my house. I will say I'm sick, which will be true, because the thought of George Brown stepping into my house will definitely make me feel sick.

Because it has all become clear. The penny has dropped, as my mum used to say. My dad likes George's mum. Arrrrrgh! He wasn't just helping her fix her lawnmower because he is a good neighbour. She wasn't just offering him a glass of beer to say thank you. Oh, no, they were both doing these things because they wanted an excuse to hang out together like teenagers. Because they wanted an excuse to destroy my life!

And suddenly, I can see myself at the wedding… and there is George all dressed up in a suit with his wild bushy hair looking like it hasn't been brushed for a month. There is my dad and his mum all lovey-dovey up at the altar and there is me being sick all over the floor of the church because it is the very worst day of my life. George Brown is my stepbrother! My life is over. My world has come to an end. A stinky, noisy end.

I can't let it happen. I won't let it happen. I'm thinking this as George and his mother and little brother arrive at the front door. George doesn't look at all happy to be here, which is good. We ignore each other. My dad and his mum do not ignore each other, though. They laugh and giggle and play with their hair the way people do when they like each other. It is embarrassing. Old people should know better. George's mum has brought over the biggest salad, enough to feed the whole street. She is just showing off to my dad. My dad has opened a bottle of wine even though he never drinks wine. He is also showing off. I want to crawl into a hole in the ground and die!

'So, Georgia, why don't you take George upstairs and play a game on the new PlayStation until the sausages are ready?' Why don't I, Dad? Because he is disgusting, Dad, that's why. Because he will be two feet away from my bedroom and I know there's a wall in between, but I don't care and you don't care either, about me or anyone except yourself and someone who will never ever be my mother. Never!

But I can't say any of this out loud so instead I just burst into tears and run up to my bedroom and hide, sobbing great big wet embarrassing tears into my pillow. George Brown is downstairs and I am upstairs bawling. Obviously, I didn't need to wait for the wedding day for my life to be over. It's over now.

I hear my dad walking up the stairs and scream at him to go away. I want my mum back. And desperately wanting something you will never, ever be able to have again is the hardest, most horrible, thing in the whole world. I miss my mum so much.

I'm blowing my nose when I hear a knock on the door. 'The sausages are almost ready.' It's George. My dad sent George up to get me! Unbelievable. I'm not leaving my bedroom. Not ever again. I can't imagine ever doing anything again. Not eating sausages, not going to school, and certainly not opening the door of my bedroom to see George Brown standing there grinning his stupid grin and planning what he's going to tell all his revolting friends.

I don't open the door, but George does. He just stands there and he's not laughing at me. 'I'm going to have a go on your PlayStation, if that's okay. Do you want to play?'

And suddenly, I'm remembering that George's dad died too. He had a heart attack. Before I can think of anything to say, George turns and walks into the spare room. I hear him turn on the PlayStation and TV and slump down onto the couch. He's already working the controls when he calls out, 'It's okay, I know what to do. I've got a plan to make sure you will never be my stepsister, Miss Princess Perfect Goody Two-Shoes Georgia White.'

I'm thinking that if it has anything to do with chewing gum or dead lizards, it will probably work. Perhaps I will have a game on the new PlayStation after all.

A close call with the K.G.B.
Hank Koopman

The ship's captain turned red with rage, cursing in Russian. I tried desperately to wipe the horrible stain off his white uniform with my hankie. With arms flailing, he pushed me away, continuing to rant at me in Russian, which I had no way of comprehending. However, I knew it was not complementary.

Donna and I had won a cruise with CTC Cruises, the major prize in a grand final of a talent quest at Revesby Workers Club in January 1980. They chartered several Russian ships to start competition with market leader P&O out of Sydney. These vessels were sub-let by a South African company with an office in Sydney to cater to the emerging Australian cruise market. Being crewed by Russian Naval personnel and a staff trained in the UK as cabin stewards from all over the USSR, the charter of these vessels resulted in considerably cheaper fares being offered to Australian customers.

MV Turkmenia was the smallest ship in the CTC inventory, with a gross weight of only 5,127 tons, not much bigger than a destroyer in the RAN. Four hundred and one feet long and a fifty-two-foot beam, accommodating approximately 150 passengers and a small crew of about eighty. It was charming in its own way for us Aussies, not to contend with overcrowding as was the case with larger ships, but oppressive for the hospitality staff, with many KGB agents keeping tight control over them.

Our cabin steward was Maria, who came from Romania and was ordered into service by the communist political system to serve for a year in the employ of the Russian navy. Her three-year-old child was placed in the care of Maria's mother and father, with the threat of harm coming to them if she tried to defect. We attempted to tip her, but she gestured frantically, saying they could not take money from passengers. A well-publicised defection occurred the previous year in Sydney, and the Soviet Union was left with "egg on its face" and increased the number of KGB agents on its ships to prevent this from happening again.

Eighteen-year-old Liliana Gasinskaya from Ukraine had defected spectacularly on January 15, 1979, from the SS Leonid Sobinov, chartered by CTC, by squeezing through a porthole wearing only her red bikini and dropping into Sydney Harbour. She swam in the shark-infested waters for forty minutes before clambering onto a Pyrmont wharf. She was granted asylum under some protest from members of parliament, who thought she got preferential treatment because she was a beautiful eighteen-year-old. The Russians tried all consular intervention to get her back, but all those protests were dashed when, on December 24, 1979, Russia invaded Afghanistan, and consular niceties became strained even more. It was into this diplomatic quagmire that a small group of Australian tourists were placed onboard the MV Turkmenia.

Our prize had to be taken on the promulgated day to fit in with the cruise itinerary. It was the third last cruise CTC lines were to make out of Sydney. Australia chose to deny any Russian cruise ships entry to its ports after March 1980 because of the attack on Afghanistan. Passengers remained oblivious to the diplomatic posturing behind the scenes; we were too busy having an enjoyable time.

Arriving at Circular Quay and seeing how small the Turkmenia was, Donna was apprehensive about the next ten days. We were shown our accommodation and had to share a shower with the cabin next to ours. This was not to Donna's liking. What could we do? We didn't pay for the cruise, so we just had to make a go of an unpleasant situation. However, things would worsen as the ship passed The Heads and headed out to sea, facing an Easterly wind and a moderate swell. Any swell would be noticeable in a vessel this size for the uninitiated to a seafarer's life.

Donna's inability to face the dining room menu on the evening of departure was understandable, and she was not the only one. I left her in the cabin with a packet of sea-sickness tablets to quell the upheaval in her stomach. It was just as well. The menu proposed a selection of traditional Russian cuisine far from appetising. During earlier cruises, complaints reached CTC head office, and some lousy publicity made them hire an Australian chef to complement the Russian cooks to ensure Australian meals were available.

I sat down next to a man and started a conversation about how we had won the cruise as a prize. He introduced himself as Paul Dixon, "but call me Dicko," he added.

"Gee," he remarked, "I wonder how many people paid to go on this cruise? There's five of us, and we didn't pay either." After further small talk and sussing each other out, including about my service in the Navy, he revealed that he was a member of the

Australian Federal Police working undercover. His family was also onboard to cloak his operation in case hostilities between Russia and Australia deteriorated.

"You'll notice HMAS Stuart will be shadowing us for the duration of this cruise," he assured me. "If anything happens, like trying to take a shipload of Australians hostage, Stuart will come alongside and take control of this ship." This news hit me like a sledgehammer. Donna and I were part of a serious political thriller.

The following day, I ventured to the flybridge early and looked astern. Just as Dicko had said, there was the grey outline of a frigate on the horizon. Returning to our cabin, I noticed Donna still had a green pallor about her, and it was apparent the pills were not going to help her seasickness. Maria slipped a notice under our door informing us that the doctor would hold a clinic to dispense an injection to cure seasickness. Donna hates injections at the best of times; this time, there was no hesitation.

A queue had formed in the narrow passageway leading to the doctor's surgery, with about thirty people seeking relief from the awful malady of seasickness. Still unsure, Donna asked a few people, "How was it?" The answer was, "You get it in the bum. But it doesn't hurt; she's surprisingly good."

"That's a relief, a lady doctor," Donna whispered as her turn came up. She entered, and I stood guard at the door. Then I noticed this huge, burly Russian pushing through the remaining patients and moving to grasp the door handle to the doctors' surgery. I sprang into action, pulling his hand away from the door. "Hey you," I yelled loudly, "You can't go in there; my wife is in there with her pants down, getting a needle from the doctor." My condescending tone inferred he must have been stupid.

"Let go my arm," he grumbled with his thick Russian accent. He pushed me aside, saying,

"I am doctor," in a surly accent.

"Well, who the hell is giving my wife an injection then?" I retaliated forcefully.

"Australian doctor," he announced as he entered **his** surgery. I commenced to do a Basil Fawlty cringe, wishing I could disappear. There had been no mention of an Australian doctor being on board, an Australian chef, or an undercover Federal Police officer with an Australian warship he could call up in an emergency. The passengers had been left in the dark about all these contingencies.

Three days later, we arrived in calmer waters around Noumea. Here, we noticed the heavy hand of the KGB escorting some crew members ashore in groups of four or five. They were not free to go ashore alone. I cannot imagine living under such an oppressive regime. On movie nights, before the main feature, Soviet propaganda films and newsreels showed how wonderful life is under communism, people working together and being happy in factories and fields.

It was noticeable that people living under a police state constantly feared being "dobbed in" by a fellow worker or superior. In addition to the Russian band, crew members put on Russian exhibition dance nights. Donna and I also performed one night as part of our remit. It was a disaster, as the band could not read our charts. It was only the Australian piano player who saved us; he was able to read our music.

Dicko and I started a routine at about six p.m. each night. We would meet on the flybridge to discuss and solve the world's problems. This evening, a beautiful sunset appeared on the skyline. Yellow, gold, and ruby red streaked across the azure blue canvas of a night sky that was developing like a coloured photograph before our eyes. We remained speechless for a while taking it all in, thoroughly entranced.

The stillness was broken by a loud "thud" coming from behind us. Spinning around, we saw a large albatross spread-eagled on the deck, knocked unconscious or dead by flying into the ship's mast, rising several feet above the flybridge. Sea legends abound that if you or your boat kill an albatross at sea, you will be doomed. These large seabirds, with wingspans up to ten feet or more, soar over the waves for long distances like a glider, without flapping their wings. I knelt and noticed his body still moving, so I presumed he was only stunned.

"We can't let him die, Dicko; it could be a disaster for us. Can you go down to the doctor's surgery and see if they could check him over in case he broke a wing?" Dicko hurried away to find a doctor. I thought I'd gather him up and take him down one deck to the boat deck, where it was more sheltered. Taking great care, I could fold his wings against his body, pick him up and carry him down the ladder. I placed him in a sheltered position behind an electric motor that lowered the lifeboats and waited for Dicko to return with the doctors. There was no movement from our injured patient; his head still flopped over.

Up to this point, I hadn't been introduced to the Captain, but now he was approaching me in his pure white uniform, about to entertain guests at his table for dinner, a long-standing sea-time tradition.

"Good evening, Captain," I rushed up to greet him, continuing with my excited diatribe, unaware that his English was atrocious. "I need to tell you, we've hit an albatross," I tried explaining it further.

"Wott?" he looked puzzled.

"We've hit a big bird," I'm flapping my arms about, trying sign language to help him understand.

"Big bird? Wott is big bird?" He was even more confused. Now, with hindsight, I wish he had not asked me that question.

Reaching down and picking up my injured patient from its resting place, I swung around to show the Captain. At that precise moment, the albatross came to, ejecting the most enormous, foulest fishy-smelling white and seaweed green shit all over his pure white uniform. He held his nose to stop the aroma from making him throw up. His face turned crimson, trying to maintain his composure. I was shocked and quickly put the bird down, only to have him fly away into the gloom. I fell to my knees and grabbed my hankie from my pocket, trying to clean up the horrible mess but only making it worse. I repeated ad-nauseam, "I'm so sorry, sir. I'm so sorry."

Flailing his arms about and cursing in Russian, he stormed off toward his quarters.

"I couldn't find the doctors anywhere," Dicko returned to the boat deck. "They must be having dinner with the Captain tonight."

"I don't think so, mate," as I explained all the gory details of what had just transpired.

"If a Russian submarine surfaces beside the ship tonight, and I go missing, call in the cavalry because the Captain has ordered the KGB to make me disappear."

First Dates and Food (more about the latter)
Brenda Slavoff

Dating in this day and age is a gamble. All right, we've checked the dating sites and done the preliminaries, and now we have arranged to meet face to face and the inevitable worries are niggling. Will the person turn up and prove they weren't just AI? Will they look anything like their photo? Are they overweight and underpaid? Or underweight and over themselves? How can we figure out the character fundamentals of our future - maybe - companion/whatever? I have only one thing to say. First dates should always take place in a restaurant.

We all need to eat, don't we?

In the old days it used to be the cinema - back row, usually - and parking afterwards to "talk". Ah, the good old days . . . forget them and forget about sex for the moment. Restaurants are safer places to talk. There are other people about, waiters and waitresses hanging around, menus to ponder and alcohol to guzzle. We don't need to juggle conversation with parrying or initiating amorous advances. And when the conversation peters out, you can fiddle with that wineglass, chew that piece of celery daintily, while thinking out your next comment such as:

"What's your family like? Your mother?" They say people become like their parents in time.

"She's dead."

"Oh, I'm sorry. What was your father like?"

"Which one?"

Time to change the subject. Onto the time-honoured question: "How many times have you been married?" At least you can work out if they are a stayer or a tryer.

"Never been married."

Oh, so he's an evader.

I don't tend to ask anyone what they've been doing lately. That will come out in due time. Whenever someone asks me what I have been doing lately, my mind goes completely blank and I answer something like, "Oh, nothing much."

Forgetting that during the past week my dog got lost, my divorce came through, my best friend entered an ashram and I bought a new car which I pranged the next day. Not to mention that I went to the

Writers Fellowship's latest meeting which is bound to get the brain cells zinging – but in my case, obviously not immediately memorable.

But food – glorious food – never lets you down. It sustains and nourishes, occupies and comforts.

Choosing something on the menu tells you a lot about your date, too. It may go something like this:

"What are you having? The ravioli looks good."

"I'm gluten free. What about you?"

"I've gone Paleo, so I'll have to choose the steak. Though it probably wasn't grass fed, and I can't have the gravy –"

"What about the chicken?"

"Full of hormones. It doesn't say organic. Do you know how they *raise* chickens these days? Are you having the fish?"

"No, I'm full vegan now as well as gluten free." It's a challenge, but life is full of challenges.

". . . Potatoes?"

"No way. Do you know they spray potatoes ten times?"

"I thought it was only nine."

"Nope, they added another time."

"A salad? I need lots of raw food on Paleo."

"Yes, I'll have that too, but without the dressing. You never know what oils they use. And no cheese, unless it's soy."

"The fish is farmed salmon, I bet. I think I'll go vegetarian tonight too."

"So . . . what'll it be? Omelette?"

"No, I'm intolerant to eggs. The eggplant stack looks good though, with mushrooms."

"Good idea; but no cheese."

"What about wine for you? I can't drink it; cave men didn't have wine in those days."

"No, they put preservatives in wine. Terrible for hay fever. Just water, please."

There you are, a conversation packed with valuable information about our date, and all we've done is choose a dish. We already know we're soul mates.

Did I say that food is King and Country and that life revolves around it? It's there, the great fact of life, love it or hate it. Think about it: it takes a lot to get it to your plate. Farmers grow it or chase it, trucks transport it and pollute long distances, high school students artistically pack it on shelves, chefs chop, cook and rearrange it.

I repeat: a restaurant is the only place for a first date. And even if the date spectacularly backfires, the joyous memory of that eggplant stack with a side salad will linger on.

Wild as
Marilyn Arnold

It doesn't take much to be wild these days.
Such a busy world, so much craziness,
all the fake news, so much messiness,
so many antagonistic views, a failing to amuse,
opinions which confuse. To be agro is normal,
everything is lawful except political correctness,
which is unacceptable. Let's take it to court –
you could be liable to pay for insulting me today!

People are wild about lots of things,
the need to be famous, the fate of a king,
climate change, domestic violence, corrupt politicians,
their footy team losing, some future petition,
all the many wars now taking place, for no-one
has learned to communicate. There seems to be
any excuse to hurl abuse, because even two people
can't agree, like you and me. Praying for peace
has taken a downturn.

Money's the overwhelming concern now,
oh, apart from the Chinese taking over, the stadium,
the coral reef, uranium mining, whether Trump will
be president again, which country has world domination,
whether islands are disappearing, the ramifications of A.I.,
Covid after-effects, whether we will all die…

there's a multitude of real concerns,
to make us wild, to keep us wild,
so many, without a doubt… so many for the world
to work out. In fact,
I'm exhausted from all those things
I'm wild about.

Happily Ever After
Marilyn Arnold

someday her prince would
    get her pregnant
clouds at the wedding
    his shining armour blinding
seven dwarves in one voice
    warned her to whistle as she
wondered if a needle
    could stitch up her future
whether she would have to
    lick up spilt milk
whether dreams die under the whir of
    a vacuum cleaner
whether happiness could
    be ironed flat
for fee fi fo fum
    she's married now
    her story's done.

Our Thirteenth Pilgrimage Year: Days Two & Three
Allan Jamieson

Terms:
henro = pilgrim
michi = trail

I first heard of the 88 Buddhist temples on Shikoku Island – and the associated pilgrim trail – sometime in the 1980's. In the 1990's, my wife saw the book *"Japanese Pilgrimage"* by Oliver Statler (publ. 1983) for sale in the Burnie library. For the ridiculously low price of $1.50, it became ours. In the 21st Century, Statler's book is still being referred to by pilgrims as a key text.

Buddhist temples have existed on Shikoku for at least 1,500 years and pilgrimages have taken place for over 1,000 years. The pilgrimage extends around the entire island of Shikoku and the total length of the trail (if walking) is about 1,200 km. It is a journey wherein the pilgrim asks for protection and fulfilment of all wishes. Even for non-Buddhists, it is considered a rare opportunity allowing deep reflection into one's life. This is an "OK" concept if you are walking, but don't try it if you are driving a car!

Only in the past 100 years has it been possible to undertake the pilgrimage other than by walking and nowadays the vast majority travel by bus or car. Many temples sit on top of mountains. We chose to walk.

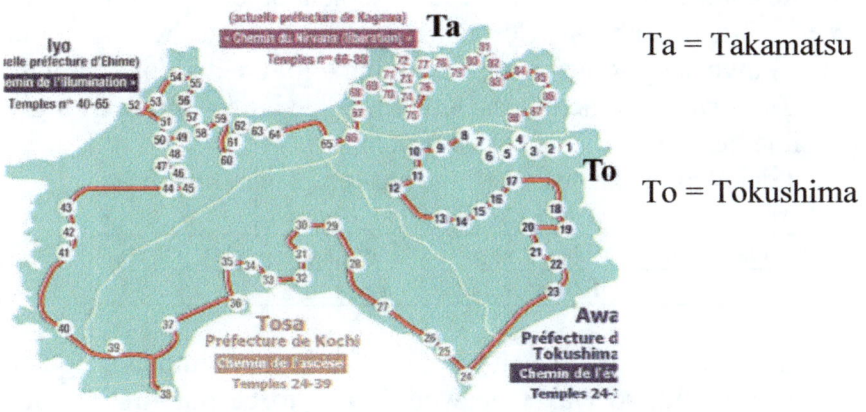

Ta = Takamatsu

To = Tokushima

I retired in July 1999 and in October, Kuniko and I decided to walk to a few temples to experience the pilgrimage. I had no ambition beyond the six temples we visited that year, but the experience prompted us to try another section of the trail in October 2000 (Year Two).

[October is the best month weatherwise to be in Japan. Two weeks is ideal because we could fully utilise a 14-day Japan Rail Pass.]

By the time 2009 came around, we had been to 67 temples in a total of 26 walking days. A reality now loomed. If we intended to complete the full pilgrimage, the remaining 21 temples would undoubtedly be the hardest to get to, simply because – so far – I had focused on the easiest temples. Also, we were now ten years older. *Not smart, Allan!*

Nonetheless, we set to in 2009 and walked to eight temples and in 2010, we walked to another five. What would 2011 (Year 13) bring?

It had always been our custom – aside from our pilgrimage – to visit some part of Japan that we had not been to before and in 2011, we had intended to visit the Shimokita Peninsula at the extreme northern tip of Honshu Island in October. Before then, though, came the massive earthquake of March 11 and the even more terrible *tsunami*. Communications with northern Honshu were problematic for several months afterwards, threatening to throw any plans I might make into chaos. What to do instead? I took another look at my plans for Year 13 and Year 14. Could we manage to visit the final eight temples – involving some serious climbing – in five days of walking?

Tough ask! Nonetheless, Kuniko agreed to try this seemingly impossible task (impossible for us, I mean).

I decided to start by visiting four temples in this order:

Day One	Day Two	Lay day	Day Three
T22	T20 & T21	Relax	T12

My 'logic' was that we usually arrived in Japan without adequate advanced training, so Day One would have to be our first serious exercise since last year's pilgrimage. Day Two would entail what appeared to be the toughest portion of the *henro michi* for 2011.

There would then follow a rest day before we tried to reach **T12**, said by most *henro* to be the real challenge.

At the end of Day One, we were very tired, having climbed 250m and walked for 4 hours at an average of 2.2 km/hr.

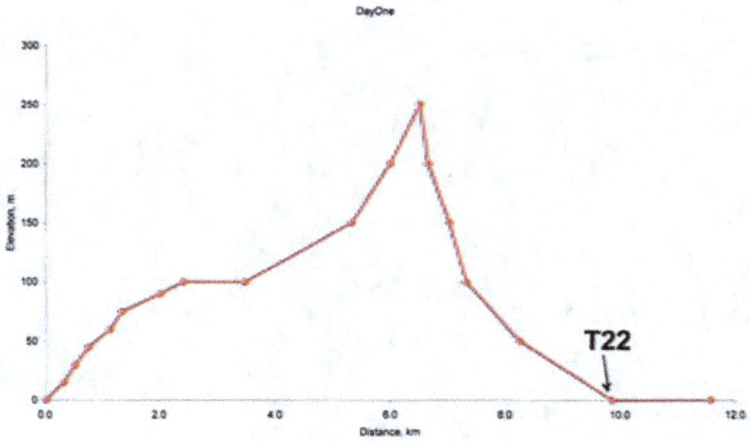

Day Two

We began walking at 0925. The *henro michi* branched off the road and soon it was up and up and up for us – a relentless climb to start the day though initially we had a good view back over the Katsuura River valley below us to show how far we had climbed.

Steps! We were often frustrated by long series of steps, in many cases too far apart and too deep to easily stride over them, though occasionally some kind individual had filled in the spaces between the steps with asphalt to smooth the way.

I was pleasantly surprised when we reached **T20** in one hour, at 1030. We had walked 3 km and climbed 500m.

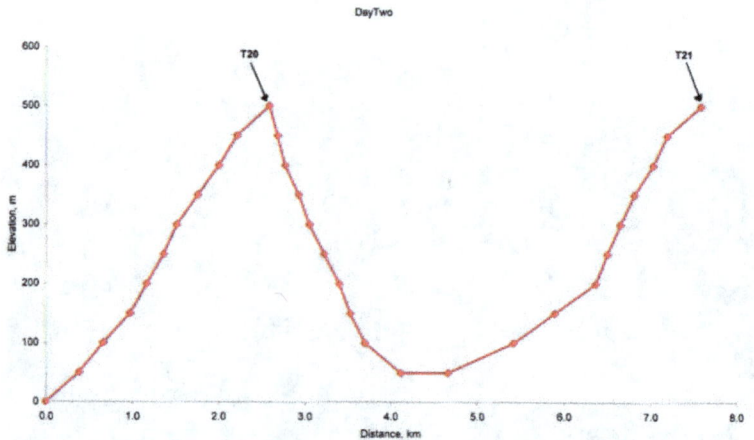

In rather high spirits, we commenced the descent to a river valley, but I had to keep reminding both Kuniko and me that the hardest part of the day's trek would be the final climb up to **T21**. I had read that the *henro michi* meandered down between farm properties, but none were seen for a long time. When we finally broke through the forest and were close to the Naka River we did walk between farms, and it made for a pleasant stroll.

What's more, it was an almost flat path compared to the descent we had just made. We could recover our breath. We came to the river and crossed on a large bridge. Just a few weeks before, the river had filled the whole valley floor and debris from this flood could be seen well above the current water level.

Many pilgrims had written of the seriousness of what lay in front of us. It was strictly 'one foot in front of the other' territory; ever upward, even if only slowly. We came to a junction – the temple car park was nearby – and it seemed we would make it: We had made it!

Temple **T21** was expansive, with large, impressive grounds. Just as well, I thought – given how hard it was to get there. We spent quite a time wandering around, recovering our breath and absorbing the ambience.

Yes, this was worth the effort!

It was only a short walk to the ropeway terminus; we had around ten minutes to wait before we could clamber aboard and descend – in luxury! While waiting, we were served an unusual but refreshing native tea.

The vista from the ropeway was impressive with mountain range after mountain range until, coming over a ridge the town of Wajiki revealed itself way down below.

We had omitted to bring any lunch that day, as I had assumed we could find something to eat and drink along the way. There was nothing and the shops at the Wajiki ropeway terminus had closed ten minutes before we arrived, so – hungry and thirsty – we had no option but to walk to the bus stop on highway 195. A ten-minute wait and we were then on a bus headed for Tokushima and our hotel. Standing room only and even that was scarce for the first 25 minutes as school kids occupied every seat and most of the standing space too. Busily thumbing their mobile phones, there was only one small group of girls who talked to each other.

All told, it had taken us 5.5 hours of walking today; an average of 1.8 km/hr. Looking back some weeks afterwards, there was no doubt in my mind that Day Two of our pilgrimage in 2011 was the toughest of all five days of walking.

The next day was our planned rest day spent in Tokushima.

Day Three

We had already walked to **T11** in 2008, so we would now walk from there to **T12** and, hopefully, we could then get down the other side of the mountain to a bus stop in time to catch (perhaps) the last bus to Tokushima for the day.

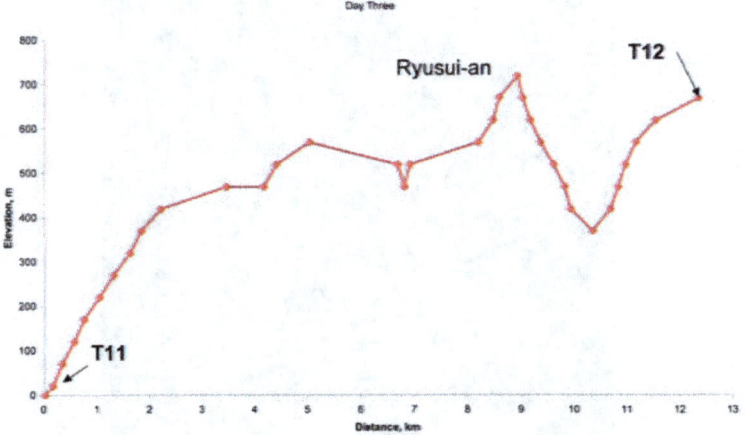

We took a taxi to **T11** and at about 1000, I followed Kuniko, who was already into the climb. The trail seemed to go up and up. There was supposed to be a ridge, a change of direction and a lessening of the slope after an hour's walk, but we noticed nothing like this.

Onward and upward, we went. Time for lunch at a place called Ryusui-an. A few other *henro* had the same idea but there was little talking as we were all exhausted and still mindful of the need to descend 350m then climb 300m up the next hill before reaching **T12**.

Down we went until we broke out of the trees and saw farms in front of us. Again, we could walk beside houses.

A small river of stones was crossed on foot, then began the final climb. Maybe we were getting fitter – we darn well should have been – as this climb seemed slightly less strenuous than the one on Day Two. So, exactly six hours after we left **T11** we arrived at temple **T12**.

I was disappointed with this temple. After the sight of **T21** on Day Two, I had imagined that a similar welcoming sight would have afforded us (it had been another difficult climb) yet the temple grounds here were rather plain to my eyes. Or perhaps it was just that I was too exhausted to take in the finer points of this temple.

I spent ¥9,000 on a taxi back to Tokushima and we sat down to our luxurious meal at a reasonable hour. Our walk that day covered 12.9 km.

The next day, we moved our 'base' from Tokushima to Takamatsu. There were still two days of walking in front of us, but YES, we did get to **T88** on Day Five.

I Wouldn't Mind
Tim Phillips

I wouldn't mind if you loved French *cinema*
As long as you wanted to watch it *avec moi.*
And I wouldn't mind if you were mooning over Gerard Depardieu
As long as *I* was the one sitting close, on the couch, *avec vous.*

And besides, subtitles are never a chore
When you're reading them together with the girl you adore
(And - when they're written in the language of *l'amour.*)

But when the credits are rolling and it finally says "*Fin*"
I'd hope that the *real* evening might then begin!

For sitting close on the couch *is* certainly good
But *mon dieu*! How it could
Be so much better *by far*
If you *didn't* then say:-

        "Well thanks for the cheese platter
        So, uh, *au revoir.*"

I wouldn't mind if you were a great mathematician
And left *me* at home to wash the dishes in the kitchen
While you lectured at uni with all your scholarly erudition.

And I wouldn't mind if I got just the *occasional* lecture
About Pythagorus' theorum or the Collatz conjecture
As long as I didn't get too many lectures from you
About my - infinitely - more limited I.Q.

And it would break me to learn that after any lecture
You were making out with some other professor
'Cause you could talk about *triangles*, and octagons, and all you both knew
Whereas I'd never know that *I* was in a *triangle* with you.

I wouldn't mind if you were a magician's assistant
Who could make my watch disappear in an instant

As long as I always got it back
After he'd pulled some rabbit out of a hat.

And that if he made *you* disappear, I could always be certain
That I could find you again, behind the curtain.

But if he wanted to saw you in half
I figure I'd have to be pretty daft
Not to learn that little trick too.
'Cause we'd need a backup plan
In case things got out of hand,
And I ended up with *two* - not one - of you.

I wouldn't mind if you wanted a caravan
And wanted to travel across this wide brown land
As long as at night we had a conjugal bed
And I wasn't confined to the trailer instead.

I won't mind if you have cats or dogs
Or keep a guinea pig in a box
And I could handle tropical fish - as they're all the rage
I wouldn't mind an elephant - as long as *I* didn't have to clean the
cage.

Hell - I wouldn't mind if you had your own animal shelter
'Cause I'll always fall for a girl with a compassionate streak
As long as you were kissing me
                         - more passionately
Than anything with fur, and claws, or a beak.

I wouldn't mind if you went bungee-jumping!
'Cause I know it *would* - certainly - get the heart pumping!
But *I* wouldn't care for such extreme sports
But each to their very own, of course.

I couldn't care if you smoke or drink
Though most illicit drugs
Would make me think,
And any meth or heroin would have to go down the sink.

I wouldn't care if you'd tattooed your neck
Or pierced your labia
But any track-marks up your arm
Would have to be another matter.

I wouldn't mind if your passion was the opera or ballet
Although many might feel those cultural forms
Might have become less relevant today.

But I wouldn't want us to argue
Like Capulet and Montague
For I have a *slight* small interest
In *one* of those more classical art-forms too

'Cause I admit I *do* love Shakespeare
So I'd love if you could appreciate the bard
Once you'd penetrated that Ye *Olde English*
(Which *is,* admittedly, sometimes pretty hard.)

'Cause in-between the sword-play
And the grand conflicts and commotions
I feel Hamlet was the first - in literature
To express the deepest existential emotions

So you'd be infinitely more likely to appeal to me
If you could resonate
With Hamlet's first, and fifth, soliloquoy.

And I wouldn't care if you were President of the United States
Although being an Aussie, I don't see how you could even enter the race
But if we *could* get around that issue of nationality
Those Yankees might benefit from a little Aussie rationality.

And it would be a first in the history of the United States
To have a woman standing in the winner's race
We could go strolling through the White House holding hands
And *you* wouldn't be the First Lady
Hell, I'd just be the *First Man*!

And the first thing that *I'd* want done
Is to say, "What's the deal out there at that Area-51?"
Do you have a *real* UFO, and alien technology and shit?
And have you back-engineered a saucer
Because, I'd really like to try an' fly it!

I'd be sayin' "Hey-no girl, you can't go up there with me
Because - hey - *you're* the President
So you've got to think about your security!
We all need you too much, and we can't take the risk
Of havin' a President up there in some alien flyin' disk.

Then I'd be searching through Area-51 looking for aliens in jars
And tryin' to find the truth - like, did we all come from Mars?
And like, "What's the truth about God and the pyramids and shit?"
Man - once I started down that rabbit-hole, I'd just never quit.

Paper Facts
Allan Jamieson

Q1. When, where and who first made paper in the way we still do today?

A It is generally accepted that in 105AD, a Chinese eunuch, Tsai Lun, "invented" the method we use today to make paper. He collected assorted fibrous material, such as plant fibre, cotton fabric, etc. and 'pulped' this mixture in water while beating the mass with wooden hammers. The mixture was then poured over a mesh screen of bamboo strips, so the fibres remained on top of the screen. After the fibres had dried in the sun, Tsai Lun had his paper.

Why put <u>invented</u> in quotation marks above? Because Tsai Lun was possibly only copying what common wasps had *always* done! Wasps make their nests by chewing up wood and plant material and mixing it with saliva. They then use this 'paper pulp' to construct their nest.

Furthermore, there is an even earlier 'claimant' though it is highly unlikely that Tsai Lun ever was aware of this. During the First Dynasty of Egypt (somewhat prior to 3,000 BC) the ancient Egyptians made their form of paper by selecting portions of the papyrus reeds that grew along the River Nile; they placed these portions down in layers; each layer lying at right angles to the one below it. They then pounded these layers with a stone. This pulped the fibres in the material and, when dried in the sun, they had their paper. While their technique was different in some ways to that used by Tsai Lun, the result was not overly different, though Tsai Lun's sheets could be much thinner than the normal Egyptian paper sheets.

On Tassie's North-West coast, you can watch a papermaker work precisely as Tsai Lun did – and visitors can make their own sheets too. [See www.creativepaper.com.au]

Q2. When was the first machine used successfully to make paper?

A. In the late 18th Century, people in France and in England eagerly tried to design a machine.

In 1798, the Frenchman Nicholas-Louis Robert invented a prototype of a machine on which paper was formed on a continuously moving wire mesh screen. The French had need of a continuous roll of paper to fill the urgent demand for banknotes after the French Revolution.

A French machine maker went into difficulties, but finally in England two brothers, Henry and Sealy Fourdrinier, engaged engineer Bryan Donkin to build a new and further improved machine in 1807.

Donkin was the only one of these pioneers to gain financial security from his work on the paper machine; by 1851, he had designed a total of 191 machines, including 83 for British mills, 105 for Europe, one for India, and two for the United States.

Q3. Which is stronger: Paper or Steel?

A You might think steel is stronger, but if you had an *equal weight* of each, the paper would be stronger. Imagine that you have a reel of paper. If you hold one end of the paper and lift it up towards the sky, you would be approximately 10,000 metres in the air – communing with passing passenger jet planes – when the paper strip finally broke. You need proof? This photo shows a 2.5 tonne Jaguar car being suspended from a single sheet of paper. [Source: *Teknisk uppkäftihet* M. Carlsberg and A. Scholander (1989) © Swedish Forest Industry]

The car is shown beside a paper machine; possibly the machine where that paper sheet had been made.

Now, would you believe me if I told you that in America in the 1930's, some passenger trains ran on paper wheels? Train engines in those days were not overly powerful and steel wheels were much heavier than those made of paper. Also, paper wheels gave a quieter ride for the passengers.

Q4. Have houses and buildings ever been made of paper?

A Yes. In the First World War, many field hospitals were made of paper. Houses in America were sometimes built of paper too during the latter half of the 19th Century.

Q5. Why should we use paper furnishings and walls in our houses and offices?

A Paper can improve our physical and mental health. Paper absorbs sound much better than glass or concrete, so hanging paper sheets – akin to a tapestry – adjacent to a wall will quieten a room and eliminate the current-day echoes that are so annoying, especially in restaurants.

Paper absorbs water from the air and can then evaporate it again, so helping to maintain the humidity of the air in a room at the optimum comfort level for living. Paper absorbs ultra-violet light more than visible light, so placing a paper screen beside your favourite reading chair will produce an illumination less harmful to the eyes when you are reading a book printed on paper.

From: A Tasmanian Epic Poem
Graeme Hetherington

(1)

These short-back-and-sides sonnets built
Of strict octosyllabic lines,
Of beats just one less than the cat's
Reddened tails, are gaol cells I'd like
To break free from but can't. Bereft
Of a honeycomb's riches, I
Still hope readers will turn each key,
Visiting all to serve the time
Needed to get the hang of them,
And having digested the lot,
The blocks they've been arranged into,
The whole grey penitentiary
The isle was once, and this book is,
Be released to freedom at last!

(2)

Till thirteen years of age reared on
The constantly wet overcast
Hell's Gates' cannibalised West Coast
Among convict-descended folk
Government propaganda called
'Residuals', though we comprised
Sixty-two percent, I escaped
As blotting paper sodden with
Memories, but only to return
At life's end to the East, where sun,
Instead of lightening, strengthens black
Squeezed out for poems, with manholes in
Ceiling thought of as trapdoors for
My ancestors to hurtle through.

(3)

(After Milton's *'Paradise Lost'*)

My matriarchal wowser-gran,
Shouting 'you devil!' dragged me from
Our sputtering one-valve wireless for
'Sooling on' with 'skitch 'em', West Coast
Old Crawler-created gaol slang,
My obsessively loved blood-red,
Bruise-blue 'Demons' against 'The Saints',
Through static making them 'The Hounds
Of Hell', that got me sent to bed
Without tea for kicking her in
The shins, for knowing as a child
That when 'Goodies' and 'Baddies' fought
My heart was with the underdog,
With Lucifer thrown out by God.

(4)

'Bit of a devil, your old man',
Hell's Gates' – formed blokes said with respect,
Though in his case mine was withheld
Since I judged him through mother's un-
Clouded stain-free New Zealand eyes,
Seeing him, of convict descent,
As Justice of the Peace unfit
To fine others when he too sped,
Gambled and drank illegally,
A style inherited from his
Great-grandfather James Sparks sent out
For forgery, rising to be
A constable whose weakness for
Low life continued as before.

(5)

(For Mervyn Peake)

Reading Peake's 'Gormenghast' replete
With hellish, gothic images,
I thought it weird his name was in
Geoffrey Blainey's *The Peaks of Lyell*,
Whose sulphur-reeking fumes I breathed
Could have Mephistophelised me,
Forming my Van Diemen's Land brain,
And even odder that the blood-
Infecting football ground on which
I skinned knees should have been at near-
By Gormanston, explaining why
I once drank from a mug with Old
Nick depicted in flaming red
Saying 'God's dead, how can I help?'

(6)

Touched by, identifying with
Faust, Mephistopheles, Christ, Job,
The Virgin Mary, Magdalene,
Gilgamesh, Enkidu, St John,
Odysseus, Oedipus, God,
Achilles, Hector, Socrates,
I write aspiring to embrace
Wide-ranging possibilities,
Shed limited, birthright Hell's Gates'
Van Diemen's Land mythologies,
Their Jim the Pieman, Gabbett, Pearce,
Authoritarian Governors,
Bushrangers, poisoner-artists as
Role models fit to form my soul.

(7)

My father's near-illiteracy
Painful to behold as he tried
To hide it making out headlines,
Or rarely struggled through a book
On Pharlap, Les Darcy, The Don,
Avoiding home-life for the pub
To slap other blokes' backs instead
Of giving me a hug as I
Watched brawling miners smash the posts
Of pub verandahs Friday nights,
His wriggling in discomfort when
It came to talk about forebears,
All meant childhood was shackled to
The deprivations of the past.

(8)

Unable to explain myself
From what little I knew about
My suppressed ancestry, I made
Up 'Aloyishus Featherstone',
Appropriately transported
For snatching a bulging purse from
Beneath a lifted petticoat
As a Duchess sat out a dance
At Windsor Castle or the like,
Imagining unearthing his
Poems stained by time done underneath
Rotting sugar sacks in a shack,
In bits and pieces waiting to
Be put together for the world.

(9)

Remembering my C of E
Masonic father breaking down,
His accusations of betrayal
When I announced I was engaged
To wed a Roman Catholic girl,
His jokes at the expense of 'Micks',
I've cast 'Aloyishus' as one,
Thinking of my forebears as priests
Who fed the London poor and were
Persecuted for their good works,
Preferring 'Paddies' as my friends,
Anything to be different from,
Revengefully defy my old
Man for failing me as a child.

(10)

Inspire me, Muse, to sing of my
Deep hatred for VDL/Tas,
My original island-home,
To explain why I've disowned kin,
The convict-blighted West Coast where,
Too sensitive for my own good
Bully-boys disfigured childhood,
Finding nothing to like in one
Who fled to Europe for his life
And stayed for over thirty years
In search of God-alone-knows-what,
Apart from Him, anywhere but
Remain on shores fatal to whales,
Seals, blacks, thylacines, transportees.

(11)

Familiar with parks in Madrid,
London Rome Athens Istanbul,
I've come to get life off my chest
In Hania, Crete, to find out in
An Epic where it all went wrong,
The public garden ideal as
An exercise yard for old lags,
A place to write, as Dante-like
I send to Hell foes, dead, alive,
To blame for my exile, a grey-
Fringed wistful gent twice split from 'Rule
Britannia' sickly wives, and at
Long last at fifty retired from
Academia to create.

(12)

Where 'Aloyishus' poems begin
And mine end I can't always tell,
As in those likening Hobart Town's
Mount Wellington, its graceless form
To Thames-side hulks looming through fog,
Or some where it's The Iron Duke,
Not just in name, but him curled up
Asleep in a heavy dark cloak
The night before he sent men to
Their Waterloo, as might an un-
Concerned, conscienceless psychopath,
Though my illustrious forebear
Was there and I was not, and on
That ground I'll credit them to him!

Letter to My Home
Brenda Slavoff

Sydney Cove,
April. Springtime at home.

My own dear Ma an' Dad,

'Tis long since last I did see you! Miles of ocean an' years an' years an' years.

I pray you be in health an' spirits an' that Johnny, Pip an' Susan be also well. They'd be grown up now, but no, how can they be? I cann't believe it. You be in my mind how I did see you last, standing in the court awaiting my sentence. Transportation. They didn't kill me, leastways not my body.

What can I tell you of the years come between us? I cann't, cause they be over now an' I be awaiting my ticket-of-leave. I swear to come home to you all! I tell the other men so an' they jeer at me: "Here be the lad who be going home soon. Take a message to me good lady, will ya?" Hardened we all be, but do not their hearts tighten at the thoughts of what they left behind? You'll not know me as the boy of sixteen who stole the watch, thinking hisself so smart. I be thin an' brown an' I don't know what my face looks like, there be no looking glasses to peer in, an' I do not wanna see what I've become. When I pass a window I look away, lest I see mesself.

But here, on the grassy slope above the homestead, a man can breathe freely. My eyes see far into the distance. It be nothing like England. The land be gently rolling, there be mountains in the distance, but it do have a harsh look. The colours be yellow an' grey in the green. The tree leaves be thin an' strange scented, hanging down as if dying in the sun. Summer be infernally hot, an' the heat feels both above an' below. How we look forward to dinner break in summer, when for a short while we sit in what shade we do find. Strange creatures be here such as you never saw, one that hops, a badger-type creature, an' a bird that laughs like a madman – or the devil! You would hate the snakes, Ma. They be fearsome creatures an' I dread having to stack an' collect wood, for the vipers love such spots. I dare not tell my fears, too many people be waiting to jeer at any weakness.

At the moment all is serene in the late afternoon sun. Blue-grey smoke comes outa the homestead kitchen chimney in thin wisps an' the breeze does stir the grasses. I can hear the dog's quiet breathing. She be a dear thing, with floppy black ears an' a twisted tail. I say she's twisted it with so much wagging, but I believe it got caught in a door once. She sits with me often an' lets me pat her. They call her Bess, an' she knows her name, for I say, "Are ye coming, my Bess?" an' she runs to my heels an' follows me up here every time. I think of old Bounder at home – is he still alive? He was a good dog. Bess is my only friend now.

Master be a silent man. He leaves us to the overseer. Master'll talk only to the overseer at the beginning an' end of day: "I want the fence rail done; how much of the corner did you cover?" The overseer works us as much as he can, but he does spare the whippings at least. Mistress says not a word to us. She sees us as so much dirt 'neath her feet, though master an' mistress live off the work they grind outa us. I see her walk down the path often, going to the kitchen. Sometimes through the open window I see her with the children, two boys an' a girl. I look down quick, cause I don't want to be noticed. The other men are usually too tired to talk much over the meal. I be the youngest an' they use me as fool of the jokes mostly. But I be not as tired as they, an' I escape to this place nearly ev'ry evening. Soon the days'll get short an' the wind'll be keen an' I won't be able to come here till spring. Sundays we don't work but we have to attend service. I don't mind, cause it reminds me so much of the church services we attended together, all of us, Susan just a littlie. Mostly as I listen I look outa the window at the endless blue sky an' the leaves stirring in the dry air.

We have little to do with the women servants. Sometimes I long to say hello as we would do at home, stop a minute, talk of weather an' such like. But I daren't. The convict girls look at you hard an' like as not say something sharp. No girl is a patch on Megan. Megan, I think of her a lot. I know she's forgotten me an' sometimes I cann't even remember exactly how she looked. But I never forget her. If you see her, give her greeting. I be coming back home. Yes, I know the men do laugh an' say "how'll you make ya money? Give us a loan, won't ya?" But I will come home. There's gold in the south, they say. Men have gone there an' made fortunes. I'd be happy just to make enough to get passage to England. It hasn't changed, has it? Things must be the same cause that's how I see 'em in my dreams at night. It'll all be the same, cause when I return I'll start right back where I was an' forget all this. I'll see you all again, I know it. Wait for me.

I have to go, 'tis nearly dark an' I must get Bess back. Come on, my girl, don't go too far, you foolish beast. Come here! Oh if only I could send a letter home! Every night I write one for 'em, don't I, girl? But I cann't write no more than you can an' there be none to write for me. Mistress wouldn't lift a thread, much less a pen, for me. Parson only tells me my sins. How can I ever let 'em know at home that I be returning? Only here, in my head an' in my heart. An' now I'll race you! Come on, steady on down!

brindle bitch
Edith Speers

she was savage.
she was real.
this is a true story,

not like the metaphorical
black dog
of depression,

or the legendary hounds of hell
or the Shakespearean
dogs of war.

she belonged
to the junkies next door.
she was never chained.

you didn't dare
turn your back on her
or she'd attack.

the only thing to do
was face her
and walk backwards

which is awkward.
then in a dream
the answer came:

no need to muzzle her
or fence her in
or tie her up

or do anything
that might harm her –
just pull her teeth.

weirdly enough
after that dream
she never bothered me.

KARMA GO COME
Meg McLaren

1

It was a hot, hot day in November when Leroy returned. The Guaracarra River still showed signs of past heavy rain and storms, rushing down over boulders and rocks, like a tawny, untamed tiger. Its yellow and olive-green waters rampaging through weeds and grasses, to finally pour into the blinding, blue depths of the Gulf of Paria.

Morning shadows were seeking shady corners as Leroy loped across the Marabella roundabout and made his way towards a tin roofed shop. Great melons, their rounded, bulging sides hot from the sun were stacked against walls the colour of sand. There were luscious yams and sweet potatoes. A couple of battered trucks were parked in front of the store. The day smelled of wet wood, steam rising from muddy streets as the sun boiled down. Leroy pushed aside the sticky strips hanging over the doorway 'catchin' flies an' gadderin' dust', and his eyes squinted to adjust to the dimness inside. The laminated counter was piled with everything from rice to tamarind balls and coconut cakes. There were loaves of Staublo's Bread and soft, white baps.

"Ah-yah-yai, Leroy! Where you come from?" A familiar voice called out and an Indian woman, her head covered with a silken sari, emerged from the dark and closely followed by a young boy. She put her arms around Leroy and kissed him on both cheeks. "I t'ought we done see de back of you, Leroy. Wha's it- one year now?"

"I bin wid me sista in Tobago, Amina…but now I'se back to stay."

He leaned on the counter, and the boy's eyes opened wide.

"How you lose yo' fingers Leroy?"

Leroy threw back his head, his laugh rough and grating, like a macaw.

"Shush Sammy."

"No, no Amina. I'se ok wid dis. Is over now. I done finish wid de drinking an' de self-pity." He turned. "Sammy, dis happen a year ago to de day. I tellin' you boy, doan you go work in de cane fields. Dey's a dangerous place. Bad people." He glanced over at Amina. "Eldica home?"

"She workin' today Leroy. She do laundry for a Mrs Dean in St Joseph's Village. You know de place?" She paused unsure whether she should continue. "De chillun' at home."

"T'ank you doux-doux."

Leroy left the shop and made his way around the corner where a primitive road meandered between monstrous trees, loud with the sound of kiskadees, and unpainted, weather-stained huts. Bougainvillea frothed over leaning fences and dark doorways, splashes of purple, pink and white. At the end of this road was a Catholic Church with a cross on top, and beyond that, the sugar cane fields, stretching as far as the eye could see.

And there, right beside the church was Number Four, so close that on a Sunday the congregation who had gathered to pray could look out through arched windows right into the yard. It was exactly as Leroy remembered. A small house sheltered under towering clumps of bamboo that creaked and cast shadows, a verandah with baskets of Boston ferns hanging from the beams, a goat tethered to a post, chickens pecking at a mound of food scraps, beating their wings, squabbling with surprise when they saw him.

The noisy household was the bane of Father McCormack's life competing as it did with his sermon, but then... there was always the hope of a conversion. "Just come to Mass on Sunday Eldica, and bring the children."

"You barkin' up de wrong tree Fada. Sunday is de chilun's bath day. Dey mus' be clean. I doan want dos pesky nuns comin' to take dem away. ALWAYS pokin' dey noses in where dey have no right to be."

Memories flooded Leroy's mind and, like peeling back the layers of an onion, each memory brought tears.

He could hear the children as he approached the house, their voices raised, argumentative. As he got closer, he heard Duane, (he must be eight now?) giving his sister instructions, as the eldest child is often wont to do.

"Put 'dese plates on de table Esme and 'den fill a jug of water from de tap."

"Do it yo'self Duane. Youse always bossin' me around."
With that she stormed out onto the wooden porch coming to a standstill when she saw Leroy. The silence seemed to go on forever, then....

"Daddy! Daddy!" Her screams brought Duane running outside…

Much later Leroy, stretched out on a hammock strung between two trees with the children curled in beside him, felt happier than he had been in a long time. They accepted his presence there as if it were the most natural thing in the world. As if he had never been away.

He tried to ignore the niggling doubt that had begun eating its way into his mind. Eldica would be home in an hour.

2

"Hola, Leroy! Wha' you doin' here? I never t'ought I goin' see you again." Eldica lowered a bundle of washing to the ground and straightened up, hands on her hips.

She was of mixed heritage, descended from an African slave who had fallen hopelessly in love with the daughter of an Indian worker. Her eyes were mesmerising, long lashed and almond shaped. Leroy felt she could look into his very soul. Her hair was dark and tightly curled, her complexion soft and dusky. He thought how beautiful she was, but did not dare to tell her so.

For the past year, when asked about his whereabouts, Eldica would hiss through clenched teeth, the tight coils of her hair standing on end, trembling with indignation, "Men! Dey come an dey go." And no one dared pursue the subject, so filled with vitriol was her voice. Then there was that worrying incident that had occurred only last week. Christmas was fast approaching and Duane dared to mention that "maybe me daddy gonna bring me a present." The ensuing cacophony of screams and shouts and the sight of Eldica chasing the boy along the mud-covered path, the whites of her eyes glistening, was still a source of conversation.

"Nooo way I go tangle wid she!" was the general consensus.

She looked at Leroy standing there, his right arm hanging at his side, its maimed paw forcing her to remember, and her stomach turned in a series of sudden drops and lurches. She felt a surge of anger as she walked up to him. The slap was fast and deadly like a scorpion's sting. She twisted around to leave, tears burning her eyes.

"Doan' go Eldica. We can sort dis out."

"I mus' go Leroy. I'se a lot to 'tink about. Watch de chil'run. Yo' see me when yo' see me."

When she reached the roundabout she climbed aboard the first bus that came along. It brought her back through the San Fernando suburbs of St. Joseph's Village, Vistabella and Sumach Gardens, that were spread around the lower slopes of 'The Hill.' They rattled past bungalows set back from gravelled driveways and manicured lawns. Humming birds, pulsating and luminous, hovered above explosions of vibrant blooms, zinnias and marigolds and hibiscus. They passed the Dean's residence, and Eldica gazed out at the familiar spreading boughs of a Flamboyant casting shade over the front porch. They disturbed a flock of parrots that crashed noisily through its branches, feathered jewels flying upwards towards a flawless blue sky.

After alighting from the bus, Eldica made her way to the rocky outcrop rising in the middle of the city. She clambered skyward up a narrow, winding track through sparse forests and bushland and found a shady spot to sit down. Only then did the tears start. The past going around and around in her head. "Thinking" she thought "Is worse than physical pain......"

3

She recalls that day last November. She remembers pushing through the cane, brutal and grass-like, thorns burrowing into her naked feet. The field is alive with insects and bold lizards, home to scorpions the size of a hand. And the Fer-de-Lance, a viper so deadly that no one could survive an injection of potent venom from its fangs.

Leroy is slashing cane in a quiet corner of the plantation. Over a hundred years ago, his father and his father's father had been transported from the banks of the Ganges, across thousands of miles of ocean, to work on the island as indentured labourers. They filled the vacuum left in the work force after the abolition of slavery, and the cultivation of cane was the basic reason for them being there. Nothing had changed. This was still all there was. Miserable lives of hard toil, poverty and subservience.

As Eldica approaches carrying in a brown paper bag, a flask of water and a bap bread spread with butter and guava jelly, she sees Robbo, dirty and unkept, chewing on a stalk of cane. His face is weathered from toiling in the burning sun, his hands wrinkled and calloused. Leroy represents everything Robbo detests about colonialism and the destructive potential of King Cane. Hate shines through the bitterness and hopelessness clouding his dark, rolling eyes. Horrified, she watches as he steps gingerly over a spiky layer of cane leaves. Holding a cutlass tightly, he moves cautiously towards Leroy. The silence is ominous, like a boil erupting.

"Hey dere monkey boy! You take my job, now I go get you!" Eldica calls out to the overseer, but it's too late. As Leroy lifts his arm in an effort to protect himself, Robbo swings down and Leroy's fingers are laid open to the bone.

Robbo flees, running as if the devil himself were at his heels. He stumbles around a corner and for a moment stands motionless in his tracks, facing the direction from which he has come. Then, as if making a decision, he keeps on running, hidden by the long spears of razor-edged blades. The toes of his feet, spread out from walking barefoot, move swiftly and soundlessly among the narrow paths.

"Why did I not see this coming?" Eldica thinks as she helps Leroy walk to the superintendent's hut. He hobbles along like a bird with a broken wing, his hand wrapped in a strip of dirty cloth in an effort to stop the bleeding.

Plantations are great places for every imaginable kind of bacteria to breed and thrive and it was not long before infection took hold. At the hospital they were adamant, the only way to prevent this contagion from spreading was to remove Leroy's fingers one by one so that the unsightly stump, that was once his right hand, could heal.

There was a lengthy court case. However, accidents were commonplace on the sugar estates and Robbo maintained it was all just another terrible misfortune. He sauntered out of the San Fernando courthouse a free man.

Leroy spiralled down into a morass of self-pity. He walked around with a slouching gait and averted his face when he saw Eldica. He seemed bent on self-destruction, helped in no small way by copious amounts of Vat 19. Then, just before the rainy season started, Leroy disappeared.

The obeah woman, who lived in a grass hut under the shadow of the 'great house' that overlooked the estate and was built on the pain and blood of slaves, came to see Eldica. Her sharp eyes and lips were blackened with Kohl. A blue turban covered her head and beads hung down around her neck.

"Girl, doan' you pay no heed to that badass Robbo." She said. "He go pay de price. Take it from me, Karma go come an' bite him on de bum!"

4

Sunset was sizzling on the horizon when Eldica returned home. Once she had stopped crying, she felt a lot better and she is hoping that Leroy has made something to eat. She loves his peas and rice flavoured with Cajun spices. She is so hungry her mouth waters at the thought. She enters the familiar yard and there he is. He crosses hesitantly towards her and she speaks gently.

"Doux-doux, tell me everything."

Then he crushes her to him and his kiss feels hot on her lips.

CONCLUSION

So…..On this very morning, on a day that will never be repeated, at about the same time that Leroy is crossing the Marabella roundabout, Robbo is walking to work through the cane fields.

He is not happy. He does not want to work. It is still dark, and from all around comes the buzzing, lively chorus of millions of insects. They had disturbed the night and would soon be silent. He thinks about his friends, on a bus travelling to Mayaro, planning their day – swimming, fishing and maybe catching a Blue Crab or two. Loading cut cane onto a bison cart does not feel like a good idea. He thinks of his ancestors, how they had suffered, and of their spirits trapped in every furrow of earth, in every ugly and brutal stalk of sugar.

He thinks of how these tough stems will be transformed…sweetening an Englishman's cup of tea. He thinks of how he hates King Cane, how it symbolises colonialism and fosters a grovelling respect for the white man.

His bare feet thud lightly on the trail and he fails to see the viper sunning itself on the path. With the speed of a stretched wire spring, it wraps itself around his ankle. Robbo feels its fangs burrow deep and the hot rush of lethal toxin as it pumps into his veins. He falls to the ground writhing in pain and fear.

Later that evening, while Eldica is waiting at King's Wharf for a bus to take her home to Leroy and the children, Robbo breathes his last shuddering breath of the warm evening air. And, in her grass hut, the obeah woman feels a tremor run through her body. She nods her head, her dark eyes sad with the knowledge of how wasted a life can be.

"Karma Go Come." She whispers.

Then silence falls over the valley of cane, over the shop where Amina and her son are sleeping, over the church where Father McCormack is saying his evening prayers, over the bus travelling back from Mayaro, loud with the sound of laughter and talk about the day's events and over the house at Number Four where Leroy and Eldica are holding their children and vowing that never again will they be parted.

Finally it casts a dark shadow over the town of Marabella and settles like a fat black crow.

NOTES…

This photo of the Marabella Plantation was taken by my father, who was a keen photographer. I am certain he would not have any objection to my using it, to illustrate my story.

- Obeah Woman: A person who practises witchcraft.
- Kiskadee: A bird of the flycatcher family. It is noisy and conspicuous, a striking mix of black, white, yellow and reddish-brown plumage.
- Doux Doux: A term of endearment.
- Vat 19:   A local rum.

Connection
Donna-Marie Koopman.

A dead bird on my doorstep should have signalled an alert. Logically, I considered that the bird might have died of natural causes or perhaps flown into the glass door a bit too hard. In some occult beliefs, a dead bird at your door is considered a bad omen. Hindsight is twenty-twenty, as the saying goes. Despite this, I couldn't shake an ominous feeling over the next few days. To cope with my unease, I threw myself into work. Additionally, to distract myself from what Hank, my husband, would call "silliness," I went shopping for last-minute Christmas gifts to help push those dark thoughts aside.

Ever since I was a child growing up, I realised my mother possessed psychic abilities, which frightened me no end. Mentioning Mr Jones, who lived down the street, was about to meet his demise. Sure enough, by the end of the week, Mr Jones had met his Maker. I tended to shy away from metaphysical things as much as possible.

On our one day off, Monday, I returned with my Christmas gifts, ensuring I had not omitted anyone. Tuesday, December 20, was a hectic day. As entertainers, December was always busy with corporate work parties and private end-of-year celebrations. Today was no exception; we arrived home late that night with three gigs crammed into the day. We showered and made ourselves comfortable in front of the television to catch up on some programs Hank had taped on our VHS recorder. This routine always had a sleeping pill effect on me, and I would doze off almost immediately.

Tonight, I opted for the comfort of my bed while Hank stayed up longer to watch his programs. I don't know how long I'd been asleep; it wasn't deep, more a dreamlike state before falling into deep sleep. In that twilight zone, I heard a pitiful wailing and screaming that jolted me back into reality. My heart was racing, and I didn't know if what I heard was imagined. However, it felt very real, especially the tears running down my face. I got out of bed and went into the living room. I wanted to tell Hank what had happened but felt he would think me foolish, so I sat beside him on the lounge, saying nothing.

He asked if I was okay. I said yes, but I couldn't get to sleep. I didn't get any real sleep that night; I just had short cat naps. I couldn't shake off the experience all night or the next day; I'd never felt like this before.

The following morning, whilst having breakfast, we heard a news bulletin of a plane crash over Scotland. We both said how terrible it must be for the families of the victims, never taking in such tragic news, as we were becoming immune to such stories at the time.

In our ever-changing world, 1988 was ending. The Iran-Iraq war concluded, and the Soviet Union finally withdrew from its war in Afghanistan. Microsoft released Windows 2.1, and Holland became the second country in the world to connect to the new medium, the Internet. Instant news was still in its infancy. Australia didn't connect to the Internet until 1989.

It wasn't until two nights later that we came home to our usual routine of showering, eating, and then watching our pre-taped shows. I told Hank, "Let's just watch the late news," which we rarely did as it was so depressing. The news reported on a plane crash over Scotland, including footage of the incident.

A terrorist bomb had downed Pan Am Flight 103 with 270 souls on board. A camera panned to the flight lounge of the airport, where families and friends had gathered, waiting to hear news of any survivors. The camera then focused on a woman on her knees, her face in her hands. She was screaming and wailing as if her heart and very soul were ripping from her body.

I went cold. This was precisely what had woken me two nights before. How could this be? I heard and felt everything this woman was going through. I was shaken to my very core.

It was then that I told Hank of my experience. He didn't scoff or ridicule me as I expected he would. Instead, he remarked, "It is often said that everyone and everything are interconnected. Somehow, some way, you must have connected to this woman."

Since this experience, my mind has become more open to things unknown and unseen.

Try a little kindness
Hank Koopman

Glen Campbell's well-intentioned song climbed the charts when it was first released in 1970 and became an instant hit. The first few lines resonated with me, mainly because I had been one of those people standing by the road with a heavy load on many occasions in my youth.

Hitchhiking has seen many cycles of public notoriety over several years. During the 1960s, when I hitchhiked around Australia, it was accepted as another mode of transport, though frowned upon by society's elite. "Flower power" people cherished the concept, and in their VW kombi vans young travellers were welcomed into the free and easy lifestyle of "the hippies".

In the 1980s and 90s, after many documented cases of abduction and murder, it was considered an unsafe practice, and only the most hardened proponents of this activity continued the tradition. However, by then, hitchhikers were not only considered prey; sometimes, unsuspecting drivers became the prey.

My process of elimination as to who I'd offer a ride to was weighed using this criterion. If the person carried a swag, he was genuine. If he was dishevelled and looked dirty with no baggage, I didn't stop. My wife, Donna, would always be wary of anyone I would pick up, yet she consistently showed empathy toward whomever I chose to offer a lift to.

As entertainers, we travelled extensively throughout NSW, Victoria, and Queensland, and this particular song was in our repertoire and formed a big part of our show and everyday life philosophy. Coming from Perth, W.A., the entertainment scene lacked the structure and sophistication of the Sydney industry. Jimmy Little suggested we use a manager to promote our bookings.

We were transported into a slick, thought-provoking operation, where we realised that an unwritten set of rules kept the cogwheels turning so that everyone carved off a percentage of a performer's fee. Managers referred acts to an agent who serviced several clubs. If the club audience received the act with a satisfactory response on the night of their performance, you would inevitably get a return engagement a few months later, usually at an increased fee negotiated by your manager. We had no say in the matter; it meant everyone would get a better reward in commissions.

A "name" act that guaranteed to "put bums on seats," enjoyed the privilege of higher fees and had the power to get agents to cancel a not-so-well-known act. We joined Actors Equity to have some say in negotiating our replacement by an agency. In this arrangement, we would appear to support any "big name" overseas act and not lose our wages.

Over time our fees increased for a 40 to 50-minute spot. The manager got a higher cut, as did the agent. We accepted any increases because our spot might only be short, but preparation for the concert could take all day. A backing band might ask for rehearsal time, and a 40-minute spot would take up the whole day if you included travelling time.

I'm referencing these facts for a reason. The general public perceives that entertainers are exorbitantly overpaid for their services and roll around in a lavish lifestyle of wealth and prosperity. Some do, it's true. However, as a whole, acts like ours worked long hours and very hard for our pay.

In the 1980s and 90s, this was how the entertainment industry in Sydney functioned: 12% to the manager and 10% to the agent.

Departing the Southern Highlands at 2 p.m., I surmised we could miss peak hour traffic in Hornsby and reach our destination at Gosford RSL with two or three hours to spare. It was May, and rain fell as we made our way along Pennant Hills Road, keeping ten kph under the posted road speed limit signs. I spotted the hitchhiker trying to find relief from the rain using a bus shelter. I pulled in sharply to the bus stop to avoid holding up any traffic in the curb lane.

"What are you doing?" Donna asked, concerned. She had kept her eye on the road in case I missed any hidden dangers from the rain.

"I'm just picking up the poor bugger hitchhiking in this rain," I stated. Donna has never been keen for me to pick up hitchhikers but understood my reasons for having a soft spot for them. He ran to Donna's side of the car as I told her to wind the window down a little.

"How far are you going," I asked.

"Brisbane," he answered.

"Get out of the rain, mate," I said, "I can take you as far as Gosford, but that's as far as we're going."

I gestured for him to get in the rear of our station wagon and out of the rain. I failed to follow my rule for picking up hitchhikers. He didn't carry a swag, only an overnight bag. I couldn't ask him to get out now; it would be impolite. Besides he might have a weapon in the bag.

I engaged my right-hand indicator and rejoined the traffic lane heading towards Hornsby. Our guest must have espied our instruments in the back of the luggage area of the station wagon and remarked,

"You're off to a gig are you?"

"Yeah", I replied, not wanting to reveal too much information to a stranger. I had been in his position before, so I knew how to direct a conversation to another person's preferences to engage on a mutual subject. I made it obvious I was needing Donna's assistance in pointing out road hazards and keeping our attention on the wet roadway through the overworked windscreen wipers.

Once we joined the Warringah Freeway, Donna and I relaxed, discussed priorities about the upcoming floorshow that night, and hoped the two new songs we'd slotted into the repertoire would appeal to the audience.

"Wow," an excited backseat passenger remarked. "I can't wait to tell my Mum a couple of stars picked me up," he continued after overhearing us strategising a plan for the concert. "Have you been on telly?" he asked excitedly.

"We're not stars," I replied, not wanting him to think we were dripping in wealth. "We're still working on it."

"Yeah? But have you been on telly?" he repeated.

"Only Bert Newton's New Faces," I commented in a matter-of-fact-way. Then I thought, let him think we're stars if it makes him happy, so I added, "And Reg Lindsays Country Homestead."

"I knew it," he began getting excited. "Country music is the only music worth listening to. I only have country music on in my rig," he continued babbling as he reached for his bag and started to unzip the top, fumbling around in it. Was this the moment we would become a news item? I moved my rearview mirror to observe what he was extracting from his bag. Is he reaching in to pull out the weapon and accost us? The bag was sitting on the seat beside him. Why hadn't he placed it on the floor like any normal person would have, instead of wetting the velour of the backseat? My mind raced. I didn't reveal any of my anxiety to Donna. Then in his hand he held a selection of several cassette boxes revealing some of his favourite country musicians.

He'd found our Achilles Heel in no time at all. He explained he was an owner/driver who had received a message on arrival at his freight office in Sydney to get home to Brisbane as fast as he could as his mother was in hospital after being involved in a car crash. His truck couldn't be unloaded immediately, and he didn't have enough cash to buy a plane ticket, so he decided the fastest way was to hitchhike.

"Couldn't you find another truck to take you back?" I asked, suspiciously?

"By the time I organised that," he said, "I could be halfway back home."

"Wouldn't a train be quicker?" Donna suggested, now showing her empathetic nature.

"Yeah, maybe. But once again, I don't think I have enough for a fare." My previous experience in telling my tales of woe to extract sympathy from a driver who picked me up came into focus. Gosford was now just ten minutes away. I thought, 'I'll catch him out in a lie'.

"How do we know you're even a truckie? You might be telling us a "porky" to get some "dosh" out of us." With a crestfallen look on his face, I immediately regretted my insinuation.

"I'm sorry you think that way," he sounded hurt by my accusation, "so if you drop me at the turn-off into Gosford, I'll continue to get another ride north. Oh, and by the way, here's my Department of Motor Transport Logbook." He flashed it my way, and it appeared to be genuine.

"If we take you to the railway station, will you buy a ticket to Brisbane and get out of the rain?" Donna asked, trying to make up for my bombastic outburst.

"If I had the money to buy a ticket, I certainly would," he replied. Donna looked at me with those pleading eyes a cocker-spaniel gets when it asks for a titbit. I looked upward and thought, 'If you see a brother standing by the road, with a heavy load, from seeds he'd sowed.' Try a little kindness.

"Right-o mate, we'll drop you at the station. Good luck, and we hope your Mum survives her injuries." With that, Donna dug into her purse and handed over our weekly shopping money: $120.00. We wished him well as we headed back into town to give our performance at the RSL.

By the time we packed up our instruments and signed autographs on the one LP we had on sale, we were heading home at about 11.30 p.m.

Tony Delroy hosted Nightline on ABC radio, which we always listened to, mainly the quiz section that kept us awake on our long drives back to Hilltop. After the news bulletins, Tony discussed items of interesting topics listeners would submit regularly during the program's first hour. Tonight would be more interesting than usual.

"The police department has warned all motorists in the Hornsby Gosford area to be aware of a fraudster, posing as a "down-and-out-truckie. Several motorists have reported this huckster, and police are on the lookout for him."

Donna and I looked at each other and sighed. We were dudded out of our shopping money about a year before near Wagga Wagga—the same scenario.

Another song came to mind: When Will They Ever Learn, When Will They Ever Learn?

A flawed strategy
Anne Layton-Bennett

Dutton thought decisive and divisive
would make him a winner
he had a slot for each group
he considered were sinners
if your skin wasn't white
you were trans or were gay
or you cared for the planet
and expressed your dismay
at the logging of trees
and the refugees' plight
you were dismissed and derided
and regarded with spite
as being 'woke' or a 'greenie'
as though it's a crime
but he misread the mood of the country
and voters, who considered such tactics
the wrong paradigm
he'd stepped onto the path of election defeat
for himself and his Party (he lost his own seat!)
so the road that he hoped
would be electoral success
was a disastrous dead end -
he'd failed to impress

© 2025 Anne Layton-Bennett

On the Cliff
Adrian Flitney

The earliest photo I have of myself is at Waldheim, Cradle Mountain. I was barely two years of age, skinny little legs in long johns, next to my 4-year-old 'big brother' in shorts and t-shirt, impervious to the cold, and my sensibly dressed older sister. Every weekend, my parents would take us to explore the Tasmanian countryside. We picnicked in the forests or beside mountain streams. This is where wild places possessed me and never let go. As a teenager, I spent solitary afternoons scrambling over the boulders of the Devonport Bluff, a rocky headland of my hometown. In an earlier era I would have been an explorer, disappearing over the horizon of some unnamed part of Australia. As it was, I became a cycling addict at 13, pitting myself against the hills and mountain passes that my native island provides in abundance.

Fast forward to age 25. I was in Europe – the hilly bits of it – on a cycling Grand Tour. Seven months, ten countries, eleven thousand kilometres. Cycling was my thing. I only ever got off the bike to hike up a mountain. I felt indestructible.

This particular story from my Grand Tour features a park bench. An unremarkable one save for its location, at the foot of the 3,100 metre peak of Mittagskogel in the Austrian Alps. That sunny autumn day, this lofty spire was my target. You may wonder how something as pedestrian as a bench can play a pivotal role in this misadventure?

I rose early, packed up my tent and was on my bicycle, pushing through the crisp morning air. Gradually, the mist rose, uncloaking the mountains and revealing a glorious chocolate-box valley. It took nearly four hours to ascend the one thousand metres of the Pitztal – the valley of the Pitze river – to arrive at the head of the road, at *the* park bench. On the way I spurned the opportunity to buy the local hiking map, not wishing to add weight to my already considerable map collection. In my experience, local trails were well marked, especially when compared to the wilds of Tasmania where signposts are few and far between. Not buying a map was a bad decision. Behind every near-death experience there is a trail of bad decisions.

I approached the bench. It was a good resting spot for lunch before the afternoon's exertions. But as I neared the bench a couple emerged from a forest track and claimed it. Sigh. In any case, I could see no sign to Mittagskogel, so I remounted my trusty steed and cycled the few hundred metres to the Pitztaler station. This is the start of a mountain railway that tunnels its way up to the ski fields on the Mittelberg Ferner, a glacier nestled among the highest peaks in Austria. I ate lunch quickly, slipped a chocolate bar into my pocket, and set out on the only walking track to be found, carrying a small day pack with my camera, a jacket, extra clothing, and a water bottle. I still could not see a signpost to my chosen peak towering above me. The track soon merged with a broader gravel trail that followed a stream tumbling through autumn-tinged shrubs. To my disappointment, the path stuck resolutely to the valley. It could have been a pleasant outing on my bicycle, but to walk? An hour passed. Ahead was more valley.

Early morning in the Pitztal, Austria

How to explain what I did next? After months of cycling, and occasionally hiking up mountain slopes, I had grown complacent but hubris hardly does justice to my decision. Was it temporary Tasmanian insanity? Shall I blame the perfect blue sky, stretching from horizon to horizon, day after day? It begged me to come and join it and share its lofty view over the peaks, valleys and glaciers.

From a kilometre's distance, I peered up a long, steep scree slope leading to a cliff face and thought I spied a breach in the mountain's defences, a narrow gully cut in the rock. I was young, fit and pumped with testosterone. I could climb that!

From the base of the cliff the stream and track beside it were the merest threads on the valley floor

An hour of steep trudging bought me to an impressive height. The track on which I had strolled shortly before, and the stream beside it, were the merest threads curving through the valley floor. The scree slope was approaching a forty-five-degree incline but above me was a cliff, steeper still. To one side, a dark and severe rock face lingered in the shadows, snow outlining cracks in its armour. Ahead there was the gully, more of a slot a few metres wide, cut in the rock by a thin stream, now only a trickle after a long summer. The sun beamed down, the faultless blue sky worked its siren call. I ate the last of the chocolate and began climbing the gully, methodically picking out secure hand- and footholds. I was careful to maintain three points of contact with the rock at all times, a technique I had learned during my teenage scrambles. It was slow but uncomplicated work. The thin streak of water was easy to avoid.

After half an hour I did something astonishing: I calmly looked down. Normally I have a strong fear of heights but on this occasion, for reasons unknown, it was entirely absent. I didn't even take a single deep breath. I just thought, 'I haven't come very far.' I peered up the gully. With my foreshortened view it was impossible to tell how far the top might be except that I was clearly not halfway, and my initial estimate of an hour's climb on the cliff was stupidly optimistic. The afternoon was already well advanced. The sensible thing to do would have been to climb down while I was still able. But I was loath to turn back, to waste such a brilliant afternoon, to admit defeat. I continued up.

The gully steepened and after another half an hour there was no looking down. Nor going down. It was so steep, footholds below one's position were too difficult to see. Despite complete absence of evidence, I thought that I might now, finally, be halfway. In any case, I no longer had a choice. The only way from here was up, so I ascended into hell.

After a further hour of unrelenting effort, reaching, grasping, pushing slowly higher, the view above me along the narrow slot in the rock looked barely different. I was in the shadows but the sun glinted over the mountain top seemingly close by. Enticing, but still out of reach!

Fear descended on my shoulders, heavier with every move. Now I was angry! Angry at the mountain for being so steep and so tall, the very things that made it attractive. Angry at myself for being so reckless, so stupid! I didn't hold back. I screamed profanities at the top of my lungs. If I was going to go into that dark night, I was not going to go quietly. Hundreds of metres above the rocky scree, any slip would have meant certain death. Not an easy end, not a moment of terror followed by oblivion. I would have repeatedly bounced from the rock as I accelerated downward. A climber who survived such a fall – finally landing in deep snow – admitted afterwards: "I was conscious all the way down. I felt my bones breaking."

The mountain now presented a new test, mocking my puny assault on its flank. A patch of last winter's snow bridged the gully, pocked with melt holes. Despite the danger that the old snow might not hold my weight, I used one such hole as a foothold, there being no other choice. The trickle down the centre of the gully had been reduced to a few drops. Higher, the drops froze on the small marks and ridges in the rock that were vital to my progress. At one point there were no ice-free footholds within reach. I carefully rested one foot on a small icy ridge, took my weight on my arms and pulled myself up until my other foot could find a firm hold. Incredibly, my foot did not slip.

Deep into the third hour, the gully finally came to a full stop. Above me, the rock was covered from edge to edge in *verglas,* a thin layer of clear ice. I bellowed unrepeatable expletives. But the ice was unmoved. Unassailable, impassable. The cleft in the rock containing my much softer body was now a rectangular cut over a metre deep. I had to edge sideward out of the cleft and round a right-angle corner, away from relative protection onto the exposed cliff face. My heart pounded in my ears. I found myself on a narrow ledge facing a section of vertical rock. There was another ledge above my head. I felt for handholds on it, placed my foot on the thinnest of marks in the rock in front of me and pulled myself onto the ledge above. Standing up, I was faced with another vertical section topped by another ledge. I repeated the manoeuvre. And then again. And again. The cliff face had peculiar human proportions. The ledges were wide enough to stand on safely, but no wider. There was always another ledge above my head, within reach. But only just.

At one point, the rock in front of me was too smooth. I did the only thing possible. I firmly grasped two handholds on the ledge above and dragged my body upward, sliding my chest onto the narrow shelf. I crouched there for a few moments, on my hands and knees, shaking with raw terror. Yet, I maintained the discipline to avoid looking down at what must have been a terrifying hundreds-of-metres drop. Then I stood, facing the rock once more. I felt for holds on the ledge above. I found a meagre foothold and continued up. I knew I was going to spend a freezing night on the summit. Yet, to let darkness fall while I was on the cliff face would be certain death.

The valley below me began to fill with mist. Out of the corner of my eye I saw the cloud creeping higher as the air cooled. Within minutes, it enveloped me in its cold, milky embrace. Visibility was reduced to a few metres but it made no difference: the few metres in front of me and above my head were my whole world. I hauled myself onto the next ledge. And again. Then, suddenly, I came to a ledge where I could stand up without holding on. In the white-out, I was barely able to see farther than my feet. But, for the first time, there was no cliff visible in front of me. I gingerly took a step forward, then another. On the third step, the ground gently sloped downward. Wow! I had reached the top!

My relief was instant and intense. That moment of ecstasy erased the pain of the most traumatic experience of my life thus far. I uncurled and grew taller. Four hours of unrelenting effort, fear and rage slipped from my shoulders and retreated into the past. Though even now, through the telescope of time, the memories of the cliff, the ice, the rising mist are as clear as the midday sky on that early autumn day.

I had emerged from hell into an ice-chilled purgatory. I was dressed in shorts and a long-sleeved thermal top. The effort had been so extreme that I was not cold despite the sub-zero temperatures over the latter part of the climb. However, I was cooling down fast. I donned all my spare clothes: two additional thermal tops, woollen leg warmers, a Gore-Tex jacket, waterproof over-trousers, gloves and Gore-Tex mittens. There had not been a breath of wind all day but I did not want my life to depend on the whim of the weather gods. After stupidly underestimating the climb, it was time to be clever. The survival instinct sharpens one's mind! In the gathering gloom, I scrambled about collecting broken rock, which lay in abundance on the summit, to make a rudimentary windbreak. In the process, I uncovered something unexpected and hugely comforting: two charred logs. Here, a thousand metres above the treeline, someone had lit a fire to celebrate the autumn equinox that had passed a few days before. Surely, they did not carry the timber up a vertical cliff; there was clearly a much easier way. If only I had a map!

After constructing a primitive wind barrier, I removed the remaining items from my backpack so I could sit on it, insulated from the frozen rock. On the climb I had been terribly thirsty but unable to reach my water bottle. Now I had a sip, keeping the rest for the morning. But, unused to spending the night in a deep freeze, I carelessly placed the bottle on the ground rather than inside my clothing. Then I sat on my pack, zipped up my jacket over my mouth and nose and pulled the hood down so only my eyes were exposed. Before this adventure, I had been disappointed in my expensive Gore-Tex jacket which let moisture through the seams during heavy rain. Now it saved my life. I pulled my knees onto my chest and wrapped my arms around them to curl myself into the smallest possible ball. Behind the veil of mist, the sun had sunk into the netherworld and the temperature plunged into deep negative.

Shortly, the mist cleared, revealing a perfect, moonless, million-star sky. It was surprisingly light: not only could I see the rock around me but also the distant peaks and the head of a glacier a short distance below. I sat and waited patiently, enchanted by the view. I felt not the slightest hint of sleepiness. Occasionally I had to unwind my tight pose and stretch my limbs. But only for a moment: I immediately started to shiver. Later, a half-moon rose, shedding more light on my mountain panorama. In the early hours of the morning, when the cold was at its peak, I attempted to light those logs. I had matches and paper – a notebook and a cycling map – but, of course, no kindling. The paper burnt furiously and the logs began to smoulder but ultimately failed to catch. The extreme cold sucked the glow from them. Still I had some welcome, if short-lived, heat, and the project served to pass the time of the twelve-hour night.

Dawn! The sun briefly won the struggle with the ragged clouds that had gathered in the valley before sunrise. I'd never been so overjoyed to see sunbeams, feeble though they were. Shivering in the frigid air, I stretched out lizard-like to bask in their rays.

Sunrise from nearly 3200m.

I felt reborn. Around me, orange rocky spires pierced a boiling ocean of cloud. During the night, no sign of human civilization was visible but now I could see a chair lift – alas not operating – stretching across the glacier below with a terminus not far from me. From this I fixed my position. Along the spine of the broken ridge, I saw a softer peak a few kilometres away: my original target, Mittagskogel. This was my route to salvation. In any case, all other directions were barred. The cliff I had climbed – I could not bring myself to go near it – to the West, the glacier to the East, and a high peak, permanently snow-capped, to the South. The water bottle that I had carelessly placed on the rock the previous evening was a block of ice. Vigorously shaking the bottle proved futile. Yet, I was alive.

It was not long before the sun withdrew behind a veil of clouds and light snow began fluttering down. My horizons diminished but the weather was not threatening. Rather, I felt cosseted by the mountain. Once moving, I finally controlled the shivering that had beset me since dawn. With exaggerated care I picked my way over the broken rock of a 3,200-metre peak, the high point of my journey. My nighttime encampment was a short distance below its summit and before long I was on slightly lower, more open ground. I drank in the dramatic, cloud-shrouded views over the glacier. Occasionally, the sun broke through with sparkling effect. I had no energy to hurry.

The mountain had one more challenge in store for me: a tongue of clear ice crossing my path from the cliff on my left to the glacier on my right, steepening as it descended to the glacier. It was far too tricky to continue upright, so with a rock in each hand to act as brakes and pushing a larger stone with my feet I slid slowly, carefully, on my bottom across the ice. About half way, my foot-rock slid away and sped down the icy slope. Careful! From then on I used my hand-rocks to laboriously cut small notches in the ice in which to wedge my feet, and crept forward, a few centimetres at a time. During the crossing, the clouds briefly parted to reveal a magnificent vista of mountains enclosing a glacial sea cut by crevasses and penetrated by a pair of isolated rocky spires. After a few seconds the clouds closed in and the vision was gone. I continued my slow progress. It took me more than half an hour to traverse about fifty metres. A mountain can be both a beauty and a beast.

I drank in dramatic cloud-shrouded views over the glacier

Once on easier ground I continued to the col just south of Mittagkogel and finally met a marked track. Two hikers scrambling along a nearby ridge were the first souls that I had seen since I left; their walking poles left at the col. Snow was falling more solidly now, blown on a light wind. I turned to take a last look along the ridge I had just traversed. The image was near monochrome: all the ledges on the face that I had climbed the previous afternoon were outlined with fresh snow. I thanked the Goddess Fortuna for holding off the snowstorm for a day, then turned to begin a steep, knee-jarring descent down the winding track that was scratched into a bare, gravelly slope. Thick cloud soon engulfed me. There was still a long descent ahead.

After a while, the track became easier. The rocky wasteland gave way to grassland and a view down the clouded Pitztal opened up. My destination was visible a few hundred metres below. More winding track brought me to civilization, two hours after leaving the col and some five hours after starting out that morning. *There* was the sign clearly indicating 'Mittagskogel.' And a few metres away was *that* park bench. If only I had arrived the previous day a minute earlier, sat on the bench, seen the sign…

If you move a blade of grass the stars shake.

In Response to Her News
Marilyn Arnold

I do not recommend this poem;
it has a smell of death,
It has the feel of stone,
It promises nothing, gives no consolation.

Do not underestimate this poem, however;
It strives to become a prayer, a chant, a cry to the gods
and, least of all, a swan-song,
least of all, a lament…

Really, this poem's only option is to
sharpen its claws
Do not expect to persuade it into memory,
Do not proclaim it – ever – finished.

It is never done – the low keening behind words,
the begging for things to be different,
for life to make it right. It is never done…
the grief to come.

My sister's nemesis is also mine…
We hear the same stealthy footsteps behind us,

There's nowhere to run.

Another year over . . .
Anne Layton-Bennett

it's the time of year when
we parcel up
twelve months of memories
and file them under
good, great or dismal

as the years pass
some will be opened
revisited, remembered,
reminders – perhaps – of happier times
of loves, and laughs and maybe tears
of days spent with friends and family

but others will stay sealed
hidden, buried in a dusty corner
the memories they hold
are of torments never told
and which are best forgotten

How to Love a Teddy
Dawn Meredith

Sometimes you are given a teddy bear as a gift.
Sometimes you get to choose one for yourself.
But occasionally, very specially, a teddy chooses you.
He might be pre-loved, with slightly worn paws.
He might smell of cupboard, or musty attic, or bottom-of-the-toybox.
But there's something about those bright eyes and wistful smile that makes you reach for him.
His cute, fuzzy face seems to say, "I like you. Take me home?"
He fits so snugly, right there in your arms.
He seems to belong with you.
And you will do anything to have him come and live at your house.
Ready?
First, you make him a part of your family.
You might even give him a nickname.
And his own place to sleep. Night Teddy!
He meets your other toys. And the dog. And the cat.
You laugh at his funny ways.
Oops!
He learns what's right and wrong at your place. How to fit in.
Wee!
If he's naughty, you have to gently remind him who's in charge.
And when he does something really silly and cheeky, you must try not to laugh.
You don't want him learning bad habits.
If he's very kind or thoughtful, he gets extra hugs and kisses and maybe a special outing.
Look at me!
But if he feels lonely, afraid or upset, you must hug him tight and tell him everything will be ok.
Come here, my fuzzy friend.
And every day, whisper in his ear - You belong here, now Teddy. I love you. I will never let you go.

Are They Watching?
Donna-Marie Koopman

In the vast expanse of the universe, I find it hard to believe we humans are the only intelligent beings. There have been hundreds of reported sightings of UFOs, but are they natural phenomena, as the cynic proposes, or are they genuine alien visitations? As many people believe, are they watching us like evolved guards to save us from ourselves, or are they watching us to protect themselves from us, making sure we never leave our solar system to become a danger to theirs?

The debate undoubtedly will go on *ad nauseam*, but there are people with stories of unexplainable incidents that have happened to them that will make some question what fact or fiction is.

Let me tell you about one of these incidents: it happened to my dad. Dad was a ganger on the trans-Australia railway in the fifties. At the time, our family were stationed at Zanthus, a camp along the line. The Nullarbor is an isolated, flat, desolate part of Australia and has quite an otherworldly feel about it. There were no handy corner shops to run to if you ran out of supplies. You made do with provisions you had bought from the "tea and sugar" train that came fortnightly delivering supplies to the camps along the line, our virtual supermarket on rails.

Flour to make bread, powdered milk, etc., had to be rationed until the next fortnight. At times, meat was supplemented with kangaroo, emu, and rabbit. Sometimes, Dad would, accompanied by one or all three of his daughters, head out of the camp to set traps, hoping to trap a rabbit or two to eke out the meat supplies.

During the week of the incident, strange lights were visible in the sky in the early hours of the morning. A couple of people witnessed them, but people being people, they dismissed them as some natural phenomenon.

On two mornings in particular, my sisters and I had risen early, as kids do. We were playing on the veranda when our eyes were drawn to the sky, and there was a round ball of bright light. It was really strange because it wasn't stationary. We came down from the veranda and stood looking up at this ball, and as we did, it would move towards us and then retreat back.

This went on for a couple of minutes, maybe more or less.

We were mesmerised but became frightened when the ball started coming closer each time. We ran in to call Mum and Dad to see this weird oddity in the sky. Of course, by the time they made it outside, it had disappeared. That happened whenever the adults came out to witness what we three girls had just seen.

Dad usually went out in the evening after tea to set his traps, which were retrieved early the following morning. These expeditions were mainly carried out on weekends, as there was little or no work to be done on the track.

The morning of the incident, Dad set out early, as he usually did, to retrieve his "catch" and traps. When he reached the site, he froze in horror; he was shocked to see the traps had been ripped from the ground. They had been twisted entirely out of shape and thrown as if in anger by some powerful force, thrown so violently that some traps were almost completely buried in the earth.

As he related the story, he told us every hair on his body stood on end. As the reality sank in, he began to feel afraid and hightailed it away from there. Dad feared nothing or anyone, so we can only imagine how frightened he must have been.

Not long after, Mum and Dad joined a group that watched the skies for unusual sightings or unexplainable events.

Are they watching us because we are so barbaric and dangerous a species, we cannot be allowed to venture from our solar system to damage another as we have ours? Leaving our junk wherever we set foot?

As far as saving our planet and the many unique, beautiful species, including us, we seem to be dragging our feet. It reminds me of a young person standing on the edge of a pool attempting their first dive; they keep hesitating, telling you; 'this time, I'm definitely going.'

In the end, everyone tires and loses interest; they don't care and stop watching.

But...... have they?.........

I am not a fish!
Adrian Flitney

I never learnt to swim as a child. I liked the beach. My father would take my brother and I often during the summer. I was confident in the water; I liked to body surf on what must have been rather small waves, but then I was rather small too at the time. I could happily stay afloat just don't ask me to swim more than a few metres.

Many years passed. I finally learnt to swim at age 28 to help a chronic knee problem. I fumbled, splashed and swallowed water as I made my way painstakingly from one end of the pool to the other. But I persevered and by the end of the summer I was cruising the lanes or along the beach like a fish. Almost. I felt so relaxed with my head under water that I accidentally tried breathing in that moist environment. Spoiler: it didn't work.

I mastered white water kayaking with the university mountain club, at least up to grade 3 – 'difficult'. Grades 4 (extreme) and 5 (you've got to be kidding) are only for the hard men and women of the sport which I decided I would never join.

I fell into solo white water kayaking sort of by accident: friends were not available at the right time, the schedule of the canoe club of which I was a member didn't fit with my free weekends. Not recommended for someone who could barely walk (those blasted knees) or even for someone who could! Yet... insert suitable cliche here about my independent spirit, 'doing it my way' etc. The logistics were managed using an electric bicycle to complete the round trip.

Now fast forward to late 2024, after close to two hundred solo trips, to a solitary expedition on the upper Mersey River. With a classic Anglo understatement I can say that I didn't have a very good paddle. However, I should state here at the outset that, despite the small possibility of an untimely demise, the worst harm that befell me on this adventure was a sore middle finger and a bruise to my left buttock.

Incessant spring rain had made this rarely paddleable section of the upper Mersey River attractive for those of a peculiar bent for adventure in the white, wet stuff. The online gauge suggested the river level was on the high side of optimum but decreasing at the time I left home. It augured well for a pleasant outing. The weather forecast was dubious but the reality was less problematic; the threatening clouds failed to live up to their promise. I entered the river just after midday, already a little hungry.

I wasn't quite 'feeling it' but I thought I would soon warm to this delightful stretch of fast flowing water. The river looked higher than expected and, to my surprise, was still rising. But on almost all rapids on this twisting path there is a choice of the difficult route on the outside of the corner or a shortcut on the inside, in quieter waters, so I was not concerned. Rapids are mainly a series of waves apart from the central Tombstone Rapid, named for the shape of the rock (below) rather than in the memory of an unlucky kayaker.

The Tombstone rapid on an earlier trip

On the seventh rapid of twenty-five (on previous trips I have counted them; ominously, the Tombstone is #13), I took the right side of a small island and found myself in an eddy, while the river took a sharp left off a large rock. To continue downstream I had to cross the main current. It is important in these conditions to lift the upstream side of the kayak by leaning downstream. This allows water to flow under rather than over the boat. I underestimated the current and failed to lean sufficiently. I was being swept sideward toward the rock and three deep breaths later I capsized. I didn't panic; as a regular white water paddler I have plenty of experience being upside-down in the water. I set up carefully for a roll which was, alas, a failure; the same happened the second time and on a half-hearted (and half-breathed) third attempt. The beginnings of panic entered my mind. I thought 'this is serious.' I hurriedly bailed out and surfaced in the eddy in a strong upstream current, holding the kayak in one hand and my trusty, battle-scarred paddle in the other. The current shortly pulled me into the main flow and then accelerated me towards the large rock, flowing with the water back into the eddy. Unable to quite reach a rock on my left, it was literally rinse and repeat, as I was pulled back into the main stream. Everything was happening quickly. I had not had the presence of mind to put the paddle into the upturned kayak to free one hand, as one would usually do in this circumstance.

Normally, after a bail-out I would eventually emerge at the bottom of the rapid into quieter water and make my way to the riverbank, but this time I was trapped in a cold and damp Groundhog Afternoon. On the third rotation, the paddle became snagged on the riverbed, bringing me to a halt as I came away from the rock. The reflected waves swept over my head, and I swallowed cold clear water, spluttering, not being a fish and all that. At the same time, the kayak had its own agenda in the strong upstream current. It ripped itself out of my hand, giving me the aforementioned sore finger. I also lost my grip on the paddle. With my hands now free, I grabbed a rock and was in a stable position but bereft of my disloyal companions, the kayak and the paddle. I was in urgent need of reunion with them both. I could see the paddle close by, just under the water's surface. I clutched at it and shortly it came free. I made a lunge for it as it rushed past in the eddy's upstream current. I had that one! But the upturned kayak, in solo mode, reached the main stream, took the left route off the rock on this occasion and continued down river into exhilarating freedom. At first, my feeling was relief too; all I had to do was catch up with it. This meant plunging into the main current, armed only with the paddle. (Do not try this at home, or in your local fast flowing river.) I rushed towards the large rock and with the minimum of paddle strokes emerged in the downstream current, successfully avoiding being drawn back into the eddy. But the kayak had a twenty metre head start.

I tried, without any real conviction, to make up the distance. It quickly became abundantly clear that I could not catch the recalcitrant vessel on its merry glide towards the next rapid. The best I could do was to get to the riverbank but by the time this realisation arrived it was already too late. For the first time since the capsize I felt real fear. I was being drawn helplessly into a series of waves culminating in a foaming giant. This was scary, even in a kayak – on previous trips I tended to avoid the last wave. I was sucked along, bounced off a rock or two, sustaining my other minor injury for the day. I broke through the last wave but the rapid was not finished with me yet. I was pulled back into a 'stopper', a region of churning water that often follows a large mid-stream rock, and held near motionless under the surface. I waited calmly for release, at least as calmly as one can in this fish-like environment. I peered up. The surface, and air, was not far, but after several seconds I realised that the river was not prepared to discharge me without some action on my part. After a random wiggle with the paddle, I broke free. Episodes like this seem to last longer than they actually do; I was probably submerged for less than ten seconds. In calmer water, and with determination to get out of the river before the next rapid, I kicked and paddle-swam to the riverbank. The kayak was nowhere to be seen.

For a few moments I sat gasping like a stranded fish that I, as mentioned, was not. Then, half hoping that the kayak might be caught around the next bend, I pushed through the frigid water along the bank. The next rapid was soon visible but predictably there was no kayak. With sad resignation, I realised the boat was gone. Even if I could get past this point, the chance of catching the kayak was slim. My car was too far downstream so I had to return upstream to my bicycle.

The road was fifty metres above me. I didn't relish the steep, forested slope but was resigned to the necessity of climbing it. Fortunately, the rainforest undergrowth was open and the soil soft and peaty which made climbing on my knee pads straightforward – I avoid normal bipedal motion due to knee problems but, ironically, walking on my knees is fine. Under my supposed drysuit I was soaked to the skin. I hurried upwards, keeping hypothermia at bay. The climb seemed to drag on with no end in sight, yet I knew I must meet the road at some point. The whole thing felt surreal. After some time I arrived at 'civilisation' – an infrequently used Hydro-road. Stashing the paddle and kayaking helmet in the shrubbery, I began to inch in the direction of my bicycle on my hands and knees.

I would have atoned for most of my sins if I had to complete the kilometre's distance this way, but a stroke of great fortune almost instantly brought a car along this usually deserted road. I flagged it down—and could they not stop for a person on their knees? After a short explanation, the two employees of the Hydro-Electric Commission gave a lift to this eccentric solo kayaker back to his electric bicycle. There remained the 'easy task' of biking back seven kilometres over the hills in my saturated outfit. I was too involved in the present task to worry about the day's misadventure. Tired and cold, I made it to my car by 3:20. Lunch had gone down the river with the kayak so I made do with a hot chocolate and a few biscuits.

I am still hoping the escapee kayak will realise roaming free is overrated and make its way home.

Into the unknown
Lesley Ririka

In 1967, the inland areas of Papua and New Guinea were still being explored, and Papua was still separate from New Guinea. I worked in New Guinea in the Western Highlands in the Jimi Valley, about fifteen minutes flying time from Mt Hagen. I worked in the Upper Jimi area in education, health, and church, but the Lower Jimi was still a 'closed' area, meaning me and other members of our team could not enter it without government permission and a police escort.

The senior nursing sister at our station was concerned about the health of the people in the area, especially the children. She applied for permission to patrol there, to enable us to give the infants and small children their basic immunizations to protect them from diseases that would reach them when the area was 'opened,' allowing anyone to establish a business or agricultural venture.

Being granted permission, we had a policeman as our guide. My employer asked me to lead the medical team, and we had all our medical and personal supplies packed and ready to go. I had done several medical patrols to the Upper Jimi, but this was different. People spoke a different language, so the little I had learned about the Upper Jimi would not be of much help in the Lower Jimi. We did not expect many people to know pidgin English because they would only have been exposed to it if they had come out of the area. Ironically, rascals (criminals) who had served a prison term were the first to become fluent in pidgin!

The medical team I had consisted of another registered nurse (a highland male) and a couple of 'docta bois' (local young men trained in basic nursing care) – who were invaluable as translators. They could speak in their language and be understood, and they could understand the reply in another language and then tell us the answer in pidgin English.

I was the first white woman to enter the area, and though people in the Upper Jimi knew me well, I wondered how people would receive me in this new locality, in the Lower Jimi. In the Upper Jimi, the walking tracks zigzagged up and down the steep mountains, but I found in the Lower Jimi, some of the walks were around the mountains; therefore, the walking was more straightforward.

Patrol officers had been through the area, so the walking tracks were well-defined and easy to follow, and basic needs such as toilets had been constructed. After several hours of walking, we came to the first village, and the policeman announced who we were and what we were there for, asking any sick people to come forward for treatment. Also, people should bring some food for us. After checking and treating those who reported sick, we went to bathe. There are important protocols to follow in the villages when bathing. Men wash upstream, and women downstream. Where there is a running stream of water piped through a length of bamboo from a creek, women must go at different times to the men. There were no walls or screens for privacy, only the rules for what time to go. I was quite nervous standing in the open having a wash, wondering if anyone would come around the corner. (they didn't). The water is cold in the Highlands, where there is often frost at night, so no lingering!

After washing and changing clothes, we sat on mats made of woven pandanus in a circle on the ground around a fire. Dinner was served very nicely on banana leaves. We provided tinned meat and tinned fish, and the village people brought a variety of cooked vegetables, predominantly sweet potatoes. These were placed in the middle and then passed around so we could select what we wanted. There was little conversation whilst we ate due to the language differences, but to everyone's surprise, the policeman brought out his bamboo flute and played beautiful lilting tunes for us.

We settled in the visitor's house for the night, sleeping on bamboo slats and using our sleeping bags. Houses were typically very low and round, with a dirt floor covered with woven pitpit. (pitpit grows like a narrow bamboo, though it is softer). Woven pitpit walls, no windows and a space in the middle of the floor for a fire at night. Rooves made from bamboo leaves sewn on a piece of pipit and layered closely together. The door was about four feet tall, so it was necessary to stoop to enter. All this, so it could be warm at night.

Patrol officers had initiated the 'visitors' house built more in the coastal tradition, still with a bamboo leaf roof and woven pipit wall, a bamboo floor a little off the ground and higher walls, a standard size door, and no windows. We were warm enough, fully clothed and wrapped up in a sleeping bag; bedtime was when it got dark, and morning was when it got light.

In the morning, we had a refreshing wash with cold water. Then we enjoyed a morning meal of vegetables similar to the meal the night before, but with the addition of a hot drink of either tea or coffee, which we had supplied, and we were ready to start the day's work. We saw sick people first, then weighed, examined and recorded all the babies and children, and then started the immunizations. I was surprised at how smoothly this went and how healthy the children were.

We calculated the children's ages by their number of teeth, their milestones, whether they could hold their heads up, sit up, crawl or walk, and where they fitted into the family. It was a slow process of using translators to answer any questions and answers. Surprisingly, people were very accepting of something entirely new for them. After finishing all the clinic work, we packed up and prepared to go to the next village, where we had another bite of vegetables.

The weather was kind to us, and rain, when it came, was usually at night, making no disruption to our progress. The second day was like the first, walking up and down the mountains or finding tracks around them. I remember coming around one corner and being faced by a local man with a machete in his hand. He frightened me at first, and I didn't know whether to run back or keep going. He was just as shocked at seeing me, a white lady by herself, in the middle of his path. Was I a masalai (ghost)? But while I was standing there, undecided, another team member caught up with me and assured me it was okay; he was returning from his garden, and I was not in any danger.

The Jimi River was narrow and deep at the base of the mountain, below our headquarters at Koinambe. A single log bridge with no handrail had been felled into place three metres above the river and five metres long. Using that crossing was a real challenge for me.

However, in the lower Jimi, the river was wider, slower, and shallower, and the bridges used to cross the chasm were higher above the water, about fifteen to twenty metres long, and made from bush vines strung across the river. The walkway of bamboo slats is placed across the vines and tied in place. This crossing had a handrail of sorts, not too sturdy and made of vines, but it was something to hold on to. We had to cross one person at a time as the bridge swung from side to side as we went across, but they were not as frightening for me as the single log with no handrail. We all crossed without mishap.

We had five stops at different villages and were received well in each one; our work went smoothly and was the first of three such patrols a month apart, as most of the early immunization required three injections/doses at monthly intervals. A different team did the second patrol, but I led the third patrol again. Villagers appreciated our return, and people were very cooperative, so it was the beginning of regular monthly patrols for medical workers.

When I returned 20 years later, after I had married Denys, seeing the development, with schools, health centres/aid posts, and churches, was amazing. Children had finished their primary education and moved on to higher education and training. One even had gone overseas to university.

However, I will never forget that first patrol, when we introduced medical work into the Lower Jimi Valley of Papua New Guinea.

Sylvania
© Dawn Meredith

"Good morning." I close my office door behind her, smile and offer the woman my hand. "I'm Donna." She regards me with cold eyes. A middle-aged woman, with greying hair and an early stoop, she is dressed plainly in a worn, cotton dress. Muttering a reply, she walks past me, past the comfortable lounge chairs carefully placed at a forty-degree angle to each other, over to the stepladder stool I use for reaching books on the highest shelf of the bookcase. She settles herself on the stool and looks around her, like a wild animal, checking for escape routes. I smile again and gesture to the comfortable chairs.

"Would you like to join me?" I say, in a friendly, non-threatening tone.

She scowls. "Nope. Happy here."

She crosses her skinny arms over her sunken chest. Her leather shoes were once very good quality. Now they are bound up with masking tape, where the sole has come away. I hesitate. Then, I wheel my office chair out from behind my desk and roll it towards her. *Not too close,* I tell myself. She watches me, saying nothing. I click my pen and turn over a new page in my A4 notebook, then lay it on my lap. She shrugs her thin shoulders and looks out the window. I check my notes nervously.

"Um, Sylvia, is it?"

"Sylvania," she growls, returning her attention to me, with flinty eyes.

"Oh, er, sorry," I say, hurriedly checking my notes. I cross out Sylvia and replace it with Sylvania. "That's a pretty name," I offer. She sighs loudly, looking at the ceiling, bored. Her skin is sallow and wrinkled, yet her file says she is only forty-one years of age. The lines on her face tell of a hard life. *What could carve so deeply into a woman's face and soul?* I wonder.

"Parole conditions," she mutters, jerking me back to the present.

I nod. "Right. And you're not happy about this, I guess."

"What would you know about it?" she demands, flashing angry grey eyes at me.

"Well, I…" I clear my throat.

"You," she snarls, flicking a finger at me. "You sit there, judging me and you know nothing about me, about my life!"

"I try not to make assumptions," I offer. *Did I just sound self-righteous?*

"You already did!"

"I apologise, Sylvania, I meant no offence." *Going really well, Donna*, I berate myself. *So worth all those years at university. Good one.* I struggle to think what to say next, what to do. I try a different tack. "So, how shall we proceed here? I'm not sure I understand how I can help you." *Put it back on her. See what happens.*

"Don't need help!" She gets up with a flap of worn clothing and heads for the door.

"Wait!" I call after her. "I have to sign you off on this."

She turns. "Is it off, or on? Make up your mind."

"Well, I…" *Did she just correct my grammar?* I consult my notes, flustered. "Please, just sit down. Wherever you feel comfortable." She remains standing, and just as I'm about to give up, she makes her way slowly back to the stool. "Your file says you were arrested, after abducting children." I look up at her briefly. Her facial expression is stony. "Can we talk about that?"

"What's there to say?"

"Well, perhaps the reasons why you felt it necessary."

"My business!" Sylvania barks. "No one else's."

"Perhaps the parents of those children wouldn't agree," I say, trying not to sound smug, just practical, rational. She mutters and turns away. Her face is red and blotchy. "Did you… feel you were helping these children in some way?" I venture.

"What would you know about it," she mutters, her eyes scanning the office gardens outside – a bleak, featureless lawn edged in concrete with scraggly bushes.

"The judge made this order because she thought there was merit in exploring this," I try to explain. "She was giving you another chance. Don't you want to avoid a long sentence in that hellhole at Dillingly?"

"Judge knows nothing," Sylvania says, then turns back to me. I am shocked to see tears glinting in her eyes.

"Is it jail time you are afraid of?" I ask. Sylvania clasps and unclasps her hands, stroking her thumb, hard. "Was it something about the children you thought you were helping?" I press her. I scan her history. "You've never been in prison before. You've never even been arrested before."

She smiles at me then, an eerie look that makes my skin instantly itchy.

"Never been caught before, have I?"

I swallow. *Am I looking at evil here? Clever, cunning, malicious evil?* But there is something sad behind her eyes and I want to dig it out and inspect it, see it in the light. I believe. I have hope. Even for her.

She folds her arms . "Forget it," she says suddenly.

"Forget what?" I find myself asking.

"About trying to save me. You're too late. Too far gone."

"But I..."

"The reasons I took those kids, you'd never understand."

"You could try me."

"Can't be bothered. Just write in that notebook that I'm sorry, okay?" She gestures irritably at my book.

"I don't know if you are." I look at her, hard. *What am I missing?*

"What do you mean?"

"Sorry," I say, feeling suddenly stupid.

She points at her chest with a triumphant grin. "I'm the one who's supposed to be sorry. Ha!"

I feel my face getting hot. I place the notebook and pen on my desk, get up and push my office chair back behind it. I can feel her eyes upon me, boring into my back. I walk over to the window.

"I often look out at this garden and wonder why someone doesn't make it nicer," I say. "It's quite depressing to look at, actually. If the effort was made, it could look lovely. And then bees would be attracted to it, perhaps even little birds," I add wistfully.

"Such a perfect little world, isn't it, the one inside your head?" Sylvania says behind me. I turn. Her lips are twisted in a grimace.

"That offends you?" I ask.

She shrugs. "Offends me? What the hell do I care?"

"Then why say it?" I challenge her. *God! We're going round in circles.*

"You're so predictable," she says gruffly. "You're all the same."

I take a breath. *Calm down, Donna.* I regard her, trying to see her with new eyes, a fresh perspective. She is teaching me something here. Counselling 101 – what influence or issues does the therapist bring into the room simply by being there? I turn back to the window to think. It's getting noisy in my head, lots of voices pushing their points of view, doubt creeping around me with its heavy, dank cloak. I am feeling a familiar helplessness, that of my nine-year-old self, struggling to understand my alcoholic mother. Trying to stay safe from her violent hands, but needing her love and approval so badly.

"Bad mother," Sylvania says quietly.

I spin. "Pardon?"

"Your mother. Addict was she?"

I stare at her, dumbfounded.

"I can see it." She nods to herself. "I can see it," she says softly, looking down at her bony hands. "I've seen that pain before."

Something hits me in the guts, like a fist. I blink back tears. *My God, what's happening here? Pull yourself together, Donna! You're the therapist!* I try to get things back on track.

"Is that what you saw in those children?"

"Go on then, deflect!" she barks. "Drag us back to my so-called crime!"

"But that's why we're here," I say, standing on the precipice of my professional confidence. "To talk about you."

She tilts her head to the side and regards me hungrily. "Why should I unburden myself to you, Donna?" She says my name so softly. Her grey eyes are older than the mountains, where I grew up, older than the river which winds around the valley of this town. I swallow again, gathering the tatters of my wits together.

"I don't pretend to know all the answers, all the…"

"Yes, you do," she counters. "You sit there with your notebook and pen and before I even speak, you've decided so much about me, based upon your notes."

"I have an open mind," I insist. "I take people as I find them."

"What a noble idea," Sylvania smirks.

"I'm hoping we can find some middle ground here," I say, mentally pushing away an image of myself slapping her.

"Why?" she snaps.

"Well, that's how I usually start. Find something we can agree upon."

"How about we agree that you're stupid?" she cackles.

I give her a patient look and wait. She scowls at me. I stand up and offer my hand again.

"Thanks for keeping the appointment, Sylvania," I say. She stands up and takes my hand warily. Her skin is soft and thin. She gives me a look I can't read.

"Giving up already?" She is swaying slightly. Then her eyes roll into the back of her head and she falls at my feet in a dead faint. I crouch beside her, reaching for her pulse and patting her face. Her pulse is flighty and uneven. "Sylvania! Come on, wake up. Sylvania, can you hear me?" I scramble to my feet and reach for my phone. Moments later, there's a knock on the door. "Come in!" I call. The medical officer arrives with her kit and takes over. A security guard is leaning against the open doorway, watching.

"Amazing what these crims will do," he says, darkly. "Just to get some sympathy."

"I hardly think this is deliberate!" I say hotly.

He smiles patronisingly. "She certainly convinced you."

I stare down at the crumpled woman, this woman, who read my ancient, deeply buried pain so effortlessly, who offered me that precious jewel beyond price – empathy.

"No," I reply. "Not this time." I share a look with the medical officer. She nods, a half-smile upon her lips. Sylvania regains consciousness. She doesn't get up, just regards me with those eyes of wisdom and loss.

"It's okay, Donna," she croaks.

I can't stop the tears this time. One plops onto her worn dress. I sniff, embarrassed. The medical officer helps Sylvania onto a chair and straps the BP cuff onto her skinny arm. As the machine buzzes, I pick up my discarded notepad and make my recommendation.

I Touched You Today
Laurence Harrould

I touched you today
No hands met
No lips pressed
Our bodies remote in space
But I touched you today.

When we said goodbye
Your eyes said it all.
We embraced, we kissed
And we touched.

In your eyes I saw the love
That we have for each other.
The caring, the yearning
The wanting that we share.

I touched you today
Not in space
But in time.

A Day in the Bush
Laurence Harrould

My wife, Danita, had been working hard and so I suggested we have a day off to spend some time amongst the trees. Not the relaxing day I had planned but total disaster was narrowly avoided.

There is a list of places to visit in Tasmania and we're working our way through it. Liffey Falls was handy and would be good to be able to check off. According to Google Maps, the road to Liffey Falls was closed. However, the National Parks website had no such message. We thought the National Parks site was likely to be the most current – wrong choice number one.

A pleasant drive in the country brought us to the road to the falls in the National Park – CLOSED!! due to landslide. According to the map there are two roads leading into the falls and so we entered the other address into the GPS and headed off, trusting our technology – wrong choice number two – BIG TIME!

Following the GPS we descended down a wet, slippery bush track which zigzagged across a steep hill. By the way, it had been raining consistently for some days now and EVERYTHING was wet, soggy, muddy and slippery.

Continuing along, the 'road' became narrower and rougher until it was a bush track barely wider than the car. As we bumped and slid over rocks, branches and other obstacles we could see the crossroad ahead on the GPS – nearly there UNTIL a tree across the road. Not just any tree but a very big one at head height so there was no way we could get the car past it. No option but to reverse back up the track. The other bit of background that I have so far left out is that it was a brand-new car. It's an SUV but not a 4-wheel drive.

I found a patch a bit further back where we could turn around but it was tricky getting there. I was driving with Danita giving instructions. As I was reversing over rocks and tree branches with more forestry close by on either side, we both had visions of our brand-new car ending up with dents and scratches. She was quite vocal in stating her 'concerns' while I was quietly panicking without saying much. Eventually, we reached the turning spot. "Turning spot" probably gives the wrong impression. It was a dent in the bush and involved a 50-point turn but eventually the car was facing back the way we'd come.

Back to trusting the GPS – wrong move number three. We didn't want to go back up the hill we had come down originally as it was very steep and windy with very tight bends. The GPS showed the road we were on going through to another straight road up ahead which we thought was the one we needed, to get onto the other access road to the falls. We followed this new one only to end up with the road we were on completely disappearing.

This time we had noted a good turning point and the road was wider, so we were able to get back around and decided we did have to go back up the original hill. There was only one problem. The road we were on was steep and there were huge ditches and mounds across it. Coming down wasn't too challenging as gravity helped. However, going back up was not so simple.

We got past the first few, which involved very carefully picking our way across the ditches and mounds by using the sides we had come down which were a little bit levelled off. Then we came to one that we simply couldn't get over - the car stopped. The logical thing was to reverse out of the ditch and mound and take a faster run at it. Have you ever noticed that when you need it most, logic just doesn't work? Putting the car into reverse did nothing – it wouldn't even go into reverse. The car is automatic and has a gear dial, not a gear stick. I couldn't change anything. Thinking it was perhaps because the wheels weren't straight, I tried straightening the steering and still nothing worked. Couldn't go forwards and couldn't go backwards. By this time, I'm having visions of spending a long time waiting for someone to turn up or to have to walk out: no phone reception of course. Also, the car is fully electric and we weren't sure of how much battery capacity we had left. So, you can't go get a jerry can of petrol and carry it to the car if you run out of 'fuel.'

Then a stroke of genius: the car is really a computer with a battery and four wheels. What do you do when you can't get your computer to do what you need? You shut it down and start again. So that's what I did. Huge relief, got it into reverse and managed to drive out of the hole we were in. As we were reversing down the hill we started hearing some very odd noises under the car and it wasn't moving properly. I'm thinking; "we've caught a tree branch and it's ripping out the underside".

Stopping at the first opportunity and climbing out to inspect the underside, in the mud, I found nothing caught under there, so what was the problem? In the process of reversing down the hill a BIG pile of leaves and other bush detritus had piled up against the back wheel and the car couldn't get over it. I cleared that away and we're off again – with a huge sense of relief.

Took a run up to the ditch and the same thing happened – couldn't get over. Nothing for it but to get a really good run up and floor it… made it over – YAYY and PHEW!

Back up the windy, slippery road. At the top we met a guy on a heavy road bike. Stopping to chat, he told us his GPS had said this was the way to Hobart. He was a lucky man… Taking a touring bike down the road we'd been on would not have been a great experience (chances are, he'd still be there).

Now that we were at the top of the hill, we decided to follow the road signs and ignore the GPS. We knew there is a charging station at Westbury and so headed there. Once we had internet signal Danita started looking for coffee shop options in Westbury – nothing. It was now after 2pm and everything seemed to shut about then or around 3. Anyway, we had brought a picnic lunch and decided at least we could find somewhere and enjoy that while the car charged. We were both really looking forward to the hot chocolate we'd brought with us.

Got to Westbury and needed to deal with the most important and urgent item – toilet break. Found the toilets which were next to the Council chambers. As it was a Sunday, the Council was closed but the toilets were open – another PHEW and! And sense of relief and a feeling things were starting to go right. However, on my way into the toilet I met a man standing outside the Council building. As is the way in Tasmania, people are polite so we said hello. He noticed my skull cap and we got talking because he was at the Council building for a Christadelphian function. Christadelphians are very pro-Israel and pro-Jewish and so he clearly wanted a deeper conversation. Meanwhile, I'm still trying to get INTO the toilet. Fortunately, Danita arrived and she picked up the conversation and I escaped.

Immediate needs having been met, we got the car set up on the local charger and there at the end of the street was a park – just perfect for our picnic. Mistake number four.

We got ourselves settled in the park at a very comfortable open-air bench and picnic table. It then started to rain – very gently – so I went and got our raincoats and hats. Just as we got ourselves properly settled it bucketed down – typical day in Tasmania… Never mind the rain. We were both so exhausted we decided to stay where we were and have our picnic in the rain. By now the hot chocolate, we were so looking forward to, was very tepid chocolate but at least it was wet and tasty. We were clearly getting some very intrigued looks and comments from other people but there was no way we could move and endured getting wet.

Having finished eating and having given the car a bit of a recharge it was time to head off. We did a bit of a drive around Westbury to see if there was still a coffee shop or something open where we could get a hot drink. Luckily, we discovered 'Love Lucy Boots.' It's more a wine bar than coffee shop but it was open and did serve coffee. Lucy, the owner, is a very loud and fun lady. We had a delightful time there and got talking to some other patrons who were headed to the same part of Tasmania as we lived so we were able to give them some good pointers about where to go when they got to Devonport. We had a wonderful time there and it felt a bit like a reward for us not losing it earlier in the day.

One thing that did happen there was when we were ordering our drinks. We usually have a large decaf mocha, extra shot, extra hot with almond milk. As Danita was going to do the ordering, she asked me what I wanted and I replied, "My usual." Lucy, thinking I was talking to her, replied that she didn't know my "usual." A few weeks later we went back there with some friends and I asked for my usual and Lucy had remembered it and other details about our visit – WOW! So, if you're near Launceston make sure you visit Love Lucy Boots in Westbury.

All in all, we had a memorable day and still have not made it to Liffey Falls. Not sure why Danita and I both develop nervous tics whenever there is a suggestion of going back there – I suppose we'll make it one day (in the middle of summer, I expect).

Tiddles
Donna-Marie Koopman

Australia's Nullarbor Plain is a flat, desolate landscape, an inhospitable part of our world. Yet, an air of ancient mystery surrounds it, almost like being on an alien planet. Sometimes, one can feel an other-worldly energy seemingly vibrating from its pre-historic landscape.

Stretching out for miles and miles, there are days one can see the curvature of the earth in the distance. It's a phenomenon caused by specific atmospheric conditions that occur in the strangest circumstances. Often, even though it's neither cold nor humid, a mist can surround our railway camp. If you wander away from the camp, it is very easy to become disorientated and lost. Many of the railway construction workers had done just that: immigrant refugees from WWII who had been sent to railway camps on the Nullarbor Plains to maintain the Trans Australia Railway. I lived there as a child, Dad being the "ganger" (foreman), and witnessed many strange and magical events that fascinated me. A dry electrical storm would cause lightning to run across the ground in a spectacular light display.

It was the weekend, and Dad usually set rabbit traps away from the camp so Mum could have some fresh meat to supplement our fortnightly food rations. As he ventured into the harsh desert landscape filled with spikey spinifex bushes, it was a beautiful clear day with high streaky cirrus clouds painting a white contrast on the azure blue of the heavenly canvas. He assured himself that he might go a little further than usual, as his last foray to trap rabbits the weekend prior had been unsuccessful. He searched for signs of rabbit droppings and warrens and was unaware of a mist enveloping the region until it was too late. On a typical day, he could use the sun to navigate his way back to camp.

Today, he had no idea where to go. Dad related this uncanny story to Mum and his three daughters when he emerged out of the unusual mist later that afternoon when we were becoming worried about his whereabouts. He always came home before lunchtime, not at three in the afternoon. He realised his predicament and decided to stay put until the mist lifted, no matter how long that might take.

Our family also had another member, Tiddles, the ginger tomcat. I'm positive he was a re-incarnated human because he was exceptionally smart. He always gravitated to Mum, maybe because she was the cook and always gave him tiddly bits of leftovers, hence the name Tiddles. I'm convinced Tiddles could understand what we said because he'd answer with mews, meows, yowls, or growls should he be angry. Was he sensing Mum's apprehension when she told us girls that Dad was late returning today? Tiddles was obviously Mum's cat, following her everywhere.

Dad found it strange when he heard a mewing call emanating out of the mist. Then there was Tiddles, tail swishing from side to side as if to say, 'Are you coming?'

"Come on, Tiddles, you lead the way home."

Tiddles turned around, and Dad followed close behind him. Out of the mist they came: Mum's cat, who most times wouldn't acknowledge Dad existed, and Dad, very relieved to be rescued by this orange tomcat Mum insisted on keeping when it was left to her by another family who was transferred to the city. Had today been different because he sensed Mum was worried? Tiddles might have received some extra titbits from Mum that week, guiding Dad back to camp. To us girls, on hearing Dad's story of survival, Tiddles was now our Hero Cat.

Some might find this story hard to believe, but cross my heart; it's true.

Certain maxims of the sister of Mehitabel as dictated to Archy***
Marilyn Arnold

i asked my sister if it all
seemed real not using the
c word; but meaning
it anyway and whether she had any
maxims for the road ahead I am trying
not to think about life she said
wothehell today is what it is tomorrow
is what it is she said life is
always toujours gai

im learning french you know as for
maxims live so that you
can stick out your tongue
at your medical oncologist

don't give up rock and roll to
dance is to enjoy the body its
breathlessness it is you know
a form of foreplay

if you get gloomy just
take a glass of wine and forget
the liver think how much
better this world is than
hell a place you can't end up in if
you don't believe in it

denial is often the only sensible
tenet of survival pretending
the future holds no threats

there is always
something to be thankful for
i already own three wigs so
i have the goods when all
my hair falls out

someone said medicine is the
science of uncertainty
In all probability announced
mehitabels sister la mort
is the only certainy however
I still have a plan of thirty five more years before I reach nirvana

which I will spend enjoying
my day to day existence as
a star in the theatre of life my plan
to be always toujours gai
dancing on the cold cobbles singing
no regrets no regrets
come what cold wind may

*** *in imitation of Don Marquis (*"Archie & Mehitabel"*), whose poems were typed up by Archie the cockroach on an old typewriter and who can't do capital letters, punctuation or proper line ends. He is an acquaintance of Mehitabel the cat, whose words he uses in his poems*

Castaway
Jennie Herrera

I was mad to sign on. Mad. A wreck in the tropics. Turquoise water. Sun. Food. Hope. Mad. And it wasn't even more money. Here I live condemned. Live? Exist. And long for that palm-fringed sand. Gorging in thought. Solitude no concern of mine.

> Silver-emerald isles
> Strung about the throat of dawn,
> Gold-hinged, shining
>> With a thousand wiles
>> For any Crusoe; profligate
>> And flush with dining
> Turtle eggs, crabs, vie;
> Fins, milk-of-nuts, soft tropic fruit
> Pungent in their season
>> I would list and lie
>> Cornucopia'd till I die
>> Softly lose my reason

And all the time the thunder of monstrous waves, grey-green billows thundering on rocks fills my ears. And the wind sighs through my head, making everything ache and tic with unearthly pain.

Shelter beckoned. It stood up above the rocks. I ran as best I could, bedraggled, soaked, sleet and rain and wind and surf, not knowing where one started and another ended and found this place. This benighted place. Still shown on maps, imperfect maps, but then no one knew all the intricacies ... And the shoddy walls were already cracking and breaking and tumbling. A place out of the wind, the ever-singing westerly, it was barely that, but I huddled in close, afraid of the surging water almost below me, and said, I said to the screaming wind, I'm safe, safe awhile, and they'll come, they'll search, admiralties need lighthouses ... if they don't care a penny for wrecks they care for lighthouses. They LIST them.
And keepers. And oil. They'll have to—

Have to. A keeper unfed. A keeper cold. They'll come.

I walk doubled over against the tempest, round and round my tiny kingdom. My kingdom and its ruined castle.

Some shriveled berries. Some shellfish cemented on. Birds. Birds. Lay me eggs. Nothing to boil them with but I'll eat and be thankful.

And the great brown slimy strands of kelp. I've tried chewing. I'll chew anything. Get down and peer into pools left by the last storm, pools in rocks. Hoping for …

Why me. Why the softest man on board. Why save me, God. But then you didn't. Not unless they come soon. I'm no Crusoe. I wasn't the hardened men up the rigging, not the captain of a hundred voyages. Mr Purser. Mr Mean. Looking sourly at the cost of hard tack. But I'm here and something will be thrown onshore this outlying isle, this bare windswept rock, with not even sufficient spars to make a raft. If I could tie wood with kelp, if I had wood, if … if …

The cold seeps through every bone and vein. I try to sleep, night by night. And blessed dreams. Little shops in a market town, men in striped aprons, women with baskets, and all carrying … all taking food, little suppers, I would accost them on the street and demand in a big voice—and wake up! The waking into a grey dawn with the sun fighting to show a glimmer. Ragged racing cloud always harried, always on the run, I know the wind never sleeps. We hoped … God, we hoped for a lull … and I'll pretend this rain is gentle village rain, up the High Street, round the corner, past the village pond, me there somewhere …

No cold attics in my airy pillowed home

Where sunburst rays are held by eaves, turned in by pearly dome; another roof beyond the billowed manor, church, Masonic hall, cloud chapels

Of cream stone, shops, bright awnings, diamond panes and shadowed lintels,

Must be a spreading place of learning, boys with lurking exciting dreams,

Construing Virgil, thinking bat and ball and waiting tea, quoting reams

Of Paradise Lost and Gained and gained and lost again

… and a door opening into warmth, the smell of … of toast over the fire … something burning but I don't care. Even black charred, I'll stretch out a hand …

And a new ship loading. Oil. Tins of … Don't think of food.

Tell yourself—

Men have lived in worse places. I don't know where but they must have. Places with no lighthouse. Places with danger …

I have a lighthouse. Its rough stone walls against my back. Built to protect poor mariners. My back hurts. My stomach shrinks. Sometimes I think I see and then I know I don't.

And all the time the thunder all around me, coming at me, echoing in my head, these southern rollers, unimpeded in a thousand miles and crashing, taking rocks, hurling, the thunder, the thunder, if I could eat, if it would being manna on the wind, throw up fish, anything, I've ceased to define food and the brackish water in pools … it's water … water … but I know it's not …

And oil for the light. A ship. A ship. More than oil. Warm. Light. Voices that aren't, that aren't, sometimes I think the wind is voices. Calling me. Seducing me. Why wait? Why hope? Don't be a fool. I was thought quite clever. My mother. Mothers think foolish things. And fail to see …

And the pain. Which is worse. Pain in my face, my feet, my ribs, my back, slipping on rocks to retrieve … and it wasn't. The blood flowed down my leg. But the hope wasn't. And a different kind of pain. Despair. They'll come. Of course they'll come.

They know there's a lighthouse here. They'll come. And I'll be here. Waiting. Skeleton thin. But waiting. Even eager.

Turn, flash, reflect and flash again; a light above—
My eyes are salt sore, filmed. I see, I *think* I see—
My mouth cracks and whispers, flares red at the corners,
My skin, like tunny-scales, reflects the agony of solitude—
With manic force, the great iron hooves
Strike the beams and struts of stable walls
Rear and curl and fight in life-denying fury
Then break free—

How can a man live forever with despair at his side. How can a man live with thunder night and day, and the swish of water running down and the screaming fits of wind, banshee wind. Live? This isn't, this is dying. Slowly. Dying to the sound of thunderous hooves tearing at the rocks beneath me, determined to destroy, demanding sacrifice in the maelstrom.

Grasp hope for what? Let go. Feel the light which is warm

and bright only in my dreams. Let me into my dreams. Keep me there. Tie me down.

> A thousand nights with lowering light
> By my elbow, and dark imps plucking at my
> Other side; in loneliness they expand and grow;
> Escape a life's conditioning; hard round the highway curves
> Lean in to their great creaking collars; monstrous beasts
> Midnight black; with threaded hames a-jangle
> Uneasy shafts ride up on rock-hollow sides
> Eyes blinded—

Why go on? Why? Who is the padre to say—to wag a finger and say Sin Sin Sin. Your precious body. My precious … my everpresent hunger, my eyes that see spume and foam but can't find sun or moon. My teeth and gums that hurt hurt hurt. Not that kind of sleek chaplain. No, I'll look elsewhere. But there's no succour there. For what is good and evil when hope is destroyed by crashing waves? Not waves. No, they're something else. Something come to life. Something coming for me.

> A leaping carriage meanly clothed in draper's black
> Its souls contained within, unsighted, sway and slide,
> The faint whistling curlew cry of the devil's legion
> In crevices of life; the beacon captures one pallid face
> As the curtains shift and part, their tassels dragging wearily—
> And still the great hooves thunder on;
> The lash and crack of well-thonged whip, keening
> High and fierce—

They're calling … aren't they calling? I thought I heard … words. Sounds that formed words. Grunts. Roars. Sealion words. If I huddle in, tight against the rough masonry, if I stop my ears, stop my ears, don't listen, don't listen … oil, memory says, oil … and men, the creak of ship's timbers, the boat cast off … oil … it isn't oil or is it … oooooeeerrr … I can't keep it out of my head … it has to be oil … and light … a flash … a comfort and I have thrown hope away … grab comfort back as it whirls away on wind and sleet … a shivering little man throwing arms after … clutching air … come back, come back … don't leave me …

A cloak and mantle flung about; "a wild
Night," the Keeper says, by faint firelight, "and cold",
I have a fire, the Tempter says, great glowing boilers down
below;
A quick leap—a soft-cushioned leap; do not stop to query—
It will come, I remonstrate, the quarter's ship; bringing oil,
Hard rations for the souls who warn the lost
Of great-maned beasts hereabouts—

Only a curlew calling. The saddest sound. But edible. If I can catch
… but curlews fly up and I can only stumble after … come back,
come back … don't leave me …

***

The survey team came on shore with difficulty and looked at the
lighthouse in its ruined state. They looked down over the rocks where
a barrel with rusted hoops was perched. "One wreck?" "Maybe
more." "What a place to strike."

They walked to and fro across the islet, its few shrubs clinging
to pockets of sandy soil, and came upon bones, half buried under sand
and debris.

"So there *was* someone. How long between the wreck and
death." They weren't sentimental men. But they felt a moment's
pity.

"Not long, I hope, or the poor blighter probably went mad,
lost hope, gave up."

One man removed his heavy woollen cap briefly and felt the
wind singing in his ears. A wind that carried thunder and fainter
curlew cries.

Little Beach
Andrea McMahon

We'll have fun! You'll have fun! That's what Lily's mother tells her, perhaps a little more forcibly than is necessary, as they pack the camping equipment for the trip to Little Beach. There's so much stuff to take. They haven't even got to packing the food and cooking utensils yet. It's not like the old days when there was just the two of them. The good ole days before her mother met Luke.

On the road, Lily is sandwiched between the twins, Winnie and Bella, waiting for the fun to start. Winnie is on her left, Bella on her right. She thought twins were meant to be close, even inseparable, but not Winnie and Bella, her newly acquired stepsisters. They like to scream and shout at each other, occasionally leaning over her to deliver a well-placed pinch or punch. All part of the fun, apparently. Lily likes her stepdad, but thinks she'd like him more if he hadn't come saddled with two annoying six-year-olds.

After a four-hour drive that would've tested the patience of a saint, let alone two unruly six-year-olds, they finally arrive at the Little Beach carpark. It's here that Winnie and Bella discover they have to walk 750 metres to the campsite with their backpacks on their backs. They are not pleased. It's hot, the forecast is for 32 degrees, but it feels even hotter. By the time everyone has had a long drink of water, polished off a packet of party lollies for energy, pulled on their packs and grabbed camping chairs, tents, toys, and fishing rods, they are dripping with sweat, especially Lily, who has been given the unenviable task of holding Winnie in one hand, Bella in the other. The twins squirm like little worms, occasionally breaking loose and sitting stubbornly on the sandy path, refusing to move until their new big sister sweettalks them into moving again with promises of collecting seashells and searching for mermaids.

The Little Beach campsite is small and peaceful. Or at least it was peaceful until the Mason-Wilson family arrived. Winnie and Bella are shrieking with excitement now they can see the sea. They want to go swimming, but tents have to be pitched first. They are not pleased. Lily ignores their pleading and goes about selecting a flat, soft spot to set up her own tent. Once the last pegs have been secured, she inflates her sleeping mat and pillow and unfolds her sleeping bag. Lily loves her little red tent. It's a cosy two-man tent that she won't be sharing with Winnie and Bella, who have been told in no uncertain terms that they will be sleeping in the big tent with their father. They are not pleased. They stamp their feet, hands on hips, lips pursed in protest, until they are distracted by a plate of cheese and crackers Luke has prepared as a child-pacifying, pre-dinner snack.

Lily is lying in her tent, eyes closed, listening to the roar of the surf, when her mother appears at the door of her tent.

'Knock, knock.' Sarah pokes her head through the flyscreen. 'Lily love, would you mind keeping an eye on the little ones while Luke and I go for a quick fish on the rocks? You never know, we might catch something for tea. They have good barbeques here.'

Sarah points to a modern barbeque hut, deliberately not looking her daughter in the eye. If she had, she would've seen sparks of anger that could've set the surrounding forest on fire. 'Maybe even take the girls for a paddle?'

Winnie and Bella, who have supersonic hearing, run over to Lily's tent shouting with delight, their little fingers grabbing at her through the tent door like stubby tentacles. Defeated, Lily caves into her mother's demands and crawls out of her tent. The twins attempt to pull her towards the ocean even before she has got to her feet.

'Hang on, you two,' she says, 'we need towels and hats and rashies and sunscreen.'

Winnie and Bella rush back to the big tent, returning with their backpacks. They rummage through their belongings, pulling out the necessary items excitedly, as if pulling presents from a Christmas stocking.

As they walk towards the beach, Lily sees it has been well named. Little Beach is a little beach. But it's beautiful. She lets her feet sink into the soft, silky sand, her eyes captivated by the tiny seashells and many-coloured pebbles that decorate the water's edge like an intricately woven shawl. To the left there is a long rocky ledge below a sheer cliff. Waves crash into the far point of the land, rising high into the sky. Lily is distracted for a moment by the alarming thought that Luke and Sarah might be washed off the rocks by a freak wave. It happens to some poor person every now and again, and Lily most certainly doesn't want it happening to her family. Not only because she would be distraught if her mother drowned, but also because she would be stuck looking after her two darling stepsisters. As an indication of how chaotic this might be, Winnie and Bella rush to the water's edge, shrieking with glee, a wave knocking them off their feet and onto their bottoms immediately. They laugh and clutch Lily's hands. The trio sit in the water side by side, cooling their bodies, the waves lapping against them.

The twins cling to Lily as a set of stronger waves pushes them around in the sand. Lily's eye catches a large barnacle and limpet encrusted rock nearby. She is beginning to understand how it must feel to have something latch onto you so tight it might never let go. She closes her eyes and imagines slipping under the water, rolling onto her stomach, and swimming through the shallows, as free and unfettered as a fish, or a mermaid, or any number of creatures of the sea. She sweeps over beds of seagrass and rocks decorated with colourful starfish. She explores hidden caves lit up by shards of sunlight. Her arms are fluttering fins now, her legs a huge tail fin that hurls her through the water at lightning speed. She passes over an enormous manta ray, swerves to avoid a cold-eyed shark. She spies a fishing line with its vicious hook and swerves past it, elegant and carefree. She is swimming through a school of small silvery fish, over a bed of bright green sea lettuce, when a familiar voice snaps her out of her dream world.

'Fish for tea tonight!'

She looks up to see her mother walking towards the water's edge holding a huge fish. The twins release their grip on her and run over to their stepmother giggling all the way. The sudden feeling of freedom is bliss. Lily slides into the water, rolls onto her back, floats in the shallows between a set of waves, before diving under a breaking wave, just one of many fish in the sea. When she surfaces her mother is standing by the water's edge waving her catch at her daughter.

'Spanish mackerel! Nothing better than barbequed Spanish mackerel. Luke is still fishing so we might even catch another couple.'

Sarah is admiring her catch as she speaks. Lily thinks of her fantasy fish slipping past the evil hook and line and smiles to herself.

'Tomorrow morning you can go for a fish with Luke,' Sarah says to her. 'We'll be getting up nice and early to see the sunrise.'

Tomorrow morning I'll be sleeping in, thinks Lily, as she pulls herself up clumsily, a fish out of water. Winnie and Bella, bored with the fish now, return their attention back to Lily, grabbing a leg each.

'Lily, Lily, look for mermaids!' they shout in unison, pulling her this way and that.

'That's a good idea,' says Sarah, encouragingly. 'I'll head back now and clean this big fella. He put up a good fight,' she adds proudly.

But not good enough, thinks Lily, as her fantasy fish swims past, skilfully avoiding enemy fishing lines once again.

'Fresh fish for tea tonight, nothing better,' repeats Sarah, as Lily spies Luke walking along the beach, his fishing net weighing heavily over his shoulder. She feels herself salivating involuntarily and knows her mother is right. There's nothing better for dinner than fresh fish with a squeeze of lemon.

Lily's fantasy fish swims past her at lightning speed. It is not pleased.

Number 47
Anne Layton-Bennett

over there is a nation
where half the population
is in a state of elation
while the other half cries
in despair, fear and dread
because four more years of bullying
of bluster and lies
stretch out slowly ahead

fooled by rambling rhetoric
and incoherent rants,
one half thought the prancing and dancing
and the dyed orange hair
suggested vigour and youth
they mistook it for strength
but what price truth
in a world that is spinning
and where it's all about winning
so facts are distorted, and so is the news
and if X marks the spot then it's probably fake
because any fib's worth telling for DT's sake

© 2025 Anne Layton-Bennett

Patterns of Nature
Kathleen Bentley

The wind moans as if in pain as it rustles through the trees,
Whispering gossip to its neighbours.
The last of the sun has sunk beneath the horizon
While a frail, pale moon struggles to climb into the darkening sky.
The last of the Egrets rise from the river,
Nestling in the trees where they vie for the best positions.

For a moment in time all is quiet. The wind holds its breath.
The clouds roll in. Dark thunderous clouds full of rain.
Suddenly water pours from the heavens with a vengeance.
A fierce wind forces itself through the trees.
Branches are torn off, leaves scatter every which way
Almost turning the trees inside out. Then silence …

The Earth rests while the pale moon wipes water from her eyes
No wind, No rain. And, as the clouds part to reveal the moon
climbing higher
The sweet smell of damp leaves and grasses fill the air.
The moon, now glowing with such intensity that it brightens up the
heavens,
Takes control, tidying up the night sky after the violent but brief
squall.
A slight breeze helps by sweeping the fallen leaves under the trees.

Nature takes time to recuperate from turbulent events,
To regain strength and move forward to a better day 'tomorrow'.
Our lives are entwined with Nature. Some may say we mimic it.
Moments of great drama with periods of supreme joy.
Yes, Nature and humankind have similarities.
Their own weather pattern if you will, but who mimics the other?

Footsteps
© Dawn Meredith

You can turn your head
And glance back upon your footsteps,
There, in the mud, the sand, the flattened grass, the snow.
See the heat rising from the prints you left behind on the asphalt.
But you cannot go back there.
Always, your feet will take you forward
Or keep you standing still, trapped in the present,
The echoes of the past ringing in your ears.

Mistakes clang like annoying brass bells,
Ever-present reminders of your failures,
Ringing out forevermore.
Acrid smoke rises from the pyres of relationships left in your wake.
Ambitions never realised. Goals never reached.
Do not listen.
Do not look.
Turn your gaze to the rising sun and walk,
Leaving your shadows and regrets behind you.

Feet do not have a mind of their own.
They are driven by our needs, our desires, our unspoken fears,
Our despair, our elation, our prideful march, our ecstatic joys.
Can Destiny guide your feet?
Who knows.
Better to have your feet obey your instincts.
Walk with purpose, into the light,
Without a backward glance at the impressions
And the jumble sale you leave behind.

Encounter with Royalty
Denys Ririka

I gave Prince Charles his first taste of pawpaw!

In 1966 when Prince Charles was enrolled for one year of schooling at Geelong Grammar School in Victoria, he came to Papua New Guinea (PNG) with a group of schoolboys for six days experience at Martyrs Memorial Boy's School. The school was established as a memorial to those who were lost in the Second World War.

We had been told of his coming arrival and there was much talk amongst the boys about his visit and jokes about what we would do. There were various special preparations like improved walking tracks and a swimming hole in the river. In those days there were no cameras or mobiles, so memories needed to be visual or story. While swimming one boy could watch another touch Prince Charles' body and each witness the other.

I was walking back from my garden house with a hoe fork on my shoulder and a bush knife (machete) in one hand and a pawpaw with the other arm. Prince Charles was walking down the steps of the Sefoa garden house, where he had slept for the night, and he walked up to me, greeted me and asked; "Is that a coconut that you are carrying in your arm?" There were a number of coconut trees around the garden house and the school. I replied;

"No, it's a pawpaw, would you like a taste?"

"Yes, thank you."

I wiped the bush knife on my trousers and cut a piece of pawpaw with it and handed it to the Prince. He enjoyed it and we discussed the differences between a coconut and a pawpaw. The watching security guard smiled.

In preparation for his visit, we had moved the stones in the river to construct a pool for swimming. I did swim with him and played ball games in that pool.

. . . .

Years later when I was in London at Lambeth conference, the bishops together with their wives, were invited to afternoon tea with the Queen and Prince Phillip at Buckingham Palace. They arranged ten bishops with their spouses in each line to meet either Prince Phillip or the Queen and Lesley and I were selected for the line to meet the

Queen. When she came to us we were introduced and she asked how we were, how we were finding the weather, and how were the church and the government in PNG? I replied;

"Fine your majesty. I hoped to meet Prince Charles."

"Oh, he is away. Why were you wanting to meet him?"

"I gave him, his first taste of pawpaw when he was at Martyr's memorial school visiting from Australia, from fruit from my garden."

"Oh, how lovely."

She shook hands with us and moved to the next couple she was to meet, but the meeting made a big impression on me. She was genuinely interested and spoke thoughtfully.

When we returned to the group of Bishops, an Indian Bishop asked,

"Can I shake hands with the hand that shook the Queen's hand?" and I replied,

"No" and moved by hand back. "I am not going to wash my hand until I return to PNG!"

The next morning, he asked me again if he could shake my hand, but I replied,

"Sorry I forgot and washed my hand this morning when I had my shower" and we both laughed.

It was a great privilege to meet the queen.

I thought I saw a sheer blue Gustav Klimt
Terry Hannan

Christian and Louise had cautiously stepped from the route number fifty-nine tram that had transported them from central Melbourne to the outlying suburb of Moonee Ponds. Christian had only become aware of this location when Louise had encouraged him to accompany her with the aim of increasing his geographical knowledge of the city to which they had recently located. The geographical experience had an additional Louise pre-defined purpose. They were to attend lunch at a 'friend of friend's' (*la amico del'amici*) home where Beatrice, the owner of the luncheon venue in Moonee Ponds had arranged the dining get together to share time with her cousin Angela and her neighbour, Gertude.

As they walked towards the luncheon venue Louise was brimming with excitement because the occasion would be a reunion with Angela whom she had not seen for several months. Louise had previously met Gertrude in Angela's Sydney house and this neighbour was a retired teacher of classical piano and recently widowed. The ten-minute walk from the tram to Angela's home transposed Louise and Christian from the local noisy, busy, time worn shopping precinct, into quiet suburban streets lined with neat Australian post-Federation cottages. Many of these had white picket fences made of moulded wrought iron and behind the fences were manicured gardens. Number seventy-three was different and had a front garden with a dense, space-filling array of flowers and bushes that was well maintained, and the foliage partially obscured the neat wooden cottage.

After entering the property through the swinging wooden gate Louise and Christian stepped onto the veranda and approached the recessed original wooden door protected by an external fly-screen door. There was no evidence of modern renovations about the building or its surrounding environment. Following Louise's activation of the electronic door buzzer the loud yapping of a small dog could be heard and then the door was opened by Beatrice cradling her beloved Possum, a Prince Charles Cocker Spaniel. Beatrice displayed a welcoming joy and did not appear as if she was resolving her recent bereavement. A chattering conversation then erupted over the persistently yapping dog, who became silenced by a tasty morsel retrieved from beneath the kitchen bench. Louise felt she was in paradise in the company of the warm, exuberant female host exuding her *joie de vivre* and revealing desire for a cooling drink. Champagne was immediately served by the recruited barman, Christian, and this facilitated the passing of time as they awaited the arrival of the remaining guests, Angela and Gertrude. Christian became enthralled by the environment, and he felt he was on the set of a French or other European drama series being shown on SBS On Demand. The wooden hallway was lined with art that was highlighted by the trilogy of sepia-coloured etchings of female nudes portrayed in high quality pencilled artwork. As the group entered the centre of the house art could be seen occupying most of the wall spaces.

Louise became mesmerised by a Picasso-like painting of a female nude on a white background, where the body contour was defined by three curved lines. She repeatedly expressed how the image was powerfully sensual and beautiful despite the apparent simplicity of the image. For Christian the house interior led to his recall of past European experiences that were accentuated when he entered the compact bathroom with its patterned walls, a standalone bath elevated on four brass moulded feet, and gold-coloured metal taps. In the bathroom a wide wooden-framed mirror was located over an ornate hand washing basin and clean washing had been hung neatly over the bath suspended on a wall-fixed wire frame creating an attractive, utilitarian and comforting space.

As the two women chatted during their coordinated preparation of lunch, Christian began his tour of the house. He noted the densely packed European-style garden through the French, glass-panelled wooden-framed doors and his attention became captured by the voluminous collection of books. In the wall-covering bookcases the shelves were cluttered with disorganised arrays of books that appeared to have no defined order or position. He noted the overflow of books on two sofas stacked high with tomes of varying historical publication dates. On a sofa stacked with books adjacent to the kitchen, Christian picked up and flicked through the apparently unread, recent publication, *"The Tattooist of Auschwitz."* In an adjacent room there was an antiquarium of rare books with the writings of Milton, Burns, Shakespeare and other historical authors and their jackets oozed physical and literary antiquity. Christian turned to his left away from the bookshelf in the cluttered reading room and became surprised by the framed painting on the wall that was partially hidden behind a high-backed wooden reading chair. He was not an art-centric person, but had become enlightened about this social stream following his regular excursions through different European countries. His recent diversion from a life in science and academia into creative writing had necessitated his research into art and history further expanding his awareness of art. What had entered his visual space was a classic Gustav Klimt portrait and he immediately became inquisitive. Was it real? How did it get there? Was it a print?

Christian began to wind up his mental machinations about the painting and formulated that this may be an Antiques Roadshow, Fake or Fortune experience? To distract himself from his fanciful ideas he continued to explore the house and despite additional distractions within Beatrice's house he found himself drawn to the Klimt artwork and based on his amateur assessments it looked genuine. The female figure in the image was typical of those seen in most of Klimt's art, *The Woman in Gold*. History indicated that the subject may have been the Austrian fashion designer, Emile Louise Flo`ge or Adele Block-Bauer a related in-law. In the painting the female is seductively semi-naked, pale skin, with exposed breasts, wearing intricate gold apparel and was surrounded by soft and sensuous colours with elements of blue. Christian became seduced by the possible provenance of the portrait.

He then used his latest version iPhone to conduct a Google search during an interruption in the lunching activities. He was acting spontaneously and did not want to appear to be a modern phone addicted individual and subsequently explained to those at the dining table the purpose of his activities on the device. From his internet searches he came to understand that most Klimt's portraits had a dominance of one colour, either gold or blue. The Klimt artwork in Beatrice's house appeared subtly, but significantly different from other portraits by the artist. In the image the woman's neck piece was a deep golden colour, not the common yellow gold, and this represented a "*Kragen*" in German. Hanging on the right side of her body, from the neck to her waist, was a sheer blue, semi-translucent, seductively portrayed piece of her clothing that may have been a nightdress or bathrobe? Christian became fixated on the beauty of the artwork and its potential authenticity.

The lunchtime dining at the antique wooden table in the kitchen dining area diverted Christian away from the artwork to the special reunion of known female friends and new acquaintances. Maintaining the ambiance of the house's European genre, Beatrice had made a Spanish style gazpacho soup which was of light density, positively flavoured with citrus and was accompanied by a strong sherry. Mid-meal Louise reminded herself of her mantra, "*one should never mix your drinks*" (she was an expert on alcohol consumption), as the sherry combined with champagne and wine, began to induce in her a state of instability. Fortunately, her sensations were not severe, and her historical experiences allowed her to safely manage the alcoholic beverages consumed throughout the remainder of the afternoon. The table conversations had been wide ranging in their subjects and did not falter in their delivery. There had been significant revelations from Beatrice and Gertrude who had become widows following painful journeys with dementia in their deceased husbands. There occurred several instances during the luncheon conversations where Christian felt eager to talk about his emerging ideas relating to the Klimt artwork. He finally succeeded in verbalising his thought streams and to his surprise the women let him speak; 'Beatrice, is the Klimt painting a print or real? If it is real, it is likely to be very valuable.'

'I don't know' was Beatrice's response. 'It had never crossed my mind. My husband surprised me when he arrived home with it when we were in Germany. He was extremely excited and indicated that it was possibly very valuable. I recall when he explained his purchase, he spoke about acquiring the painting in a flea market.'

Gertrude then spoke; 'My husband was a professor of art and music and had expert eyes for hidden treasures. With my classical piano expertise and his academic qualifications, we would tour Europe and immerse ourselves in the arts. Christian's ideas sound interesting.' Beatrice responded, 'I must apologise for my lack of knowledge about that artwork because my husband's dementia blew my world apart and many things receded from my memory.'

This interaction was followed by a short interlude where Beatrice and Gertrude shared common pathways of having husbands with dementia. Those observing their interactions noted a sense of healing appear in both women.

Exhibiting courage Christian returned to his painting theme: 'Beatrice, would you consider the challenge to find the provenance of the Klimt piece?' She replied, 'Of course. Even if nothing comes of it the experience will be a wonderful distraction and possibly rewarding.'

The remainder of the afternoon became consumed by babbling chatter until Angela and Gertrude declared they needed to urgently depart for another engagement. Louise and Christian lingered with Beatrice for nearly an hour after the two women had left.

During the next month Christian would occasionally recall his conversations regarding the Klimt artwork then finally disregarded it completely. One day he was on a tram travelling to the city and noted the unnamed SMS message in his iPhone and considered it to be another scam but could see Beatrice's name in the text. *"Hi Christian, I hope I am not disturbing you. I took your suggestions regarding the painting, simply to play the game and have fun. Guess what? Events blossomed and I am still holding my breath."* He continued reading. *"Following the lunch I contacted a group called 'freemanart' who described themselves as being 'experts' in the fine art of authentication. They have an office in Melbourne and declare their international reputation in this field."* Excitement rattled through Christian's body as he read the remainder of the long SMS which described a series of communications and events that resulted in the artwork becoming evaluated and that activity had been undertaken in complete secrecy between the company and Beatrice.

The long text message described how one day she responded to a ring on her front doorbell and when she opened the door, she saw a man in his fifties wearing rimless glasses and exhibiting an intense persona and noted on the lapel of his expensive suit the gold embroidered lettering, *"freemanart."* 'I have come to inspect the Gustave Klimt artwork. Are you Beatrice?' She responded with 'Yes' and he sought her permission to enter her home; 'May I come in? Only you and our organisation know of my presence here. I am sure you understand the importance of this arrangement.' Beatrice nodded her approval and offered him the choice of tea or coffee? A polite and barely audible reply came; 'No thank you artworks and liquid stains are not readily compatible.' For the next hour Beatrice had twiddled her thumbs in anticipation elsewhere in the house as the representative performed his tasks then beckoned her to come and talk. He spoke quietly with conviction but there was no verification of his assessment. 'With your permission would you be willing to sign this document for our company so we can have this piece evaluated internationally?' With a trembling hand, Beatrice signed the form and noted underneath his witness signature box the words Reinhold Haux. Following the signing the man removed the Klimt painting from the wall and proceeded to wrap as if it was fragile crystal.

No matter what Beatrice was doing for the next nine months, even to the point of almost forgetting about the painting, she could not stop thinking about the permutations and implications of the artwork's evaluation. At the end of nine months, she expectantly removed an official looking envelope from her mailbox that was watermarked with the '*freemanart*' logo. Inside her house she tentatively slit open the ornate envelope. Written in perfect copperplate handwriting, underneath her identification details, were the following words. "*Dear Beatrice, the company of 'freemanart' would like you to arrange a private and confidential meeting with members of our assessment board so we can discuss the conclusions of the international evaluations of your Gustav Klimt artwork. All communications must remain private and confidential. Non-adherence to this directive may negate any further involvement and support from our company. We look forward to rewarding conversations at your earliest convenience.*" Beatrice's hand reached for the partially emptied champagne glass on her kitchen bench and then Possum fully aware of her distracted state abruptly started yapping and demanding attention.

Two days in my working life
Allan Jamieson

<u>Örnsköldsvik, Northern Sweden, December 1978</u>

My whole working life was spent in the worldwide pulp, paper and forest industry, which is mainly why I made 2,700 plane flights – one flight every four days on average.

I am about to take you on one such business trip, when I had ten flights in two days and never saw a bed!

In April 1977, I returned from Tokyo (where I had lived and worked for two years) to the small city of Örnsköldsvik where I had lived the previous six years. This time, though, I was accompanied by my wife, Kuniko, who I had met in Tokyo and had married in Melbourne, in January 1976.

Kuniko had been to Europe once, as a typical Japanese tourist – Italy, France and England in six days with two half-days either side to travel from Japan to Europe and back.

December in northern Sweden was a very new experience for her. In late December, the sun is above the horizon for no more than four hours each day and the daytime temperature is regularly below zero deg. C. Though she had gained her Swedish driving licence, she had never driven on ice or snow and walking a kilometre into town to shop would not be nice either!

My company asked me to attend a business meeting at Porto Alegre in southern Brazil in the third week of December 1978. I immediately tried to figure out how I could get there and back before December 24 – *Julafton* – which is when Swedes celebrate Christmas. Indeed, Dec. 21 is even more important as it is Kuniko's birthday!

First, I thought this could be my chance to fly on Concorde. Scheduled flights between Paris and Rio de Janeiro had commenced in January 1976, however it was soon obvious to me that Concorde was attractive (arguably *justifiable*) <u>only</u> to those passengers who <u>lived</u> in Paris and who wanted <u>solely</u> to visit Rio – because Concorde's departure and arrival times did not "mesh" with those of normal jet aircraft. In my case, I would spend more time at Paris and Rio airports while waiting for connections than I would 'save' in flying time. ***Pity!***

My task was still not easy to arrange, as this time of year in Europe has always been a busy time for air travel. I did manage to secure seats on all ten necessary planes, as follows:

Örnsköldsvik (0640 on Dec. 20) → Stockholm → Copenhagen → Paris → Lisbon → Rio de Janeiro → Porto Alegre → Rio de Janeiro → Paris → Stockholm → Örnsköldsvik (arr. 2045 on Dec. 21).

From Paris to Rio, I flew in a Lockheed 1011 'Tristar' the third of the wide-body aircraft to enter airline service, after the Boeing 747 and Douglas DC10. The seating arrangement was 2-5-2 and I had secured a middle seat in one row: not my choice – the plane was full! The early Lockheed planes were not able to cover a long distance over water, so we landed in Lisbon to refuel – during which all passengers had to stay on board. Those two legs were: Paris 1800 → Lisbon 1915 and Lisbon 2045 → Rio de Janeiro 0645. That's why I spent the night of Dec. 20 a long way from a bed! The Lockheed was operated by TAP (*Transportes Aéreos Portugueses*) and I was treated to their ground crew at Lisbon cleaning the plane with all us passengers still seated. The crew were especially diligent, and they worked fast!

I arrived at Porto Alegre at 1130 and spent two hours in the business meeting. My task was to explain the technicalities of a new pulp bleaching process ('oxygen bleaching') a process that I had spent nine years researching and in implementing three of the first four full-scale oxygen bleaching plants in Sweden, Japan and America; hence it could be argued that I was THE expert.

At about 1500, I was back at Porto Alegre airport and waiting to fly to Rio, where I landed at around 1800.

The flight from Rio to Paris did not leave until 2230 so I headed into an airline lounge and had a real meal – a vast improvement on in-flight meals. I also had an interesting experience, because not far from the table where I sat was a group of people who were all focused on one member of the group – a very vivid young girl (late teens or early twenties) who was quite beautiful. Her skin was light brown, and I assumed that she was what Westerners call a *mulatta* (a girl of the mixed race that comprises around 45 per cent of the total population). From previous visits I had made to Brazil, I had concluded that these *mulattos* were generally very pretty, and clearly also quite clever, proud people.

This girl certainly lived up to this exalted status. It seemed that she was the only member of the group who would fly out of Brazil that evening; the others were there to 'see her off.'

Eventually, my flight was called. She had not left the lounge, and she did not join my flight.

The rest of my journey was uneventful, though I was quite tired when I finally arrived back in Örnsköldsvik.

Was my visit to Brazil successful? In a word, "no," but there were many such meetings that did not lead to a sale. The equipment and associated knowhow were major financial commitments by a pulp company (more than US $1 million at that time) and the benefit of having an oxygen bleaching stage in your mill was to lessen the amount of effluent entering a waterway. Not every country had strict pollution control standards in the 1970s, so the benefit was not easy to quantify in dollar terms.

[It would be easier to justify an oxygen bleaching stage if the pulp company was planning to build a completely new mill, because installation of oxygen bleaching would allow other equipment items to be deleted from plans for the new mill.]

There were only two companies selling oxygen bleaching systems at that time – both were Swedish as it happened – and neither company made a sale to the Brazilian pulp company.

French Slice
Hank Koopman

Minstrels in Paris formed a guild (union) in 1321 and were almost exclusively employed by the royal families and noblemen throughout the land. However, it became evident that not all minstrels could be employed by every noble household in France. Besides, nobles were known to pay a paltry sum for their services in the first place. Then, some minstrels were not up to par with an employer's expectations, and these would be terminated in one way or another, depending on how cruel and free from prosecution a king or nobleman might be.

Antoine's life as a minstrel in 1792 had morphed into a successful and equally safe occupation, considering the upheaval in his country caused by King Louis XVI, which made life for most commoners unbearable. Revolutionaries had started to physically retaliate against the royalist and elitist classes, who almost bankrupted France while maintaining an extravagant lifestyle after involvement in the American War of Independence.

Antoine's great-grandfather had also been a minstrel, having moved to Saint-Père-sur-Loire, next to the Loire River, a beautiful setting where his family prospered during the late 1500s. He had pleased his royal benefactor, who granted him the small holding that had since been handed down from father to son over the next two generations. As a plethora of minstrels evolved, most now eked out a living as troubadours visiting towns and villages, enacting various skills to be known for their individual skills. Some might include magic tricks or juggling. Others would become fire eaters or clowns.

In Antoine's case, music had been passed on through the family genes, and his father taught the young Antoine to play the lute early in life and project his voice into song. The village had progressed and became a town, blissfully free from political interference. The perfect idyllic lifestyle changed when the King sent his tax collectors to steal more money from those who earned an income deemed more than they deserved—yes, times had changed.

Due to higher taxes and expenses to keep his family of four alive, he needed to offer his services more often and further afield. He remembered how he managed to ride home each night and never had to stay away longer than one night at most. Angelique, his wife, understood the necessity for him to stay away from her and their two daughters so they could pay mounting taxes enforced by the King. Antoine's family was not considered poor in society but not rich enough to be acknowledged as the elite in his village. However, in other villages, his trappings, horse, and the beautiful lute slung over his shoulder might have caused strangers to have another opinion.

His songs required a chameleon existence because part of his specialisation was retelling news he might have been privy to on his travels. Careful vetting of villagers had to be considered, as every village he entered might have a specific majority of the inhabitants who were still primarily royalists or revolutionists. Antoine always had to try and "decipher" the crowd before he'd sing a condescending ditty about King Louis.

If he were summoned to perform at a chateau where a well-to-do Nobleman lived, his songs would refer to "no good thieving commoners" guillotined that day by the King's men. He had a diplomatic style and could safely navigate his persona in either camp, always inducing laughter from his audience, even during this upheaval where the nobility had set people against one another.

His popularity grew by word of mouth from village to village, but it grew amongst the elite class, who loved to hear his "ditties," which proceeded to tell of some hapless serf the King's soldiers caught stealing a stag that was the King's property.

Among the commoners, some craved to rise to the elitist status and attempted to climb the ladder to success by informing on their neighbour, someone they might have had a dispute with, which led to the neighbour being prosecuted in a kangaroo court on trumped-up charges of treason. To this end, Antoine was forever having to "pussy-foot" around and try to psychoanalyse his prospective employers and prospective audience.

He could be considered "one who sits on the fence" regarding politics. However, his primary purpose was to earn a living and provide enough money to sustain his family. It had never been in his nature to speak ill of anyone, and he and his family lived far enough away from Paris and the upheaval that came to pass in 1789 to become affected until now. It was a four-day ride from Antoine's home to reach the capital.

When the guillotine beheaded King Louis XVI on January 21, 1793, the revolutionaries had won their war. Queen Marie Antoinette was placed in captivity and put on trial by the Revolutionary Tribunal, and she was guillotined on October 16th, 1793.

Antoine thought his plight was over, the last vestige of royalty removed. Now, all his "ditties" could include everything he'd wanted to sing about Marie Antoinette and her quote about "let them eat cake," an anecdote cited as an example of her obliviousness to ordinary people's conditions and daily lives.

One thing Antoine didn't see coming was the factional split within the Revolutionary Council. They were as divided on policy changes as the Royals, and the elite were divided on "class warfare" before the Revolution. Inevitably, this started further conflict among the people who had now become inoculated to everyday executions. France had turned into a nation of blood-thirsty killers looking for any excuse to attack someone their side was against. Total madness and tribal warfare continued unabated.

It had become more dangerous to sing about a Revolutionary Council without incriminating one side or the other. Nasty, jealous people could soon drum up a crowd of supporters and accuse an innocent man of treason. Because anarchy was flourishing everywhere, he would be sent to the guillotine before a trial was set, much like lynching had been a customary solution in America. Antoine realised he had to escape this cauldron of lunacy and hysteria, deciding to head back home to his loved ones.

"That's him!" a crazed voice screamed out from a frenzied crowd, rushing over to encircle him. He distinctly noticed a fellow minstrel yell out and point at him. He had always been told by some of the elite class and nobility that his services were no longer needed because Antoine had been booked to provide entertainment for them. These re-buffs had been festering in his mind, and now here was a chance to eliminate his perceived opposition.

"I've seen him perform for the royalists denigrating our loyal revolutionary comrades," he screamed, whipping the forty or fifty followers he'd gathered into a frenzy. Antoine's worst nightmare materialised. All the years, he had been able to switch from one loyalist to another and come home to Angelique and his girls.

Now, a traitorous fellow musician was about to achieve his vindictive ends and get rid of him using this bloodthirsty crowd of deranged peasants who wanted nothing more than to witness another head roll off the platform from the guillotine. His lute was pulled off his shoulders and smashed underfoot as the unruly crowd were whipped up into a frenzy by his accuser. Antoine's jacket was torn off him and ripped to shreds.

He cried out his innocence, but his once persuasive voice was indistinguishable from the howled screams of his accusers' now demented curses and profanities. As his feet were lifted from the earth, he knew the end was near. Nothing could save him. He let out a final cry, "Angelique, I love you. Look after the children."

His neck was clamped into the aperture where the 88-kilogram blade would descend and decapitate his head. He cannot do anything; the crowd is screaming out for vengeance. The blade falls!

My head falls a few centimetres as Donna pulls the pillows out from under my head to wake me.

"AAAHHHHH!!!!!" I leapt out of bed, looking at where my head should have been if I hadn't just been aroused from my nightmare. A startled Donna then asked,

"What's got into you?" she asked, "I'm changing the linen this morning."

The Box of Lost Souls
Edith Speers

Everyone knows the horrors of share housing. Gotta be a horror show because it starts with hope and desperation. What else d'ya expect. Bound to end in tears.

Starts so cool. Move out of home, get a house with some mates. An old house, steep steps, shitty little back yard, peeling paint, dodgy electrics. Maybe the owner reckoned on a pay-out from fire insurance. If we didn't get wasted and do a trash and burn he could always torch the place himself and who'd care. We were nobody.

Why else would anyone rent to the likes of us? Especially Sheels. Shaved bald, with random rat tails, a few piercings, a few tatts, chick with no tits under an op-shop singlet, army pants splattered with paint. She got the lease. Maybe the landlord thought she was easy. She was not easy. She was hard as nails. Nobody's bitch.

Whatever. We moved in and made ourselves at home. Like home never was. Dried spaghetti on the wall behind the stove. Sheels said that's how you tell it's cooked, if it sticks to the wall. Green mould on the bathroom tiles, sink full of crusty dishes, unidentified food objects ('UFOs' said Sheels) growing alien life-forms in the fridge. You had to step over shit everywhere, wade through piles of clothes on the hall floor. Yada yada. Hope was the bait and desperation forced us into the trap, the fire-trap. But the creepy shit didn't start until Sheels started work on the box.

She didn't buy the photos. She doesn't give a rat's arse for anyone. Janis got them from the St Vinnie's. No shit, she had tears in her eyes when she spread them out on the table.

'I couldn't leave them there,' she says. 'No one knows who they are. No one wants them. It's like no one cares they're dead.'

'I used to think the olden days had no colour,' I said, picking up a black and white studio portrait. From the clothes it musta been a hundred years old.

'That's stupid,' says Sheels. 'Grass is green, sky is blue. Always has been.'

'Call yourself an artist?' says Tristan. 'Next you'll tell me snow is white.'

You never know with Sheels. Sometimes it's a simple 'fuck off,' sometimes it's post-modernist de-constructionist pre-Raphaelite surreal pointillism wank wank wank. This time she says, 'Limbo.' She's staring at the pictures so we stare at the pictures. 'A grey world,' she says, 'for the un-christened, the un-shriven, the un-dead...'

'Zombies,' says me. 'They look like stiffs. Wouldn't want to meet that one in a dark alley.'

'Lost souls,' she says. 'I'll make my container a box for lost souls.'

So that's what she does. Her art school assignment is to create a container for abstractions, for the invisible. The container as an arbitrary boundary between different places on the space-time continuum. Something like that. I'm only quoting what I can remember. Sheels disappeared up her own arse for days before she disappeared completely. She gets this cardboard box and glues old wall-paper samples all over it and cuts out the people from the photos and glues them all over the box. Decoupage and collage, she said. And the more she decoups and collages, the weirder the electrics get. Stove goes on and off by itself. Tellie changes stations. Seemed to like those SBS and ABC history shows. A clue, but we didn't make the connection. Who would?

Anyway, when she finished the box that's when the nightmares started, first the real nightmares, where you wake up gargling, a scream caught like an unburst bubble in your throat, body slick with cold sweat, heart pounding, then the nightmares where you don't wake up because you're not asleep. Janis kept hearing babies crying. Shredded her nails and her fingertips clawing at floorboards, plaster, brick-work. First just in the house, then everywhere. Cops took her to the psych ward at the Royal on an ITO. Drug-induced psychosis they said. Tristan heard voices, very gentle and persuasive, explaining why he had to break into the museum and liberate the stuffed animals to save the planet. Bipolar they said. On meds the rest of his life. Me? You know that guy I said I wouldn't want to meet in a dark alley? I met him in a dark alley. Now he follows me everywhere.

Sheels disappeared. She took the box with her. She's looking for a new share house.

Crime and Punishment
Graham Meyers

Pigs, Plods, flat-foots, even Porkus Mobilis in a certain comic strip. The epithets applied to the police are many and mostly unimaginative. But we need to remember what society was like before the advent of the organised force we have today. What I hold against them is their lack of humour – I have never met a policeman with anything like a comedic awareness.

Maybe my jokes are just not original enough. What I am about to relate is a story that is both comedic, and in its own way, tragic. The tragedy is happening to a whole society and a way of life. I was not a witness to the events, but my informant was indirectly involved.

In remote Western Australia, cross-cultural issues massively complicate law enforcement.

One of those complications is the crime of petrol sniffing. Vapour inhalation was made illegal in the early nineties and now carries a mandatory custodial sentence. This may seem harsh, but the legislation was passed at the request of the Indigenous people themselves. Its purpose is to deny the user access to petrol. The hope is that in time the youngster (and it is nearly always teenagers) might pass through the most difficult period and perhaps be able to see another, better way. I am sure incarceration saved many young lives and untold community disruption.

Forward now to an unnamed community where two brothers in their mid-teens have taken up the lethal habit. The family initially hopes that it is just a phase the kids are going through, as you would. Instead, the problem worsens. Over the next couple of years, the boys create havoc. Their antisocial behaviour starts fights, causes injuries and sparks family feuds. In desperation the parents request that the police from Laverton arrest the offenders. It is heartbreaking for any parent to do this, but they know that to do nothing will result in a slow, terrible death. They have seen many such deaths and fervently hope there will be life for their sons after prison.

The officers duly arrive in the community, parking the truck near the office as they always do. After a few minutes of formalities with the Adviser, they stroll down to the home of the offenders.

Small for their age[1] and half-stoned on petrol, the brothers are taken by surprise.

One is grabbed but he struggles gamely. In the melee, his brother escapes. The constables secure their prisoner inside the vehicle and pursue the fugitive.

He dives between houses and hides behind dead cars, but the policemen are not new to this and begin to close in. Suddenly the offender bursts from cover and sprints beyond the houses to a stone-littered flat on which stands an old wooden long-drop toilet. He dives inside and slams the door behind him. The officers, red-faced and breathless, reach the door just in time to hear the lad bolt it on the inside. One rushes to the rear of the dunny lest there be an escape route there. No, the cubicle is as solid as a rock.

Ripper! He's trapped, just like his brother in the back of the truck.

"Open the door Kumana,[2] ...we won't hurt you!"

Silence.

"Kumana, OPEN THE DOOR!"

More silence.

"OPEN THE DOOR KUMANA! ...or we'll break it down!"

This is pointless. They are both big men, and the larger of the two slams his shoulder into the door. Not designed to resist such force, it flies open with a crash, but the tiny room is empty. The policemen are momentarily baffled. Then, as their eyes adjust to the reduced glare, a slight noise causes them to look through the seat hole into the darkness of the pit. There crouches Kumana.

He has wriggled down through the seat opening and is just beyond the men's reach.

"Give us your hand, Kumana."

No chance. Kumana crouches even lower. Bloody hell, what now?

Luckily, they have tools in the truck, so one holds the hot and malodorous fort while the other trudges back to get the vehicle and its gear. They set to dismantling the wooden seat arrangement, taking it in turns to work in the tiny space. The sun beats down making the cubicle as hot as a heatwave in hell, and soon both men are sweating profusely.

When the seat has been cleared out of the way they kneel on the floor and reach down but Kumana sits tight in the bottom of the pit with his arms tightly folded, giving them nothing to get hold of.

There is no option but for the smaller of the two to climb down into the hole.

Desperately hoping it has not been used too recently, the officer lowers himself down feet first, worrying that Kumana will attack him while he is vulnerable. Fortunately, the boy has enough sense not to lash out, and when the large and previously not-long-enough arm of the law is right beside him, Kumana gives up any idea of fight. They help him up and out and into back of the truck. All in a day's work for officers on the longest police patrol in the world.

1. Chronic petrol sniffing can cause severe growth retardation.
2. Literally, "you whose name I cannot speak."

Rocky First Date
Tim Phillips

Awkward stares
Awkward greeting
Awkward hug
Awkward meeting

Shoulders bump
On way to table
Rocky first-date
Rocking table.

Ramrod straight
In straight-backed chairs
Awkward pauses
Yearning stares.

Fingers touch
Contrived as chance
Startled eyes
Avoided glance.

Hidden surges
Sudden fears
Thoughts of happiness
Dread of tears.

So much withholding
Fear of hurt
Mind is whirring
Eyes alert.

Painted face
Male bravado
Awkward progress
Getting- to- know.

Broke not woke
Anne Layton-Bennett

I wonder what made so many believe
the lies and deceit that Trump always weaves
but whatever the reason that made people cleave
or trust to his untruths and his words filled with hate
the ballot they've cast is now everyone's fate

the result is a world left in horror and shock
because the president-elect belongs in the dock
serving time for charges – and the list isn't short
he's a felon, a racist and a consummate liar
who's gamed the system of justice, it's reduced to a rort

he's screwed US democracy and everyone's caught
so whatever's to come in the next four long years
may not be so good, best cherish today
for tomorrow could bring an unthinkable fray

© 2024 Anne Layton-Bennett

The Selkie
Kathleen Bentley

The wind blew her hair across her face while her eyes scanned the ocean for any sign of the yacht or of life. The waves rolled in throwing all kinds of flotsam and jetsam onto the shore, but nothing she could recognize from the yacht.

She sighed. It was true then; there was nothing left of the *Santa Anna* nor of Jake. A tear escaped from her eye and ran down her cheek. She brushed it away this made the mythology almost believable. Jake certainly believed it to be true that the sea always claimed its own.

Watching the ebb and flow of the receding tide, tears filled her eyes. Her heart ached for the love of her life – now gone, claimed by the sea. It was then that the tears flowed. Head in hands she gave way to the feeling of utter grief until she was exhausted, then a type of peace overcame her.

She remembered all the good times shared with Jake and how he loved to enchant her with stories from ancient times: tales of the sea, ships and pirates, love stories, sea monsters, seals turning into humans and of humans turning into seals – the Selkies. She shook her head trying to make sense of it all.

Wiping her eyes with the back of her hand she recalled Jake's last words as he boarded the yacht. He said he needed to go to find out who he was. He promised to return "some-day" saying that love was a very strong emotion and that he loved her with all his heart, but she was to love again – as she had loved him. She pushed her hair off her face and raked her fingers through it.

Looking out to sea again, she turned to walk back to her car, but a noise behind her made her hesitate so she turned back. A seal was splashing in the shallows. It appeared to be nodding at her. She walked into the ebbing tide with her right hand outstretched. The seal appeared to be chatting at her. It sniffed her hand.

It was then she noticed the pendant around its neck, it was the one she had given Jake for his birthday last week. Maybe the myths of yesterday held some truth. Maybe it was possible for transformations from human to seal and back to human form. Maybe there is more in this universe that we know or can believe. Maybe we should be more open-minded. These thoughts ran through her head until she felt dizzy. She patted the seal on the head not knowing what to do, but the seal turned swiftly and swam away with a flick of its tail, disappearing into the ocean.

The late afternoon sun was low in the sky, still holding enough warmth and throwing out incredible colours across the sky. The girl on the beach walked slowly to her car and sat in it as she admired the amazing show the sun was providing for her enjoyment. She wondered whether this was in compensation for her loss. Perhaps this heralded a new beginning, a better understanding that there was much in the universe that we don't understand, can't make sense of or find it difficult to believe. We earthlings are still children within the Universe and need to open our minds to possibilities we had not considered before. We cannot dismiss out of hand anything we don't understand or find unbelievable. We may be a breath away from discovering some incredible secret of the Universe should we turn our back on what we understand as impossible. She smiled to herself. Nothing is impossible if we remain receptive to this.

September Blues
Tatiana Petrovsky

She twists and turns
like a whirling dervish swept
into a dance with demons.
"Daddy Daddy take me with you
let me jump into your arms
over and over again
don't let me fall."

Repressed memories resurface,
unbidden –
the father who left
the stepfather who used her,
playing an accordion of selfish portent
each note punched out of tune.
The boyfriend who tried to care
the husband who cried in despair

the fiend who gave her the pain
he said she deserved.

"He's so crooked he couldn't lie straight in bed"
said the sergeant, shaking his head
"If she doesn't wake up to herself
and tell us the truth
you'll get a call from the morgue."

Wrapped in a shroud
woven by Sylvia Plath
she's trapped in the spin cycle
of a faulty washing machine
over and over again.

'SHADOWS'
(One-Act-Play)
Jennie Herrera

Cast: Four men plus a very elderly man, fairly tall but slightly stooped. Their ages aren't clear as the light is dim. They are wearing black clothes with some silvery luminescent material or paint on them. Not to make them look skeletal but vague and slightly abstract. They can be short, tall, fat or thin, but need clear deep resonant voices.

Set: Completely black, walls and floors, with dim light focused on the four men. There is a double door at the back of the stage which opens into a lighter space containing a saw horse, some timber, and a large handsaw.

Time: All the play takes place under artificial light. Time is irrelevant.

Scene One

Man One: *Enters right carrying a manuscript held together by a bulldog clip. He is followed by the three other men also carrying manuscripts. They halt centre stage and begin turning pages of their manuscripts. He says:* We are all dead. The war.

Man Two: What war? How?

Man One: Any war. The big war. War equals death.

Man Three: Do we know we're dead?

Man One: Of course. We bewail the pointlessness of death.

Man Four: And the pointlessness of the lives we lived before?

Man Three: So we are merely an essay in existential angst?

Man One: No, we are dead men walking—and we want answers.
The three others look around and shake their heads.

Man Two: If this is … what is it … Purgatory … the Ante-chamber to Hell … somewhere unutterably dreary—where do we look for answers? I don't think a boy's going to come round delivering papers—

Man Three: And it is too quiet …

Man Four: But I think I can hear … I'm not sure what it might be … an engine? Can anyone else hear something?

Man One: *firmly.* There is only one person, one being, who can provide answers. God. We didn't find him in life but here we are … living proof that death is not the extinction of everything …

Man Two: Living? Well, I am willing to concede that we are in some kind of state which cannot be seen as death … not unless death is not what we once thought it was …

Man Three: What does the play say we find? Does it provide a route map to God? Does it tell us how we will know him when we find him?

Man Four: IF we find him. But I think, yes, I'm certain that noise … it must mean something.

Man One: We can't go by the play. No writer of plays has been here before us.

Man Two: You sound very definite.

Man One: Once, long ago, I was a writer of plays. I liked a plain set with cubes and balls. Semi-abstract. And I needed good light at my desk.

Man Two: How long ago?

Man One: I wish I knew. Time seems to have become meaningless … here. Was it yesterday, an hour ago, last week, years, decades—

Man Three: Centuries? I was standing on duckboards, I was looking between sandbags. I was waiting. So much of war is waiting. And then …

Man One: If we keep strictly to the play … it gives us something to grasp … otherwise …

Man Four: Nothingness. We have become nothing. With nothing we are nothing.

Man One: There must be answers. There cannot be cause without effect. Action without result. Reaction. We must … a noise cannot exist in a vacuum … it must be part of the answer … *He turns towards the rear of the stage, the others turn and go with him, the lights dim briefly then brighten slightly again.*

Scene Two

Man One *reaches out and swings the two big black doors open. The space behind the doors grows brighter as their eyes accustom themselves to the brightness. A very elderly man with a long white beard and wearing a long white robe with a golden tasselled cord at his waist looks up, still holding a saw in one hand. He lets a long* *piece of wood slide down ... He waits for them to speak. He has a pleasant smile and a mild expression.*

Man One: *Turns briefly to his companions then to the old man.* May we ask—who are you and what are you doing here?
God: You were looking for me. I can always be found. Some people call me God but I believe you might prefer to call me First Cause.
The men look at each other uncertainly.
Man One: We need answers. Life has become—unbearable without answers. Will you try to answer our questions?
God: I think I understand your questions even before you ask them. Sawing wood is very good for ... it gives me a sense of purpose ... You want to know why life had no purpose but death and mud and casualty lists and you had no chance to see your loved ones before ... this journey ...
Man One: It begins to seem that way, the purposelessness ... here we all are, dead, and our purposes have been rendered meaningless by death so we must assume that all we thought was purposeful in life ...
God: You wanted a purpose which would transcend death? You don't think that sawing some wood might help?
Man Two: *Sounding rather desperate.* All the things that sounded so grand—greater love hath no man than to lay down his life for ... well, I remember some padre had that one ... and country ... loyalty ... not letting people down ... and we were all busy laying down lives for each other but it doesn't seem to have helped much ...
God: I considered a number of purposes for life but none of them seemed quite—BIG enough. A big universe, I often contemplate it, and little people in it with guns and mean little thoughts. So I fell back on purposelessness. I thought people contemplating nothing would be driven to re-think ... many things ...
Man One: But why go to so much trouble for ... nothing?
God: *Stands up straighter and brandishes his saw. The four shades draw back slightly.* Are you questioning my purposes?
Man One: *Rather grimly.* If you like to put it like that.
God: I bring purpose to some things. The smiles of little children. Birdsong on a spring morning. The way the sun turns dewdrops into diamond necklets. You didn't respect my purposes, did you? You thought your purposes mattered more.
Man One: At the time they did. We couldn't envisage this place.

Man Two: So you did intend something with us, for us, for the world?

God: No. You could not have free will if I intended ... something ... anything. You agree that you all had free will?

They look at each other and finally say reluctantly, nearly together, It seems that way.

God: *Drily,* You think I should have intervened?

When the shades don't reply **God** *goes on*: I have limited free will in other worlds. Butterflies and birds, monkeys and fish, earthworms and sandflies ... you would prefer to change places?

Man One: It doesn't seem to matter any more.

God: *Crossly,* Of course it matters, you ungrateful wretches. The best gift of all and you can only make it meaningless. Worse, you take advantage of all of life not so fortunate, the unfree. Go away. Look for purpose. See if you like it when you find it. *He makes a shooing motion with both arms, one hand still brandishing the saw. The four shades step back.* **God** *slams the doors closed. The stage is in virtual darkness.*

Scene Three

Light gradually suffuses the centre stage and shows the four men standing looking rather bewildered.

Man One: *Shuffling through his manuscript:* I'm not sure ... isn't there something about God being Infinite Love? He didn't demonstrate much of anything—

Man Two: Impatience.

Man Three: This script isn't very helpful. We are about to be remembered. We always are. Anniversaries, wreath-layings ...

Man Four: Centenaries—

Man Two: Surely not. It seems like ... only yesterday ...

Man One: And what are they really remembering? Past campaigns, courage, sacrifice?

Man Two: *Lugubriously.* Bungling.

They all turn pages in their manuscripts, their fingers trailing down the pages.

Man Three: The ending seems rather indeterminate. Can we change it?

They all murmur apparent speeches under their breath, but different speeches so it only sounds as a low gabble.

Man One: The choice is ours—unless one of you wrote the play and feels ... possessive of its integrity ...

Man Two: Not me. But the ending *is* awkward. What are we to make of it?

More muttering and murmuring of lines by all four.

Man One: *Cautiously.* Yes, it appears to imply that we are not friends, were not friends ... That in fact we were enemies. I think the playwright had no conception of this place.

Man Two: Or too good a conception ... we are still what we were ...

Man Three: But what were we?

Man One: Nothing binds us to these words on the page. We have a certain freedom—

Man Four: Do we?

Man Three: You haven't answered my question. Is there a traitor, a betrayer, an enemy among us?

Man Two: What purpose in an honest answer? We have no choice but to share this space.

Man One: *Slowly.* As we had no choice but to share the living world? If we take that to its logical conclusion ... I'm not sure ... We were so certain we were responding rightly, it gave our lives purpose—

Man Two: And drama and meaning and direction, all that, so why are we now ... drifting ...

Man Three: We have the play, the blueprint. We have found God, that is more than many do ... We can play it to the last page or ...

Man One: Throw it away? It is not a very helpful play. It says we lacked purpose in life, that we wandered in pointless angst ... in death ... but we are not dead ...

Man Three: A typical play in other words, limited by the human imagination.

Man Two: We didn't run our lives by plays in life—

Man Four: Yes. We did. Governments, media cartels, armament barons, generals WANTING YOU, ordinary people thrusting white feathers ... clergy thinking they knew God ... we followed their scripts ...

Man One: And now ... at last ... we are free ... to choose ...

Man Three: To do what?

Man Two: *Turning pages in his manuscript.* The letters are very small, here at the end, and this light isn't strong, but here, right at the end ...

The others turn to their last page ...

Man Four: *Reads carefully:* Men divided by race, religion, class, national boundaries, family expectations ... I don't remember what my family thought ...

Man One: Or mine. A lot of talk of the Fatherland ...

Man Two: The Motherland ... but they were short by then and said, black or white, brown, it didn't matter ...

The others turn and look at him.

Man Four: *Goes on reading firmly.* Men divided find divisions purposeless in other worlds. They cross eternity ... glad of the company.

Man One: But the last line doesn't follow our experience. It says, they find God and are finally able to lay the burdens of purpose down.

Man Four: Are we? Can we? *He removes the bulldog clip and drops it, then the pages, just keeping one which he proceeds to turn into a paper aeroplane.* Perhaps I understand. A smile on a little child's face ...

The others follow suit ...

*The **CURTAIN** falls*

> Note: This piece was inspired from reading about Pär Lagerkvist's play *'The Eternal Smile.'*

Family Fractures
Tatiana Petrovsky

Her mind is an Olivetti typewriter
compact concise, polished precise
letters tapping a rhythmic dance
onto crisp white paper.
His mind is a minefield
a maze of imagined slights
an Equinoxal gale of
eccentric proportions.

Detritus follows him
flaking off a stained tweed jacket
spilling from his arm-loads of scavenged
twigs, bark and cobwebs from outside
not meant to be inside.
He agitates, he negates
her request for some
semblance of order.

He says, "You are the problem
you refuse to scream and shout."
She puts on a coat,
walks out the door.
His face contorts
upper lip curls with frustration.
Yells to her retreating back
"Your family is stuffed. You know that."

She says, "As Tolstoy said
'Happy families are all alike;
every unhappy family is unhappy
in its own way.'"
The irony escapes him.
The smell of decay soils the air
scented candles are to no avail
The fractures between them
to brittle to repair.

Expanding my horizons
Noel Davern

"What do we do now?"

We were in Prague, facing a red light and scrambling for a new plan. Our destination was the F3D Pylon Racing World Championships, a pinnacle event within the aeromodelling community. My teammate, Frank, and I were the sole occupants of what had been, up to that point, the third vehicle in our little convoy.

Frank had had enough of Prague traffic. He was a 'bushie'— a coal miner from Central Queensland. Heavy traffic wasn't something he battled with. Driving on the wrong side of the road? He seemed to have that sorted, probably found it easy—he knew all about operating machinery. The navigation was my job. Up till then, my plan had been simple—follow the others. What could be easier than that?

Prague had already overwhelmed me: the beauty, the buzz, my first real overseas trip. As we drove, I latched onto a familiar name on the road signs—Brno. That must be on our way. So my revised plan was to follow the Brno signs until we got through Prague, then find a service station and buy a map. I knew the name of the town we were heading for—Mělnik. And the name of our accommodation—Pension Wanda. We'd be right. Just have to find out where that was.

Now for a little aside. "Why not just call the others and ask them to wait for us?" That would be the logical thing to do. And, believe me, I'd be all for that option—except for that, you need a phone. It was 2003 and mobile phones were all the rage. My mate's phone worked on the CDMA network—necessary in remote areas in Australia back then—but was useless here, so he hadn't brought it. I had one that would have worked here, but I, too, had left it behind. For what I thought was an excellent reason. He had just hooked up with a new girlfriend and I figured he would borrow it to call home all the time. And he and I had vastly different ideas on 'disposable income'—orders of magnitude different. I reckoned I'd go broke paying for all his international calls. But, I now rued that decision.

Another hiccup occurred once we got our map, which was a bit of an exercise in itself as no one there spoke English, and we didn't speak Czech, or even German, which it turned out would have sufficed. The map revealed a flaw in my sense of direction. Brno was way off to the east, *on the way to Russia*. Not where we wanted to be. We had to do some backtracking, but decided to skirt around Prague. Furthermore, I discovered we hadn't actually just travelled through Prague, but *Praha*. Oh, us naïve English speakers.

Our next obstacle was a road closure. Actually, it was a bridge closure. And they have a pretty lackadaisical attitude to traffic control and detour designation in the Czech Republic. Just put up a barrier and start work. Let the traffic sort itself out. Which we kind of did.

"Keep the sun to our left and somehow get across this river." Our next hurdle was accessing the autobahn, which we could see off to our right. My plan was simple—drive along the road we were on until we come across an access road.

That plan fell into disarray when our chosen road just went straight under the autobahn and then disappeared into a roadworks site. The road was still under construction! The workers didn't seem to mind our presence. In fact, most didn't even acknowledge us, just kept on with their business. One of them finally looked at us as we drove over his compressor hose, and I lent out the window with my map and pointing fingers. His response was a smile. But he did call over someone else. His boss, I guess. He was all smiles, too. Back home, if we had driven into a roadworks site, we would have gotten a vastly different response. Anyway, this bloke didn't speak our lingo either, or us his, but after much finger pointing by me, he pointed in the direction we had come and held up some fingers, then indicated that we take a right, then more fingers etc., finishing with a bigger smile. We smiled back and went on our way. All good too; we were soon on the autobahn. Then it was plain sailing until we reached Mělnik.

Now all that remained was to track down the Pension Wanda. Easier said than done, it turned out. I knew roughly where it was, remembering back to when I looked it up on the internet—out of town off to the east. But driving around hoping for the best proved fruitless. So we stopped at a servo—that had worked last time. That old communication barrier reared its head yet again. Then I had a brainwave. I pointed at the phone book. Could I borrow that and just look up the number and call them? Hopefully, the proprietor would speak English. It would have worked too, I reckon, but … the phone books there are very local, and we weren't quite local enough! Then a beaming smile crossed the owner's face. A customer had pulled in. He rushed outside, seemingly to serve her; but no, in she came and guess what? She spoke English! Old mate didn't know any English, but he knew what language we were babbling in, and he knew his customer spoke it. We were set! And it wasn't all that far, either. We were soon back with the others, laughing as we related our adventures.

I won't bore you with the details of the racing, but, believe me, it had our blood pumping. But here are a few more anecdotes from our trip.

We had flown into Frankfurt and hired a car there for our travels. A very fancy Renault Laguna. And it had a diesel engine, which the woman serving us went to lengths to point out—don't put petrol in it. It has to be diesel!

Got it!

Then I asked, "What do they call diesel in Germany?"

"Diesel," she said with a cute smile. "It's a German word."

Touché.

Speaking of the language barrier. We ended up recruiting our own interpreter—a former Czech who was part of the USA team. His help was indispensable at the restaurant we frequented each night. And I picked up a little Czech from him, which came in handy of an evening.

Pivo, děkuji. "Beer, thank you." Pretty much all I needed to get me through the night. And let me tell you, the beers they have in the Czech Republic are something else!

Then there was the exchange rate—unbelievable! It was 2003, just prior to the Czech Republic joining the EU. One of our team members wives had volunteered to organise our lunches. Pražska sŭnka (Prague ham), salad, sometimes their spectacular špekáčky, pringles, watermelon, that kind of thing. At the end of the event we tallied up the cost—50c AUD each. For four lunches! Talk about value for money.

The banquet at the conclusion of the event? *Woowee!* What a night.

It was held in Mělnik Castle. This grandiose and famous building had been confiscated by the State during the communist era, but had now been returned to its previous owners. It was undergoing restoration at the time, and as such, some rooms were currently off limits. But not to us! As guests of honour, they brushed aside some signs (which we couldn't understand anyway) and led us past the barriers.

I was awestruck. Magnificent halls full of medieval armour and weapons. Tapestries and other artwork. Stunning furniture. The smell of the place, it reeked of history. Standing there gave me goosebumps—I will never forget it.

When the tour finished, we were led to a massive, beautifully decorated hall and, as we entered, we were handed a glass of wine by a very well-presented gentleman standing by the doorway.

"Thanks, mate. Appreciate it."

A little later, we were called to order and informed that the owner would like to say a few words. Who should take centre stage but our wine serving gent! He gave a short welcoming speech, in perfect English. I'm guessing that was the language he thought most suitable, but I'm sure just one of many that he had a mastery of. The poor French team had to make do with English on this occasion.

Then it was on to the festivities proper. What a meal we enjoyed! Seating had been allocated in alphabetical order, and Australia was front and centre. The USA was down the back, much to their chagrin.

Oh, and the results? Australia took Bronze!

The Divine Paradox
Bethamy Nader

The air in Olympus crackled with a storm of a different kind. Not the thunderous roars and lightning strikes Thor was known for, but a fervent disagreement underscored by Venus's celestial beauty.

Thor: (Booming voice) By Odin's beard, Venus, I tell you, mortals achieving superhuman feats deserve reward! A place amongst the stars, the nectar of immortality! Look at them, wrestling titans in the arena, unravelling the secrets of the cosmos, crafting words that stir the very soul! Are we to deny them the gift of eternity after such tireless effort?

Venus: (Her voice, a melodic counterpoint to Thor's) Oh, Thor, ever the champion of brute strength and obvious valour. But consider the grand tapestry! Immortality is not a prize to be handed out like laurel wreaths. It is a delicate thread woven into the fabric of existence. Granting it to every exceptional athlete, every brilliant scientist, every victorious warrior… it would unravel the very balance of life and death.

Thor: Balance? What balance is there in letting such giants of mortal achievement fade into dust? They push the boundaries of what is possible! They inspire generations! Is that not worthy of recognition beyond a fleeting moment in history? Imagine a physicist who unlocks the power to heal all disease, or a poet whose verses bring peace to warring nations. Would you watch them crumble into nothingness?

Venus: That physicist, that poet… their genius, their inspiration, flows from their mortality. It is the knowledge of their limited time that fuels their passion, which drives them to achieve. Immortality breeds complacency, Thor. Eternal life can dull the sharpest minds, wither the most fervent hearts. Would Archimedes have shouted "Eureka!" if he had ten thousand years to ponder the solution? Would Homer have crafted his epic poems if he knew he had an eternity to refine them?

Thor: You speak of complacency, but I see only potential! With immortality, these mortals could continue to grow, to learn, to contribute to the cosmos on a scale we cannot even fathom! Imagine a scientist, given centuries to explore the universe, or a philosopher, forever wrestling with the mysteries of existence.

Venus: And I imagine a world overflowing with immortals who quickly grow weary, disillusioned, and petty. Power, without the constraint of mortality, corrupts even virtue. What becomes of their victories, their discoveries, when they are no longer rare and precious? What value does beauty hold when it is eternally available?

Thor: But what of love, Venus? Surely, you, goddess of love, see the tragedy in lovers separated by the inevitable scythe of death? To grant a couple eternity together, to allow their bond to flourish unbound by time… is that not a beautiful thing?

Venus: Love is born from vulnerability, Thor. From the fragile beauty of shared moments, precious because they are finite. Knowing that time is limited makes love all the more potent, all the more cherished. To grant immortality to lovers is to risk turning passion into possession, desire into drudgery. It would dilute the very essence of what makes love divine.

Thor: You paint a grim picture, sister. Surely, we can find a middle ground. Perhaps only the most exceptionally virtuous, those who dedicate their mortality to the betterment of all, deserve such a gift.

Venus: Virtue is a fleeting thing, Thor, swayed by circumstance and desire. Who are we to judge its true form? No, the beauty of mortality lies in its transience, its imperfections. It is in facing our limitations that we find our true strength, our deepest love, and our most enduring legacy. Let their legends be their immortality.

*Thor, though unconvinced, sighed. He knew Venus spoke with a wisdom born of centuries of observation. Perhaps immortality, easily granted, was not the answer. Perhaps the true greatness of mortals lay not in escaping death, but in embracing life, with all its joy and sorrow, its fleeting brilliance and its inevitable end. The debate, like a summer storm, subsided, leaving behind a lingering question that even the gods could not definitively answer.

The fate of mortal immortality, it seemed, remained a divine paradox.

Bethamy Nader   19/11/2024

The Gift
Donna-Marie Koopman

There are more things in Heaven and Earth, Horatio,
than are dreamt of in your philosophy.
(William Shakespeare.)

Sylvia passed away in 1984, aged sixty, and had always told us she would die young.

Some call it second sight, clairvoyance, or psychic ability. Whatever it is called, it is the ability to tune into the energy field of all things, be they animals, plants, or minerals. Sylvia had always known she had the "gift."

Animals have this ability. If you have or have had an animal as a pet and studied them closely, you will have noticed that they are often aware of events before they happen. Animals have been recorded detecting diseases and even death before it has occurred. Animals have this sense, which I believe we humans had before we became so refined.

Among us, there are still those who have not lost that sense. There are gifted people who use, abuse and exploit it for material gain, taking advantage of gullible, naïve and vulnerable people, desperate for answers to their problems—a yearning to reach loved ones who have passed. The greed for material wealth in these individuals diminishes their ability to tune in, so their readings are usually inaccurate and unreliable.

Genuine psychics are very ordinary folk who accept their gifts as nothing out of the ordinary. They're as natural as seeing, hearing, and breathing; they're just another sensory perception. My mother, Sylvia, only ever used her gift to help—she felt it right to only use it responsibly in the service of others.

She trained as a nurse for the same reason: to help others. With her gift, she could tune into her healing energy without exposing her ability to sense others' needs. Genuinely gifted people keep a very low profile; they don't broadcast their gifts to everyone.

There are cynics who believe these people are crackpots because of those who broadcast and claim they can predict every future event. Those people are diminished in "reading" by being influenced by material gain; it blurs their energy, putting it out of focus. It's only those closest to these gifted ones that are aware of their special sense. My father had been one of those cynics until he met Sylvia just after World War Two.

As daughters of Sylvia, my siblings, my father, and I were very aware of Sylvia's gift of predictions. She would scare the pants off us, informing us she had run into a neighbour at the local shopping centre and had smelt the odour of death on them; they would be gone by the end of the week. Sure enough, by the end of the week....

"Mum, we don't want to know," we railed at her ominous prediction.

"Why?" she would ask, "It's only natural; it was just their time in the plan of things." Death was nothing to fear; it was just a transition, like birth, coming from your watery world and then into the world of breathing. Amazingly, people were drawn to Sylvia for advice or if they had an injury. She was the "go-to" witch doctor, as Dad called her.

Sylvia had a wicked sense of humour and saw the funny side of all this, even her death predictions. It was natural and all, as it was meant to be. There were many psychic moments, not all spooky or dire—some good as well. Someone might be worried about going for a job and not getting it. Sylvia would assure them they would—and they did. There were too many predictions to list.

For non-believers, let me tell you of one incident Dad related to me that had him convinced the "gift" was real when he came to stay with me after Mum's passing.

Mum and Dad lived in Kalgoorlie, a gold mining town in West Australia. Dad was employed in the mines, and Mum cared for me, as I was only a baby at the time.

One evening, they retired early as Dad had an early start the next morning. They hadn't been in bed long when Mum heard her name being called.

"Sylvie, Sylvie, Sylvie."

She got up, turned on the lights, and looked around the house but found nothing. No sooner had she put her head down than the voice began calling again.

"Sylvie, Sylvie, Sylvie."

She woke Dad and told him someone was calling her. They checked the interior and exterior of the house, but again, nothing. So, back to bed.

"Sylvie, Sylvie, Sylvie."

Dad recalled it going on for a further two hours. Eventually, Mum realised who was calling her, and waking Dad she said, "Dorothy's in trouble; it's her voice that's been calling me. Something's wrong."

Dorothy was a lady Mum had befriended, who, during general conversation, had told Mum of the abusive relationship she was in.

They put me in my pram and headed out toward Dorothy's house a couple of blocks away. They only travelled the street a short distance when Mum spotted what looked like a bundle of clothes in the gutter. She went to investigate and realised it was Dorothy, bloodied and beaten severely.

"Sylvie, I've been calling you for hours."

Dorothy, thankfully, recovered and left the abusive monster, moving away and starting afresh.

As I said, Mum made many predictions, but she never predicted lottery wins or racehorse winners. However, she brought a lot of comfort and help to all who crossed her path.

Author Biographies

MARILYN ARNOLD

Marilyn Arnold is a published Tasmanian writer and poet, who has been writing for over thirty years. She has won a couple of poetry awards, including the Kathryn Purnell Award, the Norma Davis Award, and the Launceston Poetry Cup.

She was inaugural president of the Tasmanian Branch of the Society of Women Writers and has long been associated with the Fellowship of Australian Writers, Tasmania, and the Tasmanian Poetry Festival committee. She also runs the monthly open mic poetry readings in Launceston, "Poetry Pedlars," which has been running for thirty-two years.

Marilyn participates regularly in poetry readings throughout Tasmania and has been a guest reader at four Tasmanian Poetry Festivals. She also runs a fortnightly poetry workshop in Launceston, which has been running for at least ten years

She has recently published two books of poetry: *"Capture"* with Carol Easton, and *"Lies, Lovers and Other Constructions - 80 poems by Marilyn Arnold"* The back of this latter book states: "These are poems about the everyday: about childhood, relationships, motherhood, siblings, lovers (and their many lies), family, travel, dementia, the spiritual journey, place, conversations stolen from others. They are semi-autobiographical, but like any life under construction, there are always lies."

ANNE BAILEY

I was born in 1952 in Campania Tasmania. I am a mother of 4 children and 11 grandchildren, (of which I raised 7 full time) and great grandmother to 14. I was a foster care for about 32 years and cared for approximately 250/300 children, long term, short term, relative carer, group home carer. As a board member of the Foster Carers Association of Tasmania it has allowed me to travel to all states and territories in Australia.

I retired in 2022 and moved to Penguin, where I enjoy being a volunteer in various local venues. I am also a member of the Lions

Club in Penguin, and I participate in many crafts. One of my favourite interests is genealogy, which I have put together into a book. I'm always hoping to pick up some ideas.

KATHLEEN BENTLEY

I retired to Ulverstone from Kalgoorlie with my husband Max in 2012 and became involved with the artist community – my speciality became pastel painting of indigenous animals plus land and sea scapes of Tasmania. I was successful in selling my art to tourists from all over the world, but then came the Coronavirus and the whole world seemingly went into lockdown. That meant I couldn't exhibit my artworks, so I turned to writing.

One story had crystallised during a cruise around South East Asia then, when CVD-19 struck, I wrote a trilogy within 18 months of the enforced lockdown. I had not written anything before but the characters seemed to speak to me, so I had no trouble writing. Of course there was research to be completed which I enjoyed. My first book *The Divided Heart*, has been published with the second and third books in process. I have had several short stories published and now I am happy to contribute some of these writings to this Anthology. I hope you find these interesting.

VAL COLIC-PEISKER

Croatian born and bred, Val Colic-Peisker has lived in Australia since 1995. In 2022 she moved to Northern Tasmania. She worked as a high-school teacher, journalist, radio presenter and producer, freelance writer and translator, and spent over 20 years as a full-time academic at four Australian universities in Perth, WA and Melbourne, teaching sociology and research methods. At the end of 2020, she opted out of full-time work in order to devote more time to her sanity-preserving activities, creative writing and hiking.

Val has published extensively, mainly research-based academic works, but also essays, feature articles and commentary in mainstream media, most recently in Tasmania's '*40 South*' magazine. Her first novel, *Francesca Multimortal* (Ashwood Publishing), was shortlisted for the Dorothy Hewett Award for an Unpublished Manuscript in 2023 and longlisted for the Tasmanian Literary Prize for Fiction in 2025. Val is an honorary Associate Professor at the University of Melbourne since 2021.

NOEL DAVERN

I am a self-published author, currently living in Tasmania, and a happy member of the Fellowship of Australian Writers, North-West Tasmania.

After spending most of my life in various locations in Queensland, I moved to Tasmania upon retirement, where I continue to enjoy bushwalking, fishing, and the beauty of the outdoors.

I received my education at the Heatley State High School, the Townsville Technical College—where I completed studies associated with my apprenticeship as an electrician—and the University of Queensland, where I earned a Bachelor of Science in Biochemistry.

Following a lifetime of work in a variety of occupations, I now spend my evenings by the fire, dreaming up new storylines.

My first book, *Ambivalence*, was self-published and marks the beginning of my writing journey.

My favourite quote is by Abraham Lincoln: 'If you know what you're doing, you're not learning anything.'

ADRIAN FLITNEY

Born and bred in Northwest Tasmania, Adrian Flitney was imbued with a love of wild places from an early age. After completing a science degree in Hobart, he worked for the Department of Science in Sydney before studying to become a quantum physicist at Adelaide University. A research position took him to Melbourne where he remained for 17 years working as a physicist, tutor, chess coach and financial trader.

He returned to NW Tasmania in 2022. Alongside his love of wilderness, Adrian developed a passion for chess as a teenager and has played competitively ever since. He has been Tasmanian champion on several occasions. He has published widely in the esoteric field of quantum games and has co-authored a book with Val Colic-Peisker entitled *'The Age of Post-rationality.'*

Adrian has recently been inspired to write about his various outdoor adventures, some of which have left him a little perplexed as to how he has managed to survive into his sixties.

LAURENCE V HARROULD

There is an old adage:
    How do you make good decisions?
    Experience.
    How do you get experience?
    Bad decisions.

Laurence Harrould has plenty of experience and uses that as the basis for his writing.

In 2024 his book *'Love Your Pain (Why Bad Things Happen To Good People)'* was published. This was enabled by the significant help he received from members of FAWNW.

He is now working on publishing *'Adventures of an Urban Nomad'*, a record of his experiences as a house-sitter in the Sydney area together with his wife, Danita, and best friend, Sancho (of the four-legged variety).

His contributions to this anthology reflect recent experiences in Tasmania and part of his personal journey from years ago.

JENNIE HERRERA

Jennie Herrera currently lives in Hobart and is President of the Tasmanian FAW. She has had some success with short stories (including winning the Max Harris Short Story Award), poetry (including the Gwen Harwood Poetry Prize) and twice winning the VIC FAW Alan Marshall Award for a novel manuscript for *The Vigil* and *Old Postcards* and the Michele Turner Award for a book manuscript about East Timor with *The Set of the Sun*. Some of her writing is available at https://jlherrera.com and her work has also appeared in a number of anthologies.

TERRY HANNAN

Dr Terry Hannan is a writer with a flair for storytelling that captivates readers from all walks of life. His short story telling has been compared to that of Roald Dahl. His background in Specialised medicine has made him a wonderful observer of people and a listener. His scientific publication background has transitioned to that of writing which spans various genres, fiction and non-fiction. These genres encompass travel journeys, intimate human encounters, and creative short story telling with thought-provoking themes. His first book of patient stories (*Bedside Stories*) was an entrant in the 2017 Tamar Valley Writers Festival. His latest publication (*The Rorschach Lens*) in 2025 was his first novel that followed characters growing up under Pinochet's dictatorship.

His background in electronic health involved building self-sustaining eHealth systems to manage diseases in Low- and Middle-Income Nations, that included forty million people living with AIDS in sub-Saharan Africa. Dr Hannan's diverse work environment has become the stimulus for his creative writing which is radically different from his scientific genres.

He was anonymously nominated for Australian of the Year in 2017 and his writings are stimulated by the philosophy of Elena Ferrante. "In every encounter there is a story."

GRAEME HETHERINGTON

In my first 13 years, I went to Rosebery, Renison Bell, and Zeehan state schools before going to boarding school in Launceston. I was a lecturer in the Classics Department of UTas for over 25 years. Given the nature of the subject matter I taught, life in Europe was more appropriate and congenial for upwards of thirty years of my adult life. I returned to Tasmania in 2013, finally settling in St Helens.

Poetry has been my mainstay since about 1970 when I had the good fortune to be incidentally mentored by sympathetic friends James McAuley and Gwen Harwood to whom I owe much.

I am the author of *'Remote Corners'*, *'In The Shadow of Van Diemen's Land'*, *'Life Given'*, *'A Tasmanian Paradise Lost'*, *'A Post-Colonial Boy'*, *'An Inherited Epic of Gilgamesh'*, *'At Large'*, *'Another Love, Another Life'*, *'The Divided Self: A Tasmanian*

Odyssey', and I co-edited *'Upper Heights and Lower Depths'* with Ralph Spaulding, a Tasmanian anthology of poetry. An epic poem takes me up in my old age. My tenth collection, *'The Persistence of History,'* essentially a response to paintings by David Keeling, was published in late 2023.

ALLAN JAMIESON

Allan Jamieson spent 29 years employed as a Chemical Engineer in the pulp and paper industry, living on four continents and visiting 21 countries for business purposes – averaging one plane flight every four days through those years. Then, from 1993 to 1999, he managed a eucalypt technology group and gained a Diploma of Elementary Plant Genetic Engineering from ANU and CSIRO's Plant Science Centre in Canberra. Allan has resided in Burnie since 1981.

He began writing books in the early 2000's. So far, he has published six non-fiction books, one novel, one novella and one compendium of short stories.

Currently Allan is President of FAWNW.
For more information, see https://fawtasnorthwest.blogspot.com/
For copies of Allan's books, email Allan at jamtin79@gmail.com

DONNA-MARIE KOOPMAN

Born in Leonora in 1949, her formative years began predominately in the hot and dusty outback of Western Australia. Her father was employed at the Sons of Gwalia gold mine, later moving to work on the Trans-Australian Railways as a ganger. It was there her limited education began. Teachers, not exceptionally well trained, some being immigrants, taught small classes of railway workers' children in one-room schools at sidings alongside the line.

Donna's education evolved mainly by witnessing life, peering out of windows, and daydreaming about imaginary scenes and stories that were germinating in her active and inquisitive mind.

Marrying at sixteen, Donna's perception of human nature became more evident when snippets of poetry and prose started appearing on pieces of paper and in scrapbooks. Donna spent the first eight years of marriage to a sailor, working several jobs she'd rather forget about.

Hank, on his discharge from the service, developed an interest in music and formed a band. Not to be outdone, those scribblings on paper and in scrapbooks morphed into songs. Self-taught, Donna developed a powerful singing voice and recorded some of those songs on a solo CD.

In 2023, through Impress Print, Donna published *Reverie*, a book of her poetry and she has started writing stories with FAWNW.

HANK KOOPMAN

Born in Holland, Hank's family immigrated to Western Australia in 1954.

In 1962, he left home and hitchhiked around Australia, gaining employment on a fishing boat in Cairns, a laundry on Hayman Island, and as a jackaroo on a Queensland cattle station.

In 1964, he joined the Royal Australian Navy and trained as an aircraft firefighter. In a Sydney pawn shop, he purchased a Hawaiian guitar, which spiralled his life in another direction. Influenced by Rob E G and Slim Whitman and the Singing Steel Guitar, he taught himself to play the instrument well enough to start up a band during his last three years in the Navy.

Hank, eighteen, married Donna-Marie, sixteen, in June 1965. Many believed the couple would not survive six months. Although several events seemed to indicate that prediction would ensue, another Power was at play.

A career in the entertainment industry followed for the next 40 years, both acting and singing. Nine years living in a mobile home, performing across Australia, as well as two contracts in America, established a not-famous but successful career. Thirteen CD titles and three biographical books saw Hank transition to his new passion, writing stories through FAWNW.

ANNE LAYTON-BENNETT

Anne Layton-Bennett is a published writer both in Australia and overseas in both print and online publications. For several years she juggled writing commitments with a part-time job in a school library and running a commercial flower growing business with her partner.

She now writes regularly for specialist magazine *The Veterinarian*, and occasionally writes features for online journal www.tasmaniantimes.com

Anne co-edited: *An Inspired Pursuit: 40 years of writing by women in northern Tasmania*, (Karuda Press) 2002, and has essays included in *An Inspired Pursuit: Volume 2*, (Tatlers) 2012; *Breaking the boundaries: Australian activists tell their stories* (Wakefield Press) 2016, and *The Fabric of Launceston* (Launceston Historical Society) 2016.

Challenged several years ago to try her hand at writing poetry, Anne also has a growing portfolio of poems – some of which have been published. She still writes letters and is currently seeking a publisher for her first book.

MEG McLAREN

Meg was born on the island of Trinidad, in the West Indies. She had a happy and colourful childhood, and her writing is influenced by these experiences. Over the years she has travelled extensively and has come into contact with many different lifestyles. She is now retired and lives in Tasmania where she is able to pursue her love of writing.

ANDREA McMAHON

Andrea McMahon writes short stories and poetry. Andrea's stories have been published in journals and collections, including *Island*, *Forty South* and the *Minds Shine Bright Anthology 2024*. Her story *The Cuckoo's Nest* won the 2023 Lane Cove Short Story Prize, and *Damselfly*, the 2020 Tasmanian Writers' Prize. Andrea lives in Hobart and has worked as a librarian and library adult literacy practitioner. More of Andrea's writing can be found at andreaswriting.wordpress.com and in her short story collection, *Skin Hunger*, published by *Ginninderra Press* in 2008.

DAWN MEREDITH

Dawn spent her childhood in England, Norway and Australia. In 2018 Dawn and her family left NSW to settle on a 100-acre farm in Northern Tasmania.

Gaining a B.Ed in Fine Arts, Dawn later trained as a Special Education Teacher and Children's Counsellor.

Dawn has authored 15 books in fiction & non-fiction, for children, young adults and adults. She has also written pieces for curriculum-based publishers such as Hodder Headline, Rigby Heinemann and Blake Education. Her most successful book to date is *12 Annoying Monsters – Self Talk for Kids with Anxiety* reaching children all over the world. Dawn has produced a wide variety of work, including the WWII memoir *The Boy Who Went to War* as well as many fantasy and scifi books for teenagers.

In 2011 Dawn was awarded a May Gibbs Literature Trust Fellowship and spent 4 weeks in Adelaide working on manuscripts and running workshops at schools and libraries. In 2016 Dawn won the 2016 SCBWI Andrea Davis Pinkney Writer Award for her then incomplete manuscript *Letters From the Dead* which was published in 2017.

In 2025 she is working on a novel for younger readers, *The Vanishing of Georgie Barrett* – her 16th book.

To order her books online, visit Dawn's website:
dawnmeredithauthor.blogspot.com

GRAHAM MEYERS

Graham grew up on a farm in regional South Australia. He tried several occupations in widely separated parts of Australia before graduating as a registered nurse in 1987. He later completed a Graduate Diploma in Tropical Medicine at James Cook University, Townsville and worked in Indigenous communities in many remote areas. These included the Torres Straits and Cape York, the Gibson Desert, the Kimberley and Arctic Canada. Since then he has worked in both inpatient and community mental health in Queensland and Tasmania.

BETHAMY NADER

Bethamy Nader is an aspiring poet and writer who enjoys yoga and line dancing.

Bethamy's recent poems and short stories are published in Women's Oasis Poetry Anthologies, and Eastern Shore Writers Group Anthologies. Her novellas with paranormal themes are available online at Amazon Kindle.

She recently studied Literary Review at Monash University, Victoria, and Harvard University, America. After finishing a Graduate Certificate in Journalism, Media & Communications and BA in English, Classics & Political Science @ UTAS and Advanced Diploma HR & Bus. Mgt. @ TAFE, TAS and Hospitality (Barista) Certificate @ Sydney, TAFE.

Bethamy is currently the Treasurer of Fellowship of Australian Writers, Hobart, Tasmania.

She is the founder and organiser of a national flash writing competition, for emerging young and adult writers, The Bethamy Nader Short Story Prize(s) Theme, *'Through the Eyes of a Mythical Creature.'*

She is currently organising collections of Tasmanian authors children's books, anthologies, and novels to start bookshelves for patients and their visitors in public hospitals throughout Tasmania.

Bethamy assists Tasmanian writers to publish their poems, stories and textbooks online using the Amazon platform.

TATIANA PETROVSKY

Tatiana Petrovsky is a published poet and writer; a passionate supporter of health, education and the environment – a protector and enhancer of wetlands of national significance.

Tatiana has won the Nairda Lyne Award three times.

TIM PHILLIPS

Tim Phillips was born and raised in Tasmania. He completed an arts degree at the University of Tasmania, graduating as a Gold Key student with majors in sociology and philosophy. He is deeply interested in the question of human consciousness and is passionate about the work of the mystic, occultist and intellectual Rudolf Steiner. He is also passionate about the work of Carl Jung and Jungian astrology as best exemplified by the work of the Jungian analyst Liz Greene. He is currently reading *Romanticism comes of age* by Owen Barfield.

DENYS RIRIKA

Born in PNG in 1951. Educated in PNG. Diploma of Theology in PNG ordained Deacon in 1984 then Priest in 1985.

In 1985 received 10th Anniversary medal for work amongst gangs in Port Moresby. Married in 1986. One of two people selected to represent Pacific Island Nations to the World Council of Churches Urban Rural Ministry (URM) Conference to present views on stumbling blocks to presenting ministry in urban and rural settings.

Bachelor of Theology in NZ 1995, then consecrated Bishop 2002, retired 2012.

In 2013 completed Rotary Water Project of installing water tanks along the north Coast of PNG after the destruction of cyclone Guba and moved to Australia in 2014.

LESLEY RIRIKA

Born in Australia 1939. Educated and completed Nursing Training in Australia and moved to PNG as a mission nurse in 1965, in 1968 completed Nurse Education course and continued nursing and nurse education until 2013.

In 1985 received 10th Anniversary medal for nursing work. Married in 1986, Diploma of Advanced Nursing Practice in NZ in 1995; returned to Australia 2013.

Publications: Nursing texts in PNG, Mathematics for Nurses, Mathematics, Anatomy and Physiology, and Microbiology for Nurse Aides.

In 2013 invested with the Officer of the Order Logohu ("OL") for service to the community through the leadership and training provided in the area of education particularly in the health-related disciplines including nursing.

BRENDA SLAVOFF

Brenda has written poetry, plays, short stories and novels. Many of them were based on the author's vivid dreams. One of her novels has been read in serial form on radio, two of her plays have been performed and she has published many short stories and poems - and all this between gardening, theatre, composing music, playing the harp and dancing the tango.

EDITH SPEERS

Edith Speers was born in Canada, migrated to Australia after university, and for many years has lived in the far south of Tasmania. Her poetry has been published in most of the Australian journals and many anthologies of the past forty years. Several overseas literary magazines have also published her poems and she has won many awards for her poetry and short stories. Three books of her verse have been published and, as the proprietor of *Esperance Press*, she has published the work of many other Tasmanian writers.

LEIGH SWINBOURNE

Leigh Swinbourne is a dramatist and fiction writer resident in Nipaluna/Hobart. His work has been shortlisted for the Patrick White Playwrights' Award, the Varuna Award and The Tasmanian Literary Prizes. He has six plays published with *Australian Plays Transformed*. Through *Ginninderra Press* he has published two critically acclaimed collections of short stories, *'The Shark'* (2011) and *'Away'* (2014), and a novel, *'Shadow in the Forest'* (2019). In 2023 he was awarded an Australian Society of Authors mentorship for a second novel. In 2024 he published his third collection of stories, *'The Lost Child'*, longlisted 2025 for the Premier's Prize for Fiction. More on Leigh's writing can be found at
www.leighswinbourne.com.au.